A GIFT FROM
GOD

JAMES A. GAUTHIER, J.D.

Order this book online at www.trafford.com
or email orders@trafford.com

Most Trafford titles are also available at major online book retailers.

© Copyright 2018 James A. Gauthier, J.D.

All rights reserved. No part of this publication may be reproduced, stored in a retrieval system, or transmitted, in any form or by any means, electronic, mechanical, photocopying, recording, or otherwise, without the written prior permission of the author.

Print information available on the last page.

ISBN: 978-1-4907-8690-2 (sc)
ISBN: 978-1-4907-8692-6 (hc)
ISBN: 978-1-4907-8691-9 (e)

Library of Congress Control Number: 2018900077

Because of the dynamic nature of the Internet, any web addresses or links contained in this book may have changed since publication and may no longer be valid. The views expressed in this work are solely those of the author and do not necessarily reflect the views of the publisher, and the publisher hereby disclaims any responsibility for them.

Any people depicted in stock imagery provided by Thinkstock are models, and such images are being used for illustrative purposes only.
Certain stock imagery © Thinkstock.

Trafford rev. 01/10/2018

 www.trafford.com

North America & international
toll-free: 1 888 232 4444 (USA & Canada)
fax: 812 355 4082

Contents

CHAPTER ONE 1
A Little Background 1
I Am a Gift from God 3
My Grandparents 4
My Parents 8
The Outback -A Place to Stay? 12

CHAPTER TWO 15
The Angel and My Birth 15

CHAPTER THREE 24
Who Am I? 24
My Early Education 25
My Love of Horses and Riding 28
Do I possess my Mother's Gifts? 31
Becoming Friends 38
The Steeplechase 45
What is an IQ Anyway? 51
Surviving Winter in the Wilderness 53
MCAT – How old are you? 58

CHAPTER FOUR 61
Medical School- Getting Prepared 61
Medical School – My First Year 64
Medical School – Second Year 66
Medical School – Delays and More Delays 70
Medical School -My Third-Year Clerkship 82

Family Medicine 86
Obstetrics and Gynecology 90
Winter Break 95
Neurology and Internal Medicine 97
Cardiology 102
Spring Break at Last 103
Obstetrics and Gynecology – Part II 106
Pediatric Medicine Part II 115
Third Year Clerkship Assessment 131
A Time for Friends and Reflection 137
My Tenth Birthday 138
What is a Miracle Anyway? 142
It's Summer Time 147
Are you asking me for a Date? 154

CHAPTER FIVE 160
My Residency 160
Planning for my Residency 161
Help Me Father for I am Lost 168
Time for Giving Thanks 172

CHAPTER SIX 180
Planning for my future as an OB/GYN 180

CHAPTER SEVEN 187
A Strong Case of Like 187

CHAPTER EIGHT 195
Epilogue 195

Dedication

Hayden, a young woman created by the grace of God, in the mirror image of her adoptive parents, and carried to earth in the womb of an angel, to be delivered and fill the void of a childless couple who could not bear children. Hayden, I pray that you continue to jump high enough to see the sun and remain in the air long enough to greet the moon, today and for the many jumps to come in your future. In your walk through life healing bodies and souls, remember that you will never be alone because God and I will be with you always.

James A. Gauthier, J.D.

ONE

A Little Background

I understand that the day I was delivered to my parents was brisk with the onset of an unwelcomed late splash of snow and freezing rain which once again blanketed the wilderness landscape. The cold, winter days were gray and dreary amidst hope that spring would arrive once again, bringing color back into the lives of those that lived in the wilderness, or what my mother referred to as the 'Outback'. The snow was still piled high along the roadways and buildings were still adorned with melting icicles reminding us of a winter not yet gone. The daytime temperature reached a warm 37 degrees, which was warm enough to melt the newly fallen snow and ice, while reminding everyone that winter hadn't loosened its grip just yet.

The Wilderness Health Outreach Medical Center was conveniently located in the middle of the 'Wilderness', which the state defined as having a population of less than 2,750 in three sections of property, or 1,920 acres of wilderness land. Some patients of the medical center traveled distances in excess of one hundred miles just to see an OB/GYN. The wilderness medical center was a full-service health care provider for everything from emergency surgery to well-baby care. The medical center was owned and operated by a private foundation that provided the funding for the staff and equipment, including an outreach medivac helicopter.

My future father is an OB/GYN and my future mother is a pediatrician and general practitioner. Together they administer the medical center health programs for the foundation and more importantly, for the patients that seek quality care for themselves or a loved one.

James A. Gauthier, J.D.

The day was 'Good Friday' and Easter was just two days away. In town, young girls walked around in their newly acquired Easter dresses, while still being clothed in layers to react to the changing weather conditions. Young boys were dressed in white shirts and some with ties as the local children excitedly awaited the joy of the Easter egg hunt and Easter surprises. Within our small wilderness community was St. John's Catholic School; the only private school in the wilderness area. It was easy to identify the Catholic school girls who wore the traditional white blouse, tie, color coded vest and plaid skirts. The boys wore black pants, white shirt and tie and of course their color-coded vest. Each grade through eighth had a different colored vest which quickly identified what grade each student was in. The only exception was for the children preparing for their First Communion Easter morning. They wore all white and you could hear parents reminding their child to keep clean for their First Communion ceremony.

In the Outback, Easter is an exciting time, exceeded only by Christmas and birthdays. My parents established a community Easter egg hunt which was held at the Catholic school on Good Friday each year. The wilderness medical center sponsored an annual coloring contest for the best colored Easter rabbit. For those children that participated in the coloring contest, the grand prize was a two-pound chocolate Easter egg and the five second place winners in each age group received a one-pound chocolate Easter egg. Every coloring participant received a four-ounce chocolate egg. Once the colored rabbits were finished and judged, the school taped a rabbit on every door where the children could find Easter eggs hidden out of their direct sight. The medical center provided five hundred plastic eggs throughout fourteen classrooms at the school, with some eggs being filled with coins and others with candy or toys. Regardless of the egg's content, my parents explained to me that the children were provided with a safe environment where they can enjoy being children for another year. Some rooms were exclusively for toddlers and then various age groupings all the way up to eighteen years of age. This year eighty-seven boys and girls participated in the center sponsored Easter egg hunt. There was one grand prize which was a five-pound chocolate Easter bunny and five second prizes of one-pound chocolate bunnies. Every child received a six-ounce chocolate bunny to take home for participating in the Easter egg hunt. My parents made sure that no child left the annual Easter egg hunt empty-handed.

On this particular Good Friday, the medical center waiting room was surprisingly empty with three in-patients in the hospital wing. The last newborn baby left with her anxious parents leaving the nursery department without babies. My parents decided that this year they would close the medical center over the Easter weekend to enable all, but two volunteer nurses and one volunteer doctor, to spend time with their families over the Easter weekend. My father explained to my mother and grandmother that he needed a break to feel human again. It had been a difficult week, especially on my father who performed eight natural births and three 'C- Sections and sadly one baby was stillborn which brought great sadness to everyone involved in the birth. The young mother could be heard crying down the hallway and there was nothing that my parents could do to ameliorate her terrible loss. I understand that the young woman's pastor tried to explain to her that it was God's will. As I read about the events of that day, I guess I wondered why God would will the death of an innocent unborn child.

I Am a Gift from God

In order to understand the miracle of my birth, you need some background on my future family and how I came into being as my parents' daughter. My name is Hayden Elizabeth Gehardi and I am a true gift from God. While I firmly believe that every conceived child is a gift from God, my birthmother was an angel sent to earth to deliver me to my future parents who could not have children except through adoption. I will start at the beginning and then welcome you into my life. I hope that when you are finished reading my story, you too will believe in angels, or at least share in my miraculous birth. This is the story about my life; well at least up to eleven years old.

James A. Gauthier, J.D.

My Grandparents

My grandparents wanted a child so badly that they tried every method available to get my grandmother pregnant. Like so many people, it was only after they accepted that they wouldn't have a child that my grandmother got pregnant. My grandmother feared telling my grandfather that she missed her cycle for fear of jinxing the pregnancy and losing the unborn child. My grandparents had three prior pregnancies spontaneously abort and my grandmother lived in fear of seeing the doctor and losing another opportunity to bring the love of a child into their lives.

My grandmother waited until she missed her second cycle before informing my grandfather that he was going to be a father. My grandfather rejoiced at the wonderful news and then dropped to his knees thanking God Almighty who, through his love and grace could make anything possible. Before this pregnancy, my grandparents felt ostracized by their friends who all had children while they remained childless. When friends congregated, the conversation generally revolved around their children's activities. My grandparents were childless and had little in common to share with others. My grandmother prayed constantly for a child and my grandfather prayed that she place her prayers at the foot of the cross and then let Jesus answer their prayers. My grandfather believed strongly in 'God's Will' and if they were to be parents then God would provide the opportunity for them. My grandparents wondered if this pregnancy was God's answer to their prayers.

My grandmother scheduled an appointment with her OB/GYN and he confirmed the pregnancy. My grandparents were excited, but remained fearful that something may go wrong and they will lose the child once again to a spontaneous abortion. At my grandparent's first doctor visit, they asked to hear their baby's heartbeat. Both of my grandparents needed to hear confirmation that there was a beating heart in the yet to be born child. The doctor used a Doppler microphone and the baby's heart was clearly heard. My grandfather listened carefully and asked the doctor "Is our child's heart alright? I hear an echo, or something that sounds different than a normal heartbeat." The doctor listened very carefully to the heartbeat and replied, "Your baby's heartbeat is normal.

You have nothing to worry about." My grandparents were thankful, but remained fearful of losing the pregnancy before each doctor visit.

At twenty weeks, the doctor scheduled an ultrasound to determine the development of the fetus and the sex of the unborn child if that information was requested. My grandmother cried uncontrollably, and when asked why, she replied, "I am afraid of what you will tell me about the ultrasound findings and that the pregnancy will not last to term. I am also afraid because of the echo in our child's heartbeat may suggest a defective heart. The doctor replied, "Let's get the ultrasound completed and I will show you your child." My grandfather stared at the ultrasound technician's facial expressions looking for the bad news yet to come. He saw the technician smile and he relaxed and asked the technician, "Did you see something? You were smiling" She replied, "Please wait and talk with your doctor." The doctor came into the examination room, looked at the ultrasound and also smiled. He explained to my grandparents why there was an echo in their unborn child's heartbeat. My grandparents feared the worst and held each other tightly when the doctor announced, "You are having twins. The echo you heard was the heartbeat of your second child." My grandparents were so excited that they looked at the ultrasound images of their unborn children for nearly an hour and thanked God that they were having twins.

The book titled 'Ian & Eli', explained that my parent's heartbeats were in perfect unison, something the doctor had never seen or heard about before this pregnancy. That is why the echo was heard. The doctor displayed the two heartbeats on his monitor, but only one was visible on the monitor. My grandparents could only smile knowing that the two identical heartbeats were the developing hearts of their unborn children. My grandparents learned that they would have a boy and girl and they quickly named their unborn children Ian and Eli Gehardi.

On my grandmother's the next visit, the doctor delivered some bad news to my grandparents. My grandmother shook and began to cry in anticipation of the indicated 'bad news' from the doctor. He explained that my mother and father's hands were conjoined and would require a C-section birth and surgery to separate their hands. My grandmother asked, "Will my children be healthy?" The doctor reassured my grandmother that the pregnancy was on track and there was nothing to be concerned about. My grandparents were grateful that their children would be born healthy and thanked God again for their unborn children. A surgeon was brought in to explain about the conjoined hands and he reassured my grandparents that separating my parents' hands was a simple procedure and both children's hands would be normal. My grandparents were allowed to sit and view the ultrasound. My grandmother pointed to my parents' hands on the ultrasound image which showed that their children's hands were definitely joined together. My grandfather replied, "Our children will be fine."

As my grandparents came closer to a delivery date, the ultrasound technician pushed the transducer across both babies and it appeared to the technician that my parents' hands briefly separated. My grandparents saw the technician's face and immediately feared that something was wrong. My grandfather asked the technician what she saw that surprised her. She replied, "Like before, you need to talk with your doctor. I'm sorry, but I cannot discuss the ultrasound with you." Her comments left my grandparents fearful that something bad was seen on the ultrasound. When the doctor came in, my grandmother was crying again for fear that something was wrong with her unborn children. The doctor viewed the ultrasound and concluded that my parents' hands were firmly joined in utero. My grandfather asked, "What shocked the technician doing the ultrasound? I could see in her facial expression that something happened. Is it bad news?" He replied, "The technician thought she saw your children's hands separate briefly and then the hands joined together once more. I looked, but I could not see what the technician saw. Please relax; your twins are healthy and it is almost time to deliver them." My grandparents would listen to the identical heartbeats of my parents and anxiously awaited their birth. While in utero, my grandparents read daily and played music for my parents.

My grandparents were musicians by choice and occupation. They wrote musical score for movies, television and commercial uses. My grandmother used her love of music to keep her calm as she quietly waited for the day to come to meet her children. My grandfather would play music with her to help my grandmother relax and keep her mind off the pregnancy.

On April 25, 1988, my grandmother was sitting and playing her flute when her water broke. My grandmother explained that she heard a sound like a breaking water balloon and she had amniotic fluid running down her legs. My grandfather yelled out, "What was that?" My grandmother replied, "It is time to head to the hospital. Today our children will meet their parents." My grandparents were excited to greet and be with their children. My grandmother said, "Nine months is a long time to wait for something as special as the birth of our twins."

My grandparents arrived at the medical center and while my grandfather checked them in, my grandmother was wheeled into the operatory where the doctor was prepared to deliver my parents by C-section because of their conjoined hands. The doctor admonished the nurses to be very careful when lifting the newborns because their hands are conjoined. I laughed when I read that one nurse carefully lifted my mother while another lifted my father. As the newborns were lifted, their hands separated and one of the nurses immediately thought she had somehow torn off my mother's arm. The nursing staff and doctors quickly realized that my parents' hands were not conjoined; instead, my parents were simply holding each other's hand in utero. The doctor expressed his disbelief that my parents could actually hold, and continue holding hands in utero, but quickly learned that my parents wanted to be together and cried if they couldn't hold each other's hands from the first minute after birth. The hospital had to place my parents in the same bed to allow them the comfort of holding each other's hand. The doctor separated my parents and they immediately cried until both children were together and holding hands once again. It was this unbridled closeness that followed my parents from infancy to adulthood.

The floor nurse did the post-delivery exam and then returned the newborn twins to my grandmother. That is when the nightmare began for my grandparents and my parents. The OB/GYN notified the medical center's pediatrician and word quickly spread about the monozygotic boy/girl twins. The term 'monozygotic' means identical. In the last one hundred years, only ten monozygotic boy/girl births had been registered making the birth of my parents the objects of medical observations and on-going testing.

The hospital pediatrician quickly reacted to my parents' birth by removing them from my grandmother to avoid any kind of bonding between mother and child. The new born twins were taken to an observation room in the hospital where certain tests were performed; like holding one baby over water and the other baby withdrew his or her feet; a pin prick on one foot was felt by the other baby and blowing air in the face of one baby only to find that the second baby reacted as if he or she experienced the same stimulus.

My grandparents became angry and insisted that my grandmother be allowed to nurse her children and change their diapers. When the pediatrician refused, my grandparents threatened legal action and they were permitted to nurse the twins and change their diapers, but prohibited from talking or interacting with the twins. The hospital kept my parents for eight days before my grandparents were finally permitted to take their children home. The homecoming was critically important to my grandparents because their friends began rumors that the state had taken away my parents for some reason leaving my grandparents childless. My grandmother especially carried the heavy burden of criticism until she could finally present her children and dispel further rumors and innuendo. I read about this time in my grandparents' lives and I realized that people, even friends, have the capacity to be hurtful by their words and deeds. One of my favorite sayings is, "Engage Brain before speaking or doing something hurtful or stupid."

My Parents

Early testing confirmed that my parents were above average in intelligence. The book "Ian and Eli" chronicles what my parents and grandparents endured due to their near identical births. My parents were tested at birth, age two, four, five, 10 and 15. Over time, it was learned that my mother and father had IQs over 160 and were amongst the smartest people in the world.

In addition to being highly gifted in intelligence, my mother and father developed skills beyond those of ordinary human development. My mother had (i) precognition and premonition, or seeing the future or a future event; (ii) remote viewing or visualization being the ability to perceive objects without actual sensory use; (iii) clairvoyance being the ability to see things without eyes; (iv) clairaudience being the ability to hear things without actually hearing; (v) alteration or healing alteration being the ability to manipulate an organism in order to heal its wounds. My mother's abilities exceeded my fathers except in the area of telekinetic abilities, or the ability to move things with the mind. My mother tried, but just couldn't do it. My father had an excellent command of telekinesis over small objects. I learned from my mother that having such gifts is a blessing and a curse.

My parents attended a school that only permitted highly gifted students to enroll. Students could direct their own education and manage their school day in any manner acceptable to the student. The school provided a psychologist who assisted students in the exploration and development of skills outside the bounds of ordinary human development. My mother and father's gifts were somewhat unique given that only four out of fifty-two gifted students had any gifts at all.

My mother's special healing gift was put to the test while on a school field trip. My mother's journal explained what happened that day. "The parking area was about two blocks from the science center entrance. Cynthia and Ian were in the first mini-bus and were walking to the science center when Cynthia did a cartwheel and challenged Ian to try to do one. My father claimed that it would be easy and he tried, but lost his balance and tumbled off the walkway and landed in front of an oncoming car which struck him. My mother was in the second mini-bus and she screamed out in pain and began to cry. No one on her bus could understand what happened to make my mother scream out in pain the way she did. My mother cried out, "Ian!" and told the chaperone, "My brother is hurt badly. I need to get to him right now." The bus door opened and my mother ran to where my grandmother was holding my father waiting on an ambulance. My mother held my father's hand and my father relaxed, smiled and said, "I love you Eli. I'm sorry for getting hurt." My mother replied, "Rest. We will get you to the hospital."

My mother said to my grandmother, "Ian may have a broken left arm and broken left clavicle." My grandmother asked my mother how she knew about my father's injuries. My mother explained that she could feel my father's pain in her left arm and left clavicle. My mother placed her hands on my father's left arm and she felt heat passing through her hands. The pain in my mother's arm stopped. My mother then touched my father's clavicle and she experienced the same heat. My mother's clavicle stopped hurting. When my father was given a CT scan, it was noted that he had a broken left radius and left-side clavicle. The radiologist noted that the breaks were mostly healed and the doctor didn't recommend casting for the clavicle and questioned if the radius needed casting since the break also appeared to be mostly healed over. The emergency room doctor asked my grandmother when the accident happened. She explained that it happened less than one hour ago. The doctor replied, "Your son's injuries are healed over sufficiently that I am not going to cast his breaks."

My father held my mother's hand and said, "Thank you Eli for healing me." The doctor asked, "What did your brother say? Did you heal your brother's breaks somehow?" My mother explained that she touched his broken bones and she felt heat flow through her hands. My mother didn't know if that healed my father's breaks or not. She replied, "I just know that when I touched his breaks, the pain I experienced in my left arm and clavicle stopped." The doctor replied, "I have heard of healers and you may be one. It may be because of your unique twin status. I don't know, but I am happy your brother is going to be fine."

As intuitively smart as my parents were, they had significant difficulty meeting and maintaining social relationships. From birth through medical school, my parents slept together, held hands most of the time if a hand wasn't being used, and they were inseparable as twins. I read that when my mother met a boy, my father's jealously would destroy the relationship. Likewise, if my father met a girl, my mother would do what she could to end the relationship. In one instance, my father met a very nice girl and she asked my father how old he was. She then asked my mother how old she was. My mother couldn't accept my father being tied down to a lower IQ girl and my father couldn't handle my mother being with another boy. My parents shared a mutual love together from birth that naturally excluded others from getting too close to either of them. My mother and father agreed that they would love and cherish their mutual relationship with a promise to be partners in life.

My parents graduated from college by challenging courses and taking the final exam for each required class needed for medical school. They both graduated 4.0 from undergraduate college without taking a single course. They were accepted into medical school and at age fourteen my parents were licensed medical doctors. It's kind of humorous that my parents were medical doctors, but couldn't drive and needed written permission from their school in order to get a job before age sixteen.

My parents practiced together in a small community medical clinic and shared a home as employees of the clinic. My father explained to my mother that the clinic's OB/GYN announced that he was retiring and the clinic needed a doctor to pursue licensure as an OB/GYN. My father wanted more challenges and decided to make the leap resulting in the need to complete four more years of an O&G residency to become a board-certified OB/GYN. Sadly, my father moved out of their little house since he would be working fifteen hours a day at the hospital and he was required to live in staff housing. My mother couldn't stand living or being alone, especially without my father, so she moved back home with my grandparents. Throughout this time of separation, my parents came to the firm realization that they had no peers capable of interacting with them at their level. The love my parents shared from birth cemented their love and future commitment to each other. Their promise to each other was to be together always and forever as partners.

My father eventually broke his promise to my mother that he would be with her after he finished medical certification as an OB/GYN. My father was offered a position to practice in a wilderness medical center that didn't have an OB/GYN for nearly a hundred miles. Babies were born with the help of neighbors and midwives; at times resulting in the death of the mother or child at the untrained hands of a midwife when the baby was turned and couldn't be righted. My father explained that he needed to take the position and begged my mother to join him. My mother considered moving, but upon further inquiry my mother discovered that there were no jobs for a family practitioner or pediatrician in the immediate area of the medical center. My mother said, "I am a doctor too and I can't go somewhere that I can't practice." My mother pleaded with my father to stay with her. My father felt compelled to accept the wilderness medical position and left, leaving my mother with a broken heart filled with anger at my father for breaking his promises to my mother. My father claimed that my mother broke his heart. Both of my parents were traumatized at being separated from each other.

My mother cried herself to sleep nightly and eventually refused to even communicate with my father. My mother closed off all communications with my father, especially when my father wrote to her about meeting a young woman with a daughter. She was pregnant with her second child and her husband had recently died. My father spoke regularly about Marsha and her daughter Celeste that loved my father as her father. My mother continued to cry herself to sleep at night knowing that she loved my father, but could never bear him a child. My mother felt inadequate as a woman and angry because the only love of her life was getting involved with a woman that could give him a family; something she couldn't do. My mother attempted dating with other physicians, but her heart and love would always be with my father.

My mother was at work seeing her pediatric patients when she began hurting throughout her body. She felt cold and wet and felt numerous areas on her body that she was sure my father had suffered an injury. My mother's left eye was blurred and she knew my father was hurt. She couldn't determine how badly and asked the clinic director for emergency leave. When the clinic director refused my mother's request for emergency leave, she quit her clinic job and asked my grandmother for help booking a flight to my father. My mother explained to my grandmother that she knew my father was hurt and it was imperative that she get to his side immediately. My mother called the Sheriff in the area and explained what she was physically experiencing. The Sheriff, being skeptical of the report, still searched the described area and found my father's four-wheel drive vehicle that had slid off the icy road and rolled causing the injuries my mother experienced. My father was taken to the medical center where he was examined, and treated.

The Outback -A Place to Stay?

My mother and grandparents arrived at the wilderness medical center and learned that my father had been in surgery. He had a compound fracture of his left leg that required pins and screws to secure the bone. He had several breaks, lacerations and contusions all over his body. My mother explained that she knew where my father was hurting because she experienced the same pain in her body.

My mother kissed my father and told him that she was going to check him for any additional injuries. Dr. Robertson, the medical center director asked my mother what she was doing with his patient. She explained, "I am Ian's sister and I am a medical doctor with bio-alteration or healing skills. I intend to examine my brother for injuries." Dr. Robertson replied, "Ian has been fully checked and he didn't want voodoo medicine in his hospital." My mother explained that she had considerable pain in her left eye. Her vision was blurred and she suspected that my father suffered from a detached retina. She wrote down her diagnosis and added intracranial hemorrhage above his right ear. My mother touched her head and explained, "Ian has a slow bleed right here. She located two hairline fractures of the right femur and right fibula." My mother reviewed her diagnosis with the attending physician who claimed that they found everything. A CT-scan recheck confirmed each of my mother's diagnostic conclusions.

Dr. Robertson then asked my mother what she was doing. She replied, "I am going to try to heal the intracranial hemorrhage followed by the broken bones. Ian will need surgery to reattach the retina as I cannot heal that." Dr. Robertson watched my mother hold her hand on my father's head while my father held my mother's other hand for his own personal comfort. My mother took about ten minutes and said, "The hemorrhage should be repaired. Please do a CT scan and verify that the bleeding has stopped." My mother then healed the minor breaks in my father's legs. The CT scan verified that the intracranial bleeding had stopped and the bones were mending quickly. Dr. Robertson asked my mother, "How did you do that?" My mother replied, "My brother and I are near identical twins. I have some ability to heal him. I have had limited success with others and it is a gift that I was born with." My mother then suggested that the center contact an ophthalmologist to complete the retinal reattachment ocular surgery. My mother held my father and reminded him of her absolute love for him and her desire that they be partners in life.

As my mother held my father's hand, Marsha arrived in my father's hospital room with her daughter Celeste. My mother heard Celeste say, "Daddy Ian". My mother watched my father accept a kiss from Marsha and Celeste and then she politely introduced herself as Ian's sister. Marsha replied, "Ian has told me all about you and him. You are truly identical twins." Marsha then explained how much Celeste loved Ian. As Marsha talked, it was all about Ian and Celeste. My mother asked Marsha, "What about you and Ian? I don't hear you discussing your relationship with Ian. From what Ian said, your husband recently died." Marsha replied, "Yes. He died and I was pregnant with our second child. That is where I met Ian. He has turned out to be a good friend for me and Celeste." My mother asked, "Nothing more than friends?" Marsha explained that one husband was enough. She liked Ian as a friend, but she has no desire to get married or develop a long-term relationship. My mother replied, "Thank you for being honest with me. Have you told Ian how you feel?"

Marsha replied, "No. We hadn't discussed marriage or anything and I felt that just being friends was working out well. I don't think Ian has any interest in marriage anyway as his favorite discussion topic is always talking about you and his commitment to you, whatever that may be." Marsha asked my mother if she knew that Ian's life revolved around her. My mother replied, "We are identical twins. Our lives are so inextricably interwoven that we can't see life without each other's involvement; and yes, as strange as it may be to you, I absolutely love Ian and I know that he loves me."

My mother and grandparents remained with my father for the five days that he was in the hospital. My father gave my mother the key to his home so my mother and grandparents had a place to live while there. My mother and grandparents arrived at my father's house and discovered that every room in the house had numerous pictures of my mother or both my mother and father. My mother smiled and asked my grandparents, 'Who is this girl?" My mother was so happy that my father truly loved her as she had always loved him. My mother cared for my father at home and in six weeks he was able to remove his casts and move around. My mother bathed my father and they reaffirmed their love for each other on a daily basis. My mother and father discussed their relationship and affirmed that they wanted to be partners in life as well as partners in a medical practice. My mother asked, "You do mean like husband and wife?" My father replied, "Whatever you want to call it. I want you in my life, always."

My father recovered and my parents began looking for job opportunities for my mother. It didn't take too long to realize that the local medical offices were fronts for doctors vacationing, hunting and skiing at the wilderness ski resort. My parents contacted the foundation representative for the Wilderness Health Outreach Medical Center to inquire about opening up another clinic. When the representative discovered that the doctors having practice rights at the medical center were fictitious, he offered the administration of the medical center to my parents. Along with management of the medical center, the foundation that owned the medical center provided a medivac helicopter to improve wilderness health care when roads were impassable. Both of my parents, and my grandfather, learned to fly the helicopter and received their pilot's licenses.

TWO

The Angel and My Birth

The day was April 6, 2007, also known as 'Good Friday'. The medical center waiting room was unusually quiet and empty. The Easter egg hunt was underway at St. John's Catholic School, suggesting a possible reason for the empty waiting room. My grandmother concluded that everyone stayed home due to the adverse weather conditions, or possibly in anticipation of Easter two days away. Regardless of the reason for the quietness, my grandmother appreciated the quiet as she looked forward to getting home and fixing dinner for the family. My mother had purchased a twenty-three-pound ham for Easter dinner and many dinners to follow. As in years past, my grandmother blanketed the dining table with ham, mashed potatoes and ham gravy, mixed green, fruit and Waldorf salads, cooked carrots and peas, dinner and croissant rolls and apple, pumpkin and cherry pies. My grandmother took great pride in her ability to prepare inviting holiday meals for the family.

My grandmother was sitting at the admission's desk daydreaming of a warm summer day when the flowers and tree leaves would return once again, while making up her last-minute shopping list of items needed for Easter dinner. Outside the snow and freezing rain continued to fall covering the recently cleared steps into the medical center with more ice and snow. My Grandmother looked at the icy steps and called maintenance to put out more rock salt. My grandmother returned to looking outside as she watched the snowflakes fall. Her quiet vision was abruptly interrupted when a young, very pregnant woman appeared on the center's entry steps wearing a wet nightgown without shoes or a jacket. The young woman's appearance startled my grandmother for a few seconds when she got up and opened the door for the young woman who she described as, "Quite pretty with hair down to her waist and very pregnant."

My grandmother welcomed the young woman and asked, "Do you have an appointment today?" The young woman replied, "Yes. I am here to deliver this child." My grandmother asked her for any identification for her wrist bracelet. The young woman produced an identification card with a picture on the front and explained that she had no other identification. The picture may have been of the young woman several years earlier in life because it failed to look like the young woman she greeted. The card had the name 'Michaele' and an address. The second name was blurred by the wet outdoors. My grandmother politely asked, "Where are your clothes and shoes? It is freezing out there." My grandmother explained that she asked the young woman to be seated and she grabbed a warm blanket for the young woman to cover up with. She smiled at my grandmother and said, "Thank you, but I am not cold. I am here to deliver this child."

My grandmother was getting concerned and asked her about insurance, next of kin, and who the birth father was for the birth certificate information required by the state vital records program. The young woman just smiled and repeated again, "That is not necessary. I am here to deliver this child." My grandmother was about to call security when the young woman turned to her and said, "It is time for me to deliver this child." The young mother was more assertive causing my grandmother to call my father. He alerted his medical staff of an incoming delivery and told my grandmother not to worry about the demographics. His nurse would handle it while he examined the young woman. Within minutes an orderly arrived and transported the young woman to the delivery room. My grandmother whispered to my father, "I think she might be on something. She keeps saying, 'I am here to deliver this child.'" My father asked, "Where are her clothes?" My grandmother replied, "She just appeared on the entry steps wearing the nightgown and nothing else."

My father's surgical nurse asked the young woman to remove her wet nightgown and put on a surgical gown. My father did his pre-delivery examination and concluded that the baby was positioned such that he would need to do a C-section delivery. My father explained why she would need a C-section and she replied, "Thank you. I am here to deliver this child." The surgical nurse said, "Excuse me, but I need your next of kin and the birth father's name for the birth certificate." The young woman smiled and reassured the nurse that everything would be fine once she delivers the child. The surgical nurse asked, "You keep saying that you are here to deliver this child; are you a surrogate for someone that isn't here right now?" The young woman asked, "What is a surrogate?" The nurse explained that a surrogate is a woman impregnated with the sperm and egg of another and she carries the baby to term for someone else. The young woman replied, "I am." The nurse asked, "I am what?" The young woman repeated, "I am here to deliver this child. I am ready." The nurse asked for a birth date and received the same response, "I am here to deliver this child."

My father walked into the operatory and did a final check and reaffirmed to himself that the young woman's child would need to be delivered by C-section. She replied, "I understand and I am ready to deliver this child." My father's surgical notes state he obtained her consent and then alerted the operatory nurses and anesthesiologist and prepared to do the C-section. The surgical nurse looked over the paperwork and asked, "What's this?" She was looking at a squiggle on a signature line and commented, "That isn't a signature." My father replied, "That is all we have. I need to deliver this child regardless of how she signed the consent form."

The young woman touched my father's hand and smiled before saying, "I am here to deliver this child. I am ready." My father wasn't sure about the young woman and her statement of readiness to deliver this child. My father did one more check of her vitals as the anesthesiologist prepared to put her under. My father turned to Dr. Morrisi and said, "We're ready." The anesthesiologist told the young woman that he would put a mask on her and she was to count backwards from ten. She smiled and said she was ready as she began counting backwards. The anesthesia was started and the young woman's heart stopped immediately. A code was called for an emergency crash cart and my father decided he had to deliver or lose the child. My father did the C-section delivery while two other doctors tried to revive my birth mother. The attending doctors certified the time of death and the fact that my birth mother had no heart or brain function.

My father asked Dr. Morrisi, "What happened?" Dr. Morrisi replied, "Even if she was allergic to the anesthetic, she would have experienced some difficulty and I could have neutralized the anesthesia and taken a different route. No one just dies, especially where all life function ended instantaneously when I began to administer the anesthesia. I am of the opinion that there wasn't a sufficient quantity of the anesthetic in her to have caused what happened. She just died and I have no idea why." My father asked the nurse to attend to the newborn girl and set her up in the nursery. Please notify one of the pediatric neonatal nurses that we have a baby in residence. I want two nurses attending to the newborn. My father explained that the birth mother died instantly and the hospital will need to use alternate breast milk or formula depending on the needs of the newborn.

My father asked for the young woman's identification and then called the sheriff to determine who lived at the address stated on the young woman's identification card. The sheriff reported back to him that the address was a vacant lot. My father asked him if he had a missing person report for a Michaele something. He replied, "Not locally or on any national data base." The local sheriff arrived at the medical center and took fingerprints of the young woman to try to identify who she was from the NCIC database. The sheriff took several pictures and labeled her a Jane Doe assuming that her name, Michaele, wasn't any more accurate than her address. The Sheriff commented that the picture on her identification didn't even look like her. He looked around and no one disagreed with the Sheriff's conclusion. My father directed an orderly take the young woman's body to the morgue once the sheriff was finished with pictures and prints. The medical examiner notified my father that he wanted to do an autopsy to determine what happened and requested my father maintain blood and DNA samples from my birth mother and from me.

My grandmother heard what happened to the young woman and explained to my father that she just appeared on our frozen steps, bare foot and without a coat. My father looked at the security video footage and he couldn't explain where the young woman came from. He put in his notes, "She just appeared." The Sheriff looked at the security video and said, "It beats the hell out of me."

My father sent DNA samples to the local lab for a rush analysis which usually took a week or longer to get the results. However, the lab processing the young mother's DNA reported to my father that the DNA sample was contaminated and the lab needed a new sample for Jane Doe.

The lab explained to my father that the tested DNA represented both male XY and female XX sex chromosomes. My father replied, "That's not medically possible." The lab went on to explain that there is no DNA relationship between the birth mother's DNA and the child's DNA. Again, my father said that is impossible unless she was a surrogate for an unknown party.

My father pulled together a medical team to reexamine Jane Doe and collect the new DNA evidence. The orderly that took Jane Doe to the morgue reported to my father, "She's not there." My father asked, "What do you mean, 'She's not there'." The young orderly replied, "She is nowhere in the morgue. I checked everywhere." My father recalls asking, "Where else could she be?" He called the county medical examiner, but he didn't have the body of Jane Doe; neither did the Sheriff. My father turned to his staff and said, "She couldn't walk out of here so find her." Following an exhaustive three-hour search of the medical center, and questioning all the staff, the only thing they found that Good Friday was the hospital surgical gown the young woman was wearing in the delivery room. My father filed a missing body report with the state and county and turned to my grandmother and said, "I can't do anymore." My father was heard for the rest of the day asking, "Where could she have gone? Deceased patients do not walk out of hospitals." Given the missing body, the county coroner ordered the DNA evidence sealed until the body was found.

My mother could sense that my father was more than distraught. My mother had been reviewing the survey results concerning the quality of care offered by the medical center and was excited to tell my father the good news while she tried to reconcile my father's despair. My mother hugged my father and said, "I bring great news from our survey." My father replied, "I'm sorry Eli, but I can't deal with that right now." My mother replied, "I know you are distraught. I can feel what you are feeling. Please sit down and talk with me." He replied, "There isn't really that much to talk about. I just killed my first patient. A young mother died as I prepared to deliver her baby by cesarean section." My mother asked, "What was the procuring cause of her death? Is it something you did or failed to do?" He replied, 'It is nothing I did or didn't do. The anesthesia was administered and she died instantly. We verified that she had no heart or brain function"

My mother asked, "Where is the birth father?" My father replied, "I don't know. We had very little information on the young woman. She told my nurse that she was unmarried without known family anywhere. According to mom, and our security film, the young woman just appeared on our clinic steps. She was barefoot and wore a nightgown, but nothing else. The young mother said, "I am here to deliver this child." The wording was what was strange. She wasn't there to deliver her baby. Instead, she was there to deliver this child as if she was a messenger or surrogate. She had an identification card, but we quickly learned from the sheriff that the name and address were fictitious. No one knows who she is or where she came from. She just arrived here." My father went on to explain, "My nurse asked her what her name was for the surgery chart. The young woman replied, "That isn't important. I am here to deliver this child." I may be way off course, but her demeanor, innocence and smile, manner of dress and facial expression was almost angelic in my personal opinion. The child she was delivering may be a gift from God since humans don't walk out of a hospital after death; but for whom? My father experienced an entire range of emotions when reviewing the day's events and he had no idea how to locate my natural family, much less reconcile what had transpired in his surgery center.

Millie, the surgical intake coordinator said, "It was as if she was on a mission to deliver the child to someone else. She never claimed it was her child or that she had any interest in the child. She was there to complete the delivery only." My mother replied, "Angels do exist and she may have been an angel bringing a gift from God like you said." My father replied, "Maybe! I have to wonder if she was an angel. When the orderly went to retrieve her body from the morgue, her body was missing and a search only turned up her hospital gown."

My father was so incensed at losing a patient, and then losing the patient's body, that on his first day off from the medical center he did some research and found, not in medical journals, but in a book about angels that angels from Heaven are hermaphrodite, meaning male and female. Angels are God's creation and angels exist to serve God at his will. My father remembered the male/female DNA and that only deepened the mystery of who my birth mother was. Could she have been an angel from God delivering me to my parents that could not bear children? *I wonder.*

My father said to my mother, "We need to notify Child Services and have them arrange for foster care for the female child while her family is located. I have taken some blood for DNA testing if needed. At this point, no one knows who the mother was or where she came from."

My mother was very curious about the circumstances of my birth. If the young mother was delivering the child to someone, then who was the intended party? My mother felt drawn to the nursery where she claims she saw the most beautiful baby girl lying in the nursery bed and she immediately fell in love with me. My mother thought I looked a lot like my parents did at birth. She explained that she didn't understand why exactly, but she instantly bonded with me. I would intently stare at my mother and she wondered what I may be thinking. I recall my mother telling me that my parents stared at my grandparents the same way. My mother couldn't keep her eyes off of me as she held me and said that she loved me with all her heart. My mother took the day off and she fed me and personally cared for my needs. My mother held me and said, "I am to become your mother." My mother's premonition saw my parents become the adoptive parents for me. My mother accepted that I was a gift from God to fill their lives with the love of a family that my mother couldn't otherwise provide.

My mother asked my father what he thought about adopting me. She explained that she already saw them as my parents and reassured my father that she had enough love in her heart for him and for this baby girl if you are interested in becoming a father. My mother said, "You and I are partners, but we will never have children other than through adoption. I have already bonded with Hayden and I already know that we will become her parents. She is beautiful and looks a lot like us when we were babies. I can't wait to show Hayden to mom and dad." My father replied, "I would like being a father, but do understand that my life would still revolve around you first."

My mother contacted Child Services to determine what would be required to establish a temporary foster home for me. My father confirmed that they would jointly adopt me if the opportunity arose. My mother and grandmother used the helicopter and went shopping for baby things to meet the foster home requirements and when the state foster care inspector checked our home, my parents had everything needed to get approved as my foster parents. Once approved, my mother released the nurses that would have staffed the neonatal unit over Easter.

My father asked my mother where she came up with my name, 'Hayden'. My mother replied, "I liked the name. It fit the little girl that I immediately fell in love with at the medical center. Her full name will be Hayden Elizabeth Gehardi. If you don't like that name, then what is your idea?" My father replied that he liked the name Hayden Elizabeth and commented that they would refer to me as 'Hayden' and wait and see what transpired over the six-month adoption waiting period. My father warned my mother, "Please do not get too attached to Hayden just in case her family is found and they take Hayden from us." My mother replied, "Hayden is our child. She looks like us and I know that she will be smart like us. I see you and me as parents of Hayden and I have no doubt about my premonitions. My mother contacted Child Services to make sure that they understood that my parents wanted to adopt me when permitted.

My mother and father flew us home where I would meet my grandmother and grandfather. My grandmother commented, "Hayden looks a lot like you and Ian at birth." My mother said that she already saw my parents adopting me. My grandfather replied, "I hope so. I would love to have a granddaughter." My grandfather held me and said, "Hayden looks at me like you kids did at the same age. I feel like Hayden is looking through me as if she was trying to communicate with us."

I was five days old and read that I was a wonderful, happy baby. My grandmother gave my parents the night off to relax while she held me and recalled what it was like when my grandparents finally held my mother and father in their arms. My grandparents prayed that my parents' desire to adopt me happened so they would not be without any grandchildren.

My parents did their first real date as partners. They had discussed being partners most of their lives and on this particular night, my parents drove to the top of the highest hill in the wilderness, stood outside holding each other and dedicated their love and their lives to each other and of course to me too.

My parents informed my grandmother that they would be partners in life and in love. My father stated, "Neither of us has found someone that has the intellectual capacity to maintain our interest. We have always loved each other and you and dad have always known and understood how we felt about each other." My grandmother asked, "What about children?" My mother replied, "We are going to adopt Hayden. She will become our child. I am going to have Ian perform a tubal ligation so I can't get pregnant." My grandmother was a little startled and suggested that my parents sit down with my grandfather and explain their intentions." My father replied, "I will gladly let Dad know about our plans. I think Dad will be supportive, but even if he isn't too supportive, Eli and I are prepared to live our lives together with or without your blessing. I'm sorry Mom, but it is our life and our decision." My parents spoke to my grandfather who was fully supportive and commented, "You have held and loved each other since conception. I am not surprised that you have chosen to share your lives together as one. I hope you get to adopt Hayden so you too are blessed with a family." My mother commented, "Hayden is our child. My premonition confirms that she will become our adopted child. I also see Hayden as being as intelligent as we were as children. Look at Hayden; she is truly a gift from God and as best I can determine, she was delivered to us by an angel. She is God's blessing on our unique lives and fills the void of our inability to have children.

My parents and grandparents read to me daily, did counting, showed colors and shapes and began my early education within days of my birth. Six months passed quickly and my parents received word that they could adopt me. The act of adoption completed my journey that I believe started in Heaven when God, my Father placed me in the womb of Angel Michaele.

THREE

Who Am I?

I wrote this stanza when I was five years old. The stanza represents who I am, or at least was at age five.

Who am I?

I exist because I am Hayden Elizabeth Gehardi.
I exist because, even though I was adopted, I am the mirror image of my parents.
I exist because I am the daughter of Ian and Eli Gehardi and the granddaughter of Hans and Lisa Gehardi.
I exist because I am master to my dog Mitzi and my horse Tempest.
I am the best friend to Teri who makes my life complete, wholesome and fun.
I am, because I find pleasure in the morning sunshine as it brightens my bedroom window and welcomes me to another day.
I am, because I feel comfort from the warmth of the morning Sun.
I am, because I find joy in performing my daily chores and completing my study goals.
I am, because I find love and acceptance from my mother, father and Mitzie.
I am, because I am very smart and work hard at being smart.

I am, because I cherish each day as if it was my last.
I am, because I know then when the Sun sets on my life, I will be at peace with our Lord, Jesus Christ.
I am because I will accept others despite the fact that I may have a different opinion.
I will make time daily to listen with my ears while quieting my mouth. I will open my mind and my heart before opening my mouth and saying something stupid or hurtful.
I will find time to love and be loved by my mother and father. I will ride Tempest and soar like the wind as we together master the field.
I will become a great medical doctor. I will be compassionate and supportive of others. I will heal the sick and find a cure for hopelessness.
I will give when I would rather receive.
I will exist for I am Hayden.
Morning Sun, upon me I feel your warmth and see your light.
Morning Sun, be with me today and remain until night.
Morning Sun, shine brightly so others may find your warmth and light.
Morning Sun, be with others and remain until night.
Good evening Moon, I see you in the night.
Good evening Moon, I see your light
Good evening Moon, I find delight knowing that you will remain with me until morning light. Hayden

My Early Education

I am fortunate to be the child of my parents. My parents and grandparents all participated in educating me at home. My parents firmly believed that I was gifted and they purchased for me all forms of educational materials from phonetic readers, counting, shapes, colors, music notes, and games. From birth, my parents or grandparents read to me for a minimum of two hours every day. My parents and grandparents played music and I came to appreciate music and developed a desire to master music and musical instruments. They would also count numbers and show me primary and secondary colors. To me, learning is how I play and relax. I learned early on that I enjoyed stimulating activities and direct interaction with my family.

I was one of those babies that abhorred a dirty diaper; be it wet or soiled, I made sure that the problem was resolved in short order. My mother explained to me that when I had a dirty diaper, I would frown or scowl and lacked my happy face. When changed into clean clothing, my smile would quickly return to say thank you. In light of my disgust for a dirty diaper, I potty trained at fifteen months and by twenty months I began selecting the clothes I wanted to wear for the day and tried to dress myself. At times my mother and I disagreed on the proper wear for the day, but for the most part I was allowed to care for myself as well as I could at that age. My parents encouraged independent thought and decision-making skills. My father's response to many of my issues growing up included such phrases as, "Who is responsible and who should be accountable." In most cases the answer was me.

At age two, I received a child's computer with learning activities and several musical instruments including a plastic recorder and a child's size flute. I learned how to hold the recorder and flute and I enjoyed trying to sound out music from parroting my mother or father when they played a primary musical note. I would carefully observe how my mother's hands and mouth moved and I tried to mimic her motions with little success until I learned the primary music scale from my grandparents. At two and one-half, I could play Yankee Doodle on the recorder and I could recognize the sound of the notes in the primary scale. At two, I could sit and listen to my parents and grandparents play music as I sat motionless watching their eyes and hand movements.

My day as a child was involved with learning activities instead of creative play. My mother reviewed shapes, colors and measures as I poured various products from one measure to another. By age three I could identify fractional parts. My mother would cut my food into two parts and explain what a 'half' was; then quarters and finally thirds. At age three I learned to measure kitchen products, like a half cup of sugar or a teaspoon of salt. My mother and grandmother were natural teachers and everything we did, from identifying the day each morning, to the date was a learning process. My favorite activity was counting my steps when we went to the store, park or wherever I could walk. I learned to count until I had to stop walking. My grandparents had me singing the musical scale and by four years of age I could read music and play the flute and beginning violin.

My parents have always asked me open ended questions requiring thought and rarely asked questions which garnered a 'yes' and 'no' type answer. By way of an example: My mother would ask, "Is this a good time to put away your reading book so we can do some writing?" This type of question permitted me to control my life and my learning activity timeline. If my mother had said, "It is time to put away your reading book" what she did was take away my discretion concerning what and when to study. I much preferred being asked in a manner that respected me as an individual. I started early on setting small goals and no one but me understood the steps I was engaged in to meet those goals. At a very early age I found that open ended questions solicited thought where closed questions ended the thought process. *It's something for you to think about when you interact with your own children.*

As a child, I liked what independence my parents allowed me to experience as I sought to control my own personal environment. I have been a neat freak since the earliest time I can personally remember. I learned from my father that everything has its place and that is where it should be returned. I was a unique child in that I kept my room and activity areas neat and organized. I cannot recall a time when my mother needed to remind me to clean my room, make my bed, or clean up my lab. In mentioning my lab, one afternoon when I was four years old, I mixed vinegar and baking soda and created a small eruption. I wanted to impress my father when he came home with my latest experiment. I had formed a makeshift mountain and to make the eruption more exciting, I poured in a full box of baking soda and poured half of the bottle of vinegar. I looked at my father and said, "Watch this." My mixture didn't erupt; it blew up and distributed my box of baking soda all over my lab area. My father replied, "Nice explosion. I am assuming that since you created the mess that you would like the responsibility of cleaning it up too." I replied, "Of course. It was my stupidity because I used too much baking soda and vinegar to impress you." My father replied, "I'm impressed" and he left me to clean up my mess. My point is that at an early age, it was incumbent on me to take responsibility for my actions and my mistakes. The ultimate lesson I learned was 'bigger isn't always better'.

By age four, I could read and write stories and I had a good grasp of grammar and spelling. I learned quickly how to use 'Spell Check' on my laptop and by five I could type more than twenty words a minute on my laptop computer. I was reading elementary reading books and children's literature and I focused on elementary biology, zoology and chemistry. I had a small lab in my bedroom that allowed me to perform various experiments like my baking soda mountain. At four years of age, I could add, subtract and multiply two-digit numbers and I had an excellent grasp of fractions. I worked on my school work at least ten hours a day through age five. I loved school work. It was how I relaxed and I had no one to play with where we lived in any event.

My Love of Horses and Riding

My parents owned two gentle mares and at age three I rode frequently, initially bareback with a lead rope and then with an English or western saddle. I used a mounting block to mount and dismount Midnight. I loved riding and by age four I was able to have Midnight sidestep, back up and walk the trail course set up at our barn facility. At age four, I could walk underneath Midnight and he would turn his head down to look between his front legs to see where I went. When I finished riding, I used my small step ladder and washed and brushed Midnight. My mother usually offered to assist, if for no other reason than to speed me up, but I would insist on taking care of my horse. My last act would be to give Midnight a hug and a carrot for a fun day.

I loved horseback riding as much as I loved to study. I enjoyed the fresh air and usually met someone around the barn that would offer to ride with me. My love of horses led my parents to purchase two more horses so we could do family riding activities. Often, I was the object of other rider's and guests' attention when they would see me laying on Midnight's back reading one of my textbooks. I usually tried to blend fun and study together so I bored of neither activity. At four years old I tried to carry my horse gear, including my saddle. It was hard, but I could get my gear to the lock up part of the barn where saddles and tack was stored. One afternoon it began a heavy rain. I grabbed Midnight's light sheet and I put it over both of us until the rain stopped. One boy at the barn yelled, "Hey stupid, the rain sheet is to go on the horse's back, not your head." I replied, "How true, but my horse and I are dry. You are soaked. Think about your statement and guess which of us should be considered 'stupid'. I apologized all the time for my sharp tongue, but I loathed statements that lacked thought or were intended to embarrass or hurt someone else. I liked another saying, "Engage your brain before opening your mouth."

My riding barn opened up an equestrian field and placed low fences all around for our horses to jump over. The fences were only a foot high, but when you are four years old, jumping a one-foot fence with a 1,800-pound non-jumping horse can certainly lead to a disaster. My second run around the small obstacle course stopped Midnight in his tracks and sent me flying over his head. I held onto Midnight's reins and that caused me to land on my right arm and it hurt. I was too small to remount Midnight on the field so I humbly walked him back to the horse barn and my mother examined my arm. She concluded that I broke the right-side radius. My mother held my arm for five minutes and the pain left my arm and I felt fine. My mother healed my broken arm that day. I would be a few years older before I fully understood my mother's miraculous healing ability. My mother asked, "Is it time to finish up?" I replied, "Not until I make it around the obstacle course one time with a perfect ride." I rode for the next two hours because none of my rides met my definition of perfection. I finally surrendered my horse to the barn and we flew home. My favorite line for my mother was, "Thank you for allowing me the opportunity to …" My mother knew I was a perfectionist and she gave me considerable latitude to do things my way if age appropriate.

My mother introduced me to the Steeplechase on her computer. She knew that I wanted to jump fences and felt I might like to pursue membership in the Steeplechase organization in our area. I checked my laptop and found that Steeplechase was popular near where we lived. My mother flew me to a Steeplechase event and I was in awe of the jumpers clearing six-foot National Fences and water hazards. I wanted to jump and join the Steeplechase riding events and my parents purchased a big gelding jumper I named Tempest. Tempest was about two hands taller than Midnight, but the real test of size was the eight-foot step ladder I needed to get onto Tempest's back. I looked down the first time I mounted Tempest and I wanted off. My mother and I looked at other jumpers that were listed for sale, but my heart and mind kept returning to Tempest. He was tall, black and a beautiful jumper with leg muscles that bulged as he walked and ran. I decided that I would get used to the riding height and we bought Tempest. I asked my mother, "Where do we board Tempest? There are no stalls in the barn." Mr. Derington, the seller, replied, "The best way to destroy a jumping horse is to lock the horse up in a small horse stall. Thoroughbred Jumpers need open space to run, jump, and kick up their heels and roll in the grass. Please never lock up your horse. My field is only ten minutes away and you can board Tempest there for $200 a month. He indicated that he would return tempest to the field. He told me that when you want to ride Tempest, blow this whistle." I blew it once and Tempest turned and looked at me like he was a little angry at my whistle blowing.

I attempted to sign up for the northeast Steeplechase competition for beginners. The fence height was two feet for qualification. If I rode five runs at the beginner level and placed fifth or above, I could move into the intermediate level that jumped three and four-foot fences. The ultimate was professional jumping at the six-foot fences. I stood in line for about ten minutes feeling excited to ride in the beginner event. I had been jumping one-foot fences and I figured a two-foot fence was nothing to worry about. When I stepped up to register, I was almost five and the individual accepting registrations turned me away. I was angry and cried until my mother suggested I speak with the event coordinator instead of the registration person. She and I met with the sponsor and I explained my jumping and riding experience and after considerable pleading, I was allowed to do one ride in this event. If I fell off my horse, I was finished for the year. My mother hugged me and said, "Here is your opportunity to shine. I will pray you and Tempest do well."

I received a lot of jokes from the other participants. They asked which pocket I kept my ladder in so I could mount my horse. I politely replied, "I use the same mounting block that I just saw you use to mount your little horse. Tempest makes your horse look like a pony." The man replied, "I hope you fall on your little ass." I replied, "I hope I do not fall; however, if I do, watch me because I am not a quitter and I will place in this event." I was ready to mount Tempest when a man put his hand on my butt as I jumped. His additional force threw me over the side of Tempest where I was caught by the unfriendly man. He chuckled and said, "I knew it. She can't ride." I asked for no help mounting my horse. If I can't mount my horse, I shouldn't be riding him either."

My first ride was near perfect. My second ride was almost the same, but in my third ride, Tempest stalled at a water hazard and I rolled off him into the water hazard. I walked back to finish the run and avoid a disqualification. The adults were laughing at me because I was soaked from head to toe. I took off my riding helmet and water poured out of it too. My mother held my horse and I changed into dry breeches and a dry shirt. I had to wear my number jacket or forfeit. My next two rides were perfect and I placed fifth overall. Not my best, but for my first event, I was happy to place fifth out of fourteen riders. I finished the season in third place and qualified for three foot fences the following season.

Do I possess my Mother's Gifts?

On a quiet Sunday morning near my fourth birthday, my mother and I were sitting on the bed going through color flash cards for primary, secondary and tertiary colors. My mother held up a red card and I said, "Primary color"; the next card was blue – also primary'; before my mother could show the next card, I said "Green-also primary". My mother asked me how I knew the next card was green. I replied, "I just knew it was. There are only three primary colors that when mixed create secondary and tertiary colors. My mother asked if I could name the secondary colors. I replied, "cyan, magenta and yellow." My mother asked what tertiary colors are. I explained that when secondary colors are mixed you end up with tertiary colors.

My mother was curious if I had any perception or premonition skills like she possessed. She picked up five toys and asked me to tell her what toys she was holding behind her back. I looked around and correctly identified all five toys. My mother was so excited that she grabbed my father and told him that I may have my mother's ability of remote viewing.

My father decided to test me. He put all the toys on the floor and then had me turn my back while he picked up five toys. My father held the toys behind his back and asked me to identify the toys he was holding. I correctly identified all five toys. My father told my mother that she may be right about my abilities. My father asked me how I knew what objects he held in his hands. I replied, "Like Mommy's game, I looked at the toys left on the floor and determined which were missing and those are the ones that I said were in your hands." My mother asked me, "Then you didn't see the toys in your head?" I replied, "No, I just saw what was missing." My father asked me if I wanted to play another game. I replied, "Yes! I like games."

My father wrote twenty numbers on a piece of paper with five random numbers in four rows. He showed my mother and me the paper for ten seconds and then put it away. My father asked me to fill in the twenty blanks on the paper that he handed to me. I wrote all twenty numbers in the locations found on the original paper. At that point, my parents concluded that I had a photographic memory. My parents tested me on five more memory tests, one being a children's card matching game. I turned over the matching cards as if I could see through the card stock. My parents began to wonder what other skills I may possess.

My grandparents were excited to hear about my abilities. My grandfather asked if he could work with me on developing my musical talent and music appreciation. My grandfather explained that he was teaching me the basics just like he did for my parents. My mother taught me how to hold my recorder and she would play a tone to let me hear the note from the flute in comparison to the recorder. It didn't take too long and I had graduated from the recorder to the child's flute. By age four, I could read most sheet music and play the flute like my parents. However, if someone was over to our house, I would play Yankee Doodle on the recorder just for fun.

My mother believed that I was, or would be academically brilliant just like her and my father. She wrote three numbers on a piece of paper. She showed my grandmother the numbers and then she folded the paper and stuck it in her pocket. My mother said, "I have written three numbers on a piece of paper." Before my mother could finish, I replied, "I know. The numbers are 3 8, and 9." I was correct. My mother followed up asking, "I am thinking of three numbers under 100. What numbers am I thinking about?" I wrote, "12, 17, and 34." The numbers were exact.

My grandfather asked to test me. He wrote three numbers onto his hand and then closed his fist. I correctly identified all three numbers.

I had a real affinity towards learning. I didn't care what I was learning; I just wanted to learn. I would soak up knowledge like a sponge always seeking more information to stimulate my brain. My mother held me and said, "I don't care how smart you are, you are not going to have your childhood ruined by being subjected to scientific observations or ongoing psychological testing like your father and I were subjected to."

My parents decided to purchase me a small puppy to play with. It was to be a surprise and help remind me to be a little girl and enjoy life. My father would say, "There is more to life than studying." My parents went shopping and I stayed with my grandmother and practiced my music. I could see the puppy in my head and I told my grandmother that my parents were buying me a little puppy. I stood in the window waiting for my parents to land and I would see my puppy. My mother was the first in and her hands didn't hold a little puppy. She saw my head droop as I sat down on the sofa and said, "Oh well!" My mother asked my grandmother, 'What is wrong with Hayden?" My grandmother replied, "Hayden was sure that you and Ian bought her a puppy. Hayden stood at the window waiting for you to return home. She has been dead set on you returning with a puppy for her to play with."

My mother sat and held me. She asked, "What made you think that we were going to get you a puppy?" I replied, "I thought I saw you and daddy buying me a little puppy." My mother asked, "Can you describe the puppy you saw in your dream?" I replied, "It wasn't a dream. I just saw the puppy. It is very small, curly white hair, has one brown ear and one brown foot and is really cute. I thought I was going to have a puppy to play with."

I crawled into my mother's arms and appeared so disappointed until my father walked in with the puppy. I screamed, laughed and giggled as the puppy kissed my face and jumped all over me. I looked at my mother and said, "I told you I saw you buy me a puppy." My mother handed my description of the puppy to my father. It was a perfect description suggesting once again that I had certain clairvoyant or premonition skills and remote viewing skills just like my mother. My father asked, "How can that be?" My mother replied, "I don't know."

With our birthdays coming, my parents wanted to give me a chance at having a fourth birthday around other children. My parents selected a restaurant that had children's characters walking around the tables, clowns making balloon toys, singing and otherwise having a good time. We arrived by helicopter and the hostess asked whose birthday it was and my parents pointed towards me and said, "Hayden is four years old." My grandmother then told the hostess that my parents were celebrating their birthdays too. The hostess gave each of us a birthday crown and then asked for my parent so she could stamp my hand and my parent's hand with the same stamp. My parents replied, "We are Hayden's parents." The woman replied, "How can that be. You are identical twins. She can't be your daughter. We have an Amber Alert for a missing four-year-old as the hostess walked away calling the police. My parents didn't know what to do so we waited for the police to arrive.

The police arrived and my parents showed them a copy of my adoption papers. He said, "I understand, Hayden is your daughter. Why did your twin brother tell the hostess that he is the girl's father?" My mother replied, "Because he is her father. We both adopted her. If you look on the adoption papers, you will see both of our names. The officer asked my parents for identification. The officer asked me if I was related to Ian and Eli Gehardi. I replied, "They are my parents." My grandparents replied, "We are their parents and Hayden is our granddaughter." The officer thanked us and then asked the patrons in the restaurant if anyone knew who flew in on the helicopter. My father stood up and said, "Officer that is our helicopter." He replied, "You can't park it there. Next time it will be locked down until you pay a sizeable fine. The heliport is two blocks down the road." He then asked, "Why do you need a helicopter anyway?" My father politely explained that he and my mother were medical doctors and we use our helicopter for medical emergencies and family transportation. The officer said, "That's different. If you put a 'red cross' on the port side window, then there are no parking restrictions other than common sense and FAA regulations that you must abide with."

The hostess was so embarrassed that she refused to service our table. The manager apologized and offered a free meal for our birthdays and the inconvenience. My father replied, "I just wanted a nice birthday with children for my daughter." My mother looked down and asked, 'Where is Hayden?" Sheer panic ensued as my parents searched the restaurant looking for me. In one of the back corners a clown was making balloon hats and I had wondered off and joined the other children waiting for a hat. I received my hat and returned to my parents and told them that I was having fun with the kids in the singing circle. I invited everyone to come and watch. The clown had the children clapping and making animal sounds to his various songs. When he paused for a minute, I asked, "When can I see the little bear?" The man replied, "What bear are you talking about? We do not have a bear." I replied, "I saw a little bear in the restaurant and I want to see it please." The man looked at my parents like I was a nut. I kept looking around the restaurant for the little bear when my father said, "Hayden, it is time to leave." I replied, "No. Not until I see the little bear." I had never been disrespectful to my parents, but I wanted to see the little bear and no one was going to prevent me from seeing it. I was holding my father's hand when the front door to the restaurant pushed open and in walked a little brown bear cub. Patrons screamed "Bear" and stood up. I couldn't see so my father put me on his shoulders. The little bear walked around and then left the restaurant as a patron held the door open. I said, "I told you I saw a little bear."

Bear night confirmed in my mother's thoughts that I had premonition abilities and my mother planned on doing a little more testing of my gifts of remote viewing. I heard my father say, "Just keep it fun. I do not want Hayden treated like we were treated."

My mother replied, "I promise to treat the tests like a game. My mother, grandmother and I flew into town. We stopped by a store and my mother purchased a series of perception and visual discrimination activities. She explained to me that many of the activities selected were ones previously given to my parents at my age.

My mother had me put Mitzie away in my room so she wouldn't bother me when we did the games. My mother explained that she would be giving me a series of activities to test my perception and visual discrimination skills.

[*Test* One] Hayden, on this paper is one-hundred letters and within the page is a single word. Please find the word.

[*Result*] I found the word 'bird' in four seconds.

[*Test Two*] Hayden, here is a sequence of colors and numbers. The first color is red. Find the pattern of colors and numbers that repeat while growing.

[*Result*] I took twenty-six seconds and found red, 3, red blue, 10, red, blue green 17. I had the pattern and received a kiss from my mother.

[*Test* Three] Hayden, I have four two digit numbers on my paper. I want you to write them down and add them up.

[*Result*] I correctly wrote three of the four numbers correctly.

[*Test Four*] Hayden, I have written down a number. What is it?

[*Result*] I correctly identified the number 81 as written.

My mother explained at dinner that she repeatedly had dreams about me being her daughter, not by adoption, but through the grace of God. I had heard my parents discuss my birth, which my parents called 'miraculous'. I didn't have a good understanding why, but I did understand that I was delivered to my parents by an angel of God.

My mother came home early from work to do more games with me. My mother had explained to me that her heart and my father's heart beat in an identical rhythm. My mother brought home her stethoscope that had a USB cable connection to her computer. My mother monitored her heart beat and I could see it appear on the monitor. My mother listened to my heart beat and explained that all hearts beat in a particular rhythm unique to the individual and as we listened, my heart rhythm appeared on the computer screen. I watched my heart beat when my mother superimposed her heart beat with mine on the screen, but only one heart beat was visible. My mother checked herself and then rechecked me. Both of our heartbeats were identified and recorded. My mother merged the two beats together again to show me each of our heart rhythms and the same problem occurred; just one heartbeat rhythm was actually visible on the screen. My mother checked my grandmother and grandfather and I could see each heartbeat. They were not in unison like my mother explained how hers and my father's hearts beat in unison. My mother put her heartbeat with my grandmothers and both showed separately. When she tried me and her again, there was only one heartbeat. My mother said, "Let's wait for your father and we will check him."

My father walked into the house and was immediately grabbed by my mother to lay out his heart beat with hers. Only one heartbeat showed. My mother added me and there was still only one heartbeat. After an hour of checking, my parents came to the realization that my heart beat in exactly the same rhythm as their hearts. My mother asked, "How can this be?" A complete stranger's daughter with developmental skills like I have and her heartbeat is in sync with our heartbeats. My mother teared up and said, "Ian, Hayden is a part of each of us joined together by God and then sent to earth by an angel to fulfill our desire to have a family." I am now absolutely convinced. I believe that Sir Arthur Conan Doyle stated, "When you have eliminated the impossible, whatever remains, however improbable, must be the truth." Hayden is of our being, created by God, and she is our biological child.

My mother explained to me that I was a gift from God. My biochemistry and blood type were identical to my parents. I looked like my parents and I knew I would be smart like my parents. My father held me and concluded that the medical evidence confirmed that I was a part of each of my parents." My parents were even more curious about my birth, the young woman that arrived to deliver this child, and what happened to her. My father reminded my mother that my birth mother's body was never found and he firmly believed that the young woman was an angel and returned to Heaven when her assigned task was completed.

My father said that he wanted to put to rest the question if I was of their bodies, or if I was a child of another. He explained, "I want all three of our DNA tested for consanguinity. This test will affirm or dispel Hayden's being of our bodies once and for all. If she is truly a gift from God, then her DNA should be in equivalence to our DNA. When the DNA results were returned, I watched my parents' faces and my mother and father cried and held me closely to both of them. I asked, "Is there a problem with my DNA?" My father explained that my DNA was a 99.892 percent match with my parents. My parents were a 100 per cent match which is common for identical twins. According to the results, my body chemistry is almost identical to my parents. The DNA testing confirmed that I was of the same kinship as my parents and my body was of their identical bodies. I was more than an adopted daughter. I was my parent's daughter, created by my Heavenly Father from their bodies and sent to earth in the womb of an angel. How that happened will always be a mystery unless you believe as my family does that angels do exist and God sent an angel to deliver the child he created to my parents that couldn't have children. When my grandfather heard the results, he commented, "When God made Eve, he took a rib from Adam. God could take a part of each of you and then create Hayden in the same manner that he created Eve. We all know that God's abilities are unlimited.

My mother decided to do some further testing on our ability to relate to each other. My mother held an ice cube in her right hand and watched me open my right hand and look. I looked at my mother and said, "That's cold."

My mother tasted lemon and I puckered up my face as my tongue moved in and out of my mouth. My mother asked me if I tasted sweet like candy. I replied, "No, sour."

My mother was really curious and asked me what she had in her hand. I replied, "Toy dog" which was correct. My mother couldn't wait to let my father know about my abilities. When my father learned about the test results, he too concluded that I was a gift from God. It was a wonderful thought being a gift from God. I liked being a little different, but then my parents were a little different as well and it is okay to be a little different now and then.

Becoming Friends

Life in the outback had some drawbacks. Our nearest neighbor was more than a mile away. There was little opportunity for children's activities in town which is why the 'bear restaurant' became my family's go to spot so I could be with other children. I was almost five years old, but for me it was home schooling all the way.

I was outside brushing Midnight, my riding and trail horse, when a large truck and a motor home drove down our road. I was surprised to see the motor home stop and pull into our driveway. Gary and Melody Stern, and their five-year-old daughter, Teri was in the process of constructing a new home next to ours. In the outback, the term 'next to' is about 1,000 feet away, but within eyesight. I heard Melody explain to my mother that they were residing in their motor home until their house was built. My mother invited the adults in for coffee and Teri helped me brush Midnight and put him in his temporary stall until my parents could return him to the horse barn. Teri expressed her desire to ride a horse and I received permission for her to sit on Midnight and I walked her around our yard. Teri asked me if we had any more horses and I let her know that we had four horses total. Three are boarded in the club stable and my Steeplechase horse is kept in an open field. Teri asked, "What is a steeplechase?" I explained that the steeplechase is a different type of riding where the rider and horse jump over different height fences and obstacles." Teri asked, "How big are your things?" I replied, "The obstacles are called fences. I am qualified to jump three-foot fences and this year I am going to qualify for four-foot fences." Teri replied, "That is over our heads. Aren't you afraid of falling off your horse?" I replied, "I have fallen numerous times already, but that is part of the challenge, especially when you are ready to jump and your horse isn't. I have gone over my horse's head and backwards as I rolled over his butt." Teri asked, "Did you get hurt when you fell off your horse?" I replied, "I have broken my arm once, but mostly my injuries have been in the form of embarrassment and humiliation."

I asked Teri if she would like to watch me ride the next time I run the steeplechase course. Just watching me ride excited my friend Teri. I explained that I would be riding to qualify for four foot fences this season. Teri looked up and said, "You would be way up there. Isn't it scary?" I replied, "Not scary to me because I enjoy the adrenalin rush when my horse leaps through the air and we complete a jump with my butt still in my jumping saddle."

I put away Midnight and invited Teri into my bedroom for some hot chocolate and cookies my grandmother made that morning. Teri commented, "You have a microwave in your bedroom?" I replied, "I need one to reheat my food while I am studying. I often forget to eat because I enjoy studying. As we sat drinking our hot chocolate, Teri began looking around and asked, "Is this all your bedroom?" I replied, "It is, but it is also too small. I need more space for a larger lab and more book shelves." Teri replied, "I don't even know what all this stuff is." I smiled and said, "That stuff as you called it are my toys, games and study center. I am homeschooled."

My mother offered to let the Sterns park their motor home on our property until they could safely move their motor home onto their own lot once the property was cleared. My mother looked at me and Teri playing with Mitzie and said, "I don't think the girls will object to you camping out here for a while." My mother also invited the Sterns to dinner and was pleased that they accepted her invitation. My mother looked at me and quietly said, "I really like them so far." I replied, "I like Teri. She is my age and Mitzie likes her too."

The adults were having coffee while Teri and I played in my bedroom. I heard my father land our helicopter on our landing pad in front of the house. Teri asked, "What is that noise? I replied, "My father just landed in our helicopter." I heard my mother say, "Here is Ian now." Melody asked, "In a helicopter?" My mother explained that the helicopter is the safest means of travel, especially in winter when our roads are covered with snow and compact ice."

Gary stood up to greet my father. My father entered the room and Gary shook his hand before realizing that my father was an identical twin to my mother. He asked, "Hayden called you mom and you dad, but you are apparently identical twins. How is that possible?" My mother replied, "Ian and I are near identical twins. We have chosen to live together and we adopted Hayden together. That is why Ian is her father and I am her mother." Melody uncomfortably shuffled in her chair and asked, "You are not like husband and wife, are you?" My mother replied, "It would take me a week to explain my relationship with Ian. We treat ourselves as partners and Hayden's parents." Melody replied, "I'm sorry, but I have to ask, "Do you sleep with Ian?" My mother politely replied, "I don't think that is any of your business. My apology, but Ian and I are wonderful parents to Hayden. We are together because our IQs are 160 and Hayden's is 144. We tried relationships with others, but Ian and I are intellectual equivalents and we have loved each other since we were born. If we offend you, then we are sorry that you feel that way. We are good people and I hope Hayden has the opportunity to play with Teri."

Melody replied, "My apology. I guess it is all right. It is something we need to get used to. In the meantime, I see that Teri and Hayden are having fun playing with Hayden's dog." Teri ran up to her mother and said, "Hayden and I are having so much fun with Mitze. She kisses us on the face and likes to play with us. Can we stay longer please?"

Our new neighbors turned out to be very nice people. Teri and I played at each other's houses and my grandparents would walk me over to Teri's house, or walk Teri home. Teri was my only friend in the outback. I liked playing with her and she liked playing with dolls and doing imaginary play; something that I had never done as a child. Teri's mother purchased some old dresses for us to play dress up. We would dress up in a long dress and wear high heels and a funny hat. Teri also had numerous board games that we liked to play together. It all seemed a little silly to me, but my friend liked to play dress up and I accommodated her method of play.

Teri liked playing at her house more than mine. My bedroom had a wall of books, two microscopes, slides, and workbooks for all subjects. I had a desktop computer and a laptop for when I wanted to sit outside and work. Teri asked me what I do at home for fun. I replied, "I mostly read and study. I ride my horse and of course, I play with Mitzie every day."

I was excited to show Teri my school books. Teri could read basic readers and she read to me. She picked up some of my literature books and asked if I read these books. I replied, "Every one of them. I love to read." Teri asked me about my math workbooks. I was doing exponential functions and algebraic equations. Teri looked at my math books and said, "I don't understand anything in there." Teri picked up my algebra book and showed her parents what kind of math I did. I heard her mother say, "I don't think so. I think Hayden is pulling your leg. I walked out behind Teri and mentioned that I was almost done with the workbook and would start geometry in about a month.

I took Teri's hand and said, "Let's play." Teri replied, "Play with what? All of your things are for learning stuff." Teri's dad had been looking at my algebra book and he asked me to solve the problem he selected. He wrote out a long equation with multiple exponents in fraction form and asked me to reduce the fractional equation to its simplest form. He smiled and said, "I will give you thirty minutes to answer." I looked at the problem and said the answer in simplest form is 1. He asked me how I knew the answer so quickly. I replied, "Anything to the zero power is one." I giggled, because this type of game I liked to play. I factored each problem and did the proof for the quadric formula which surprised Teri's father.

My father offered to show Teri's parents my bedroom; that is if it is alright with me. I said, "Sure, come on in." Melody looked at me and said, "Don't worry, we won't mind if your bedroom is messy." Teri's parents couldn't believe the things I had in my bedroom. In addition to my personal library, I had work platform, two computers, a stethoscope, two power variations of microscopes' a full slide pack of samples for the microscope, an autoclave, Bunsen burner, helium and oxygen lines, a refrigerator, an academic and music section. Teri's parents kept looking around and asked, "Where is the TV?" and then asked how my parents had the time to supervise me in my bedroom activities. My mother replied, "We don't own a TV and Hayden is very skilled in what she does and we don't worry about her too much." Hayden understands the products she works with and we have absolute trust in her." Melody commented, "Hayden's room is spotless and organized." I replied, "I like everything to be in its place."

Teri looked at her mother and said, "Look at Hayden's reading books." On my bookshelf were literary classics followed by scientific journals; academic workbooks and everything else. Teri's mother replied, "Good God, I wasn't reading these books until high school and college."

My mother was having coffee with Melody when she explained about some of her gifts that I also shared. My mother talked about her healing skill and how she healed my father several times and me once when I fell off Tempest and broke my arm. I am a person that watches people's eyes to see what they are thinking. I could tell that Melody didn't believe my mother had healing skills. That afternoon Teri pretended to be my steeplechase horse, Tempest, and she jumped off our porch and broke her arm. My mother checked her arm and indicated that there was a hairline fracture above the wrist. My mother offered to try to heal Teri's break. Within minutes, Teri was back to normal and Melody started to be a little more accepting of who we were.

My mother asked me if I wanted to play a couple games before we returned to playing outside. I replied, "Fine. You know I like games." My mother asked Melody to write three numbers on something and put it in her purse. My mother said, "Hayden, what are the numbers?" I was correct. My mother encouraged Melody to ask me a question. She replied, "Okay Hayden, what do I have in my purse." I was correct on eleven of twelve items. Teri said, "Hayden, guess my number?" I replied, "A Million Bazillion." Teri said, "How did you do that?"

My mother told Melody about my unique birth. When my mother said that they truly believe an angel delivered me to my parents, Melody rolled her eyes and replied, "Yeah, right." I could see absolute doubt in Melody's eyes and her doubt in the tone of her voice. My mother explained that a complete stranger appeared at the medical center wearing nothing but a white nightgown. Outside was freezing rain and snow and the young woman was barefoot, without a coat, and just standing on the steps to the clinic. My mother asked if the young woman had an appointment, but all she would do is keep stating, "I am here to deliver this child." Ian had to do a C-section and the young woman died instantly when the anesthetic was dispensed. Ian delivered her baby; our Hayden. Ian took DNA samples from Hayden and the young, unidentified mother. When the lab sent back the DNA results, the lab concluded that the birth mother's DNA samples were contaminated because the DNA structure was both male and female. My mother went on to explain that what was even more unusual is that none of Hayden's bio-chemistry and blood was even close in proximity to the birth mother confirming that Hayden's birth mother was either an angel or a surrogate. I heard Melody say, "I am sure that she must have been a surrogate. Angels? Really?"

My mother explained, "Even more unusual, Ian ordered the young woman's body to be returned to the operatory to take new DNA samples. The orderly reported, "She isn't in the morgue where I placed her body." After a complete search of the medical center, the only item found was the surgical gown she was wearing. Her body has never been found. Melody said, "I find this incredible." I replied, "If you want incredible, please keep listening."

Ian and I wanted to get a good DNA reading from Hayden. At this point, Ian and I began to believe that the young woman was an angel bringing Hayden to us since we can't have children. When our DNA results were returned, Ian and I are 100 percent alike which is common for identical twins. Hayden was 99.892 percent of our DNA. Medically speaking, Hayden is of our blood and our bio chemistry. The DNA results would be an absolute medical confirmation that Hayden is our natural child. One more point; at rest, Ian and my hearts beat in perfect unison. If I put my heart beat on the computer and overlay Ian's, you will see one heartbeat. I overlaid Hayden's heartbeat and her heartbeat is in identical unison to our own hearts. Now tell me that Hayden isn't our natural biological child created in Heaven and carried to us through an angel.

Melody asked, "I would like to see your heartbeat and Hayden's heart beat." I looked and Melody's skepticism was obvious. She didn't call my mother a liar, but her expression and intonation sounded like she was. My mother put her heart rhythm on the monitor and then overlaid mine. We were exact and in perfect synchronization. My mother said, "If Ian were here, his would also be one single line. Melody asked if she could put hers and Teri's on the monitor. When my mother overlaid their heartbeats, they weren't even close to matching. My mother did mine and hers one more time and a single heart beat was seen and heard. Melody concluded that my birth was unusual, but wasn't convinced of the concept of an angel of God being my birth mother. My mother said, "I forgot to mention one more important event following Hayden's birth. We researched male and female chromosomes and according to literature on angels, they are hermaphrodite or male and female. The original DNA evidence confirmed that the birth mother's DNA sample was male and female strongly suggesting that Hayden's birth mother was in fact an angel.

Melody said, "I'm sorry Eli, but I just can't buy the angel thing." Melody sat for a minute and then asked, "What did you say the young woman's name was?" My mother replied, "I believe it was Michaele something. The last name was unreadable; at least that is the name on the identification card she produced. Her picture didn't look like her either." Melody wrote out "Michaele" on a piece of paper and asked, "Did you make this observation?" My mother asked, "What observation?" Melody erased the 'e' on the end of the name and then asked me, "What does that spell?" I replied for my mother, "Michael". Melody said, "This is very unnerving." Did you know that Archangel Michael is a messenger angel for God?" I heard what Melody said and I grabbed my laptop and looked up the Archangel Michael. According to the Biblical information source, Michael was one of the seven Archangels and specifically a messenger angel carrying out God's will.

My mother explained that she referred to the birth mother as "Jane Doe" and never had reason to look back at the name given. My mother said, "I feel a little foolish." My mother held me and asked what I thought about the possible disclosure of the Archangel Michael that brought me to them. I looked at my mother and thanked the Archangel Michael and God for creating me in my parents' image and then delivering me. That evening, I took extra prayer time to thank God for sending me to my parents through Archangel Michael, the angel of God.

I felt really special after discovering who my birth parent really was and that I was created in Heaven by my Heavenly Father. I concluded that my birth mother didn't die on the delivery table. Instead, she completed her mission and returned to Heaven. I often feel like I have an angel looking over my shoulder holding me accountable for the life I received at the will of my Father, God almighty who through him all things are possible; even the birth of a very special little girl whose intended parents could not bear children. To me, there is no other reasonable explanation for how I am truly of my parents' bodies and mind.

The Steeplechase

My mother and Melody were having coffee when I noticed the time and mentioned to my mother that I had to be on the Steeplechase field for practice at 4:00 p.m. My mother looked at her watch and said, "I can't believe I forgot your practice. If you do not attend to your practice runs, the association will deny you participation in the qualifying field events." I replied, "Teri, sorry, but I have to get ready to practice on the steeplechase field. My qualification round is in two weeks and if I don't score high enough in practice, I will not get into the qualifying round." I looked at my mother and said, "We had better hurry. I need to get Tempest and I need to change into my breeches." My mother said, "Hayden, please hurry so you are not late."

Melody explained to my mother that she grew up around horses. She saw my horse out front and saw the horse trailer on the side drive. She said, "Maybe while you and Hayden are getting ready, I can load up Hayden's horse." I quickly yelled out to Melody that the horse out front is my riding and trail horse. Tempest is a thoroughbred gelding jumper that is boarded near the steeplechase competition field. Teri asked, "Hayden, can I come and watch you ride Tempest." I replied, "I don't mind, but when I am preparing for my run, please do not talk to me. This year I am clearing four-foot fences and I need full concentration." Melody asked if she could tag along too. My mother replied, "The more the merrier. Just don't talk with Hayden if she is preparing for her run. To Hayden, this is very serious business." Melody said, "I will keep my mouth shut."

I walked out of my room wearing my white breeches, high English riding boots, and my shirt and jacket with my assigned association number. I had my helmet in hand; something my father calls my 'Brain Bucket'. My mother looked me over and said, "You look complete. Remember, you are jumping four foot fences this year; not three like last year." Teri asked to carry my helmet and crop. Melody looked at her watch and asked, "How are you going to get Hayden's horse and be at the event by 4:00 p.m.? My mother replied, "By helicopter of course." This was Melody and Teri's first helicopter ride and they couldn't stop talking about it.

We arrived at Milner Pond Horse Ranch and Teri asked me, "Where is your horse Tempest?" I pointed to a horse clear across the field and said, "Watch this." I blew my whistle and Tempest came running. I quickly brushed out Tempest, saddled him and then walked Tempest to the equestrian field and registered with eight minutes to spare. Just like last year, I was the youngest rider and my experience level was referred to as intermediate. I had to qualify five times at the intermediate level before I could try to qualify at the six-foot fence professional level.

I informed my mother that I was fifth out of the start line. My mother suggested that she and Melody get some coffee because it will be about twenty minutes before I made my first run at the course. Teri insisted she stand with me and Tempest, which was a little irritating as I was trying to focus on the field and my competition. I listened and heard "Next up in stand-by, number 32, Tempest ridden by Hayden Gehardi. Hayden is the youngest jumper to enter the field this season." I explained to Teri that I needed to be on the start line on time or I would be disqualified. I asked Teri to stand back as I mentally prepared for my run.

I kept in the back of my head that my qualification score would be the best three out of five runs. I patiently waited and was told to go. I cleared the first three four-foot National Fence hurdles and easily jumped over three water hazards when Tempest hesitated on the next jump which resulted in me being thrown off my horse at approximately twenty miles per hour. Fortunately, the grassy field is softer than dirt. I felt humiliated and walked back to the stand-by line waiting for my next run. My white breeches were marred with green grass stains and dirt, but it was my ego that hurt the worst. My mother quickly checked me over and I was fine and ready to go on my second run which was flawless except my breaches split in the back. Fortunately, I bring several pair of breeches to every competition. My mother and Teri held a blanket and I quickly replaced my torn breaches and remounted Tempest. Melody was standing near Tempest and she commented about the muscles in Tempest's legs. I replied, "He is a jumper and I work my horse hard to develop and maintain those muscles. Next year I am going to start six-foot fences if I do well this year."

I was impatient to get my third run in when everything shut down and a golf-cart type ambulance drove onto the field to recover an injured rider. The man was hurting in his neck and it appeared that he broke several bones when his horse rolled onto him. The accident postponed the qualifying round by nearly an hour. My mother wanted me to eat something, but I reminded her that I never eat until the competition is over. The injured man reduced my field to 9 participants. Only six would qualify for the next round.

I heard static over the PA system and the announcer ordered all intermediate jumpers to return to the stand-by area. Because of the delay, the sponsor drew names for the order of competition. My name was first. I was told to get my horse in the ready box. I patted Tempest and prayed he would protect me as we soared through the obstacle course. It is as if I was asleep because it was a blink of my eye and we were over the finish line with another perfect score. I had no idea where the time went. I mentioned what happened to my mother and she insisted I eat some protein or I might get hurt. I grabbed my mother's ham and cheese sandwich and took a bite and replied, "I ate!"

I carefully watched my competition and had to remind Teri several times to please be quiet when I am evaluating the field. Teri replied, "Hayden, don't get so mad. It's just a stupid horse event." To me it was more than an event; being successful in all I do is important to me and I personally strive to be the best I can be at everything I do. I smiled as two more riders were disqualified leaving seven in the qualification round. I had to do well or I would be competing over three-foot fences again this year. I was called and Tempest did magnificently. I had another flawless ride, but then, so did the other competitors. On my last and final qualifying ride Tempest knocked down one fence lateral and we finished. I expected I would be stricken, but the next rider fell off on the second fence and the last rider fell in a water hazard leaving me in fourth place. I was thrilled that I qualified.

Teri walked with me back to where Tempest was boarded and we took turns washing and brushing him. Teri asked me, "Why doesn't Tempest live inside the barn like most horses?" I replied, "Thoroughbred horses need the natural environment to be free, run and kick their hooves in the air. Tempest can't do that in a barn. The best way to destroy a jumper is to lock him up in a small barn stall. When Tempest is outside and it is cold I put one of three types of horse blankets or sheets on him. I slapped Tempest on the butt and he ran across the meadow and joined up with other jumpers as he kicked his rear heels high in the air. When Tempest reached the grassy field area, he rolled onto his back and looked a little silly to Teri. I explained that Tempest was relaxing after a hard day at work.

Teri liked watching me ride and jump. She held her hands up as high as she could and commented, "Did you know that Tempest jumps this high, pointing to his reins." I replied, "From up here where I am seated, one might think my horse was trying to jump over the moon." I helped Teri mount Tempest and she quickly said, "Help me down Hayden. This horse is way too big for me." I explained that Tempest was almost two hands taller than my riding and trail horse. He is big and he is strong so be careful that he never steps on your foot.

The following Saturday I was entered into the Association's qualification ride for the upcoming season. I was in group two, which included all prequalified riders over four-foot fences. I was somewhat surprised that there were fourteen prequalified riders like me. The riders came from five different states just to qualify for the season. In the catalog for qualification riding, eight riders would be qualified to ride the field and one would be a back-up in the event of an injury to a horse or rider.

I carefully watched the riders in positions two through five and each rode the field perfectly in my opinion. I hugged Tempest and asked him to run like the wind and soar like an Eagle. Tempest came in on the fastest time and a perfect ride. Teri and my mother congratulated me on a near perfect ride. I replied, "It is Tempest that needs to be congratulated, I am just along for the ride."

On the second round, I was jumping the six-foot water hazard and I fell off Tempest landing on my head and back. I was dazed, but I felt I was alright. Tempest walked over to me and put his head down so I could grab his reins and remount. I think Tempest was wondering why I was sitting on the ground instead of my jumping saddle. It took me four tries to remount Tempest. I knew in the back of my mind that I had to do it myself and finish the run or I would forfeit qualification. I am not sure how I did it, but I jumped and found myself seated and ready to go. I couldn't have help or I would be disqualified, but something boosted me onto my horse that day. I thanked my guardian angel and I finished the field to avoid disqualification. I received a lot of "Too bad" and "Bad luck" to "I thought you were a little young to be in this qualification event." Of course, that ignited my competitive spirit and I replied to all the riders, "Don't mess up because I am coming behind you and I am not going to make any further mistakes." I heard laughs and comments like, "We'll see how you do."

True to my word, I finished my last five rounds without error and I qualified for the season in fourth place which was acceptable. I received kudos from the other riders that previously mocked me after I fell in the first round. I walked Tempest over to where my mother and Teri was sitting and replied, "I qualified!" My mother replied, "Did you have any doubts?" I replied, "When I fell off of Tempest in the first run, I thought my participation in the Steeplechase events for this year was over. Fortunately, Tempest performed magnificently and I kept my butt in the saddle."

Teri developed an acute interest in riding horses, but then, most girls love to ride. My mother allowed Teri to ride her horse; a polite mare that worked well with any rider. My mother flew Teri and me to a riding barn where we could simply ride and have fun. Over the day, Teri learned a great deal about how to manage 1,800 pounds of horse under her butt. Melody watched Teri and commented, "I suppose now we will need to buy Teri a horse." I replied, "Teri can ride one of my parent's horses unless both of my parents go riding. Two weeks later and Melody asked me and my mother to check out three mares that they found for sale. We visited all three horses; had Teri sit on the horse and then ride the horse around the corrals. Teri chose a calm four-year-old mare and agreed to purchase her following a positive vet check. Teri excitedly boarded her horse, Jackson next to Midnight.

I had fun teaching Teri about English and Western riding. Melody took me and Teri shopping for English riding boots, breeches, helmet and gloves. Teri wanted western wear, but when the total was figured on her English riding gear, it was already over $945 and the western wear would have totaled another $1,200 and those prices were exclusive of the English and western saddles that were more than $1,300 apiece. Melody said, "So far we have $3,800 for Teri's horse; $1,520 in English and western riding wear, $380 a month boarding fees, $1,384 for an English saddle and Teri had to have a western saddle at another 1,140 used. All that cost and Teri can't even ride yet." I promised to teach Teri English and Western riding at the stable.

Throughout the summer I competed in Steeplechase events and taught Teri how to ride. By the end of summer, I took fifth place for the season which was where I expected to be. I needed this season to make the jump to six-foot fences next year. Teri was doing exceptionally well in both English and Western riding. Melody and Gary watched Teri ride and they concluded they had made the right financial decision to purchase a horse and riding gear for Teri. I knew it was the right decision because I could ride with Teri on our trails and we had something to do that we both enjoyed.

Summer seemed to disappear much too quickly this year. It was predicted to be another cold, snowy winter. I reminded Teri and Melody that they needed to purchase one or two horse blankets for the winter. I suggested a light weight and a heavy weight blanket and I explained when one over the other should be used. Teri asked, "Why does my horse need a blanket since she is inside the barn?" I replied, "Because it gets very cold in the barn." My mother and I took Teri to the barn after the first snow to check up on our horses. Teri commented, "It is really cold in this barn."

Fall meant back to my studies. I went shopping with my mother for more advanced school textbooks and I needed more products for my chemistry and biology studies. Our town was small, but one of the communities' most popular stores was the corner drug store. The owners devoted one fourth of the store to educational products and toys. We could generally find most of the science supplies I needed at this store. My mother understood me well and would point me in the direction of educational supplies and I could select what I would need for the next school year. If the store didn't have what I needed, they ordered it for delivery to my home. Across from the science and school supplies was an old-fashioned ice cream parlor where my mother and I could sit on counter stools and enjoy an ice cream cone. I arranged for Teri to join me for ice cream and she loved the old-fashioned ice cream parlor and its spinning stool seats.

I sat at the convenience table and reviewed my educational goals for the coming year. I needed geometry and trigonometry workbooks, charting pads, macro biology and chemistry, and a United States history book. Most of my research was on line and I take a national test annually to measure my academic progress. At age six, I was already testing higher than our high school graduates. In my spare time, I studied systems of the body, bones and bone structure including ligaments, and any other information that was necessary to satisfy my personal annual learning goals.

The guiding light of my educational goals was the MCAT or Medical College Admission Test. I knew that I would be tested on my knowledge of science, reasoning, communication and writing skills and I kept my focus on my goal of taking the MCAT before my tenth birthday. I am fortunate because my parents are both medical doctors and they can explain something if I am confused. I typically used three hours of study time daily preparing for the MCAT while the remainder of my time was spent preparing to take the G.E.D or General Equivalency Diploma so I could enter college early.

What is an IQ Anyway?

My last IQ, or Intelligence Quotient, was completed when I was two years old and many of the testing parameters were subjective observations. At six, I could take the full adult Stanford-Binet test which is designed to measure knowledge, quantitative reasoning, visual-spatial processing, working memory and fluid reasoning. I can also take the Wechsler Adult Intelligence Sale which also tested for the same things as the Stanford-Benet test. Like my parents, I felt it is good to have two tests to add validity and reliability to my IQ scores. I asked my mother to schedule me for both tests. I would like to take one test in the early morning and the other in the late afternoon; unless we sleep over and test the next morning. My mother decided that we would get a hotel room and sleep over so I would be fresh when taking each test. The testing facility was located in our state university. My mother and I flew there in our helicopter and we decided to arrive a day early so I had a full night's sleep for both exams. My mother and I arrived at the testing facility and I was immediately challenged since I didn't look old enough to take the adult intelligence test. In fact, I was two months early, but the proctor accepted my mother's statement of my personal qualification to take the test.

I was escorted into a large testing room where at least one hundred desks were lined up in straight rows. I was told to empty my pockets and surrender all personal property except jewelry and clothing. There was one other person being tested that day. The proctor announced that I would have three hours to complete the test. I raised my hand and asked, "If I am done early, may I turn in my test and leave?" The proctor replied, "I wouldn't worry about that. No one that I have tested has ever finished the test within the allotted time." I replied, "Thank you and waited for my test." The proctor insulted me by asking if I was sure I understood the big words in the test and if I would be comfortable taking it verses the child version." I replied, "I am ready for the adult level tests." I received the test and turned it in forty-eight minutes later. The proctor asked, "Did you give up?" I was a little agitated and I sneered at him and said, "No. I finished the test." I handed him my test and walked out. I looked back one more time to express my frustration over the proctor's negative remarks. My mother saw me and asked, "What took you so long?" Unlike the proctor, my mother knew me well.

The following morning, I took the Wechsler Intelligence test. This time a very friendly and supportive woman was the proctor. She bugged me too by saying, "Honey, just do your best. This is a big test for such a young lady." My insides boiled up a little as I repeated for the third time that I was ready to take the test. She patted me on my head and said, "Good luck and don't get disappointed if you don't know something. Just skip it and move on to your next question. I was ready to scream out when she handed me my test. I finished in fifty-two minutes and explained to my mother that I was held up by the proctor.

I talked with my mother about her IQ and my father's IQ at 160. I expressed my hope that I would test well. My mother commented, "You are our daughter and part of us. Of course, you will do well on the tests." My test scores arrived a week later and I anxiously opened both envelopes. My averaged IQ score was 144 which my mother explained is very good. I began receiving applications from MENSA and other gifted schools and programs. I wasn't interested in sitting around listening to someone brag about their IQ score. If I wasn't studying, I was riding, playing with Teri, or swimming.

Teri and her family stopped by for dinner and music. Melody asked my mother how my IQ testing turned out. My mother replied, "Hayden did just fine, why?" Melody explained that she had been doing some thinking about Hayden, angels and her likeness to us as adoptive parents and wondered if Hayden also shared our IQs. My mother replied, "Hayden did very well." Melody, not willing to let it drop asked, "How did she do? What was her score? I would suppose that she didn't get close to your score. My nephew is a near genius and his score was 114." My mother explained that the tests no longer use terms like 'Genius'. Hayden's combined score was 144. Under current guidelines 130-144 is very advanced and was formerly very gifted. Your nephew would be considered 'High Average' under today's scoring guidelines.

Maybe I am a little rude, but I watched Melody's eyes turn in and her voice became a little terse when she suggested that Teri may not be bright enough to interact with me because of my big brain. Teri and I heard what Melody said and Teri started crying which caused me to cry too. Teri pleaded with her mother to let her play with me. Melody responded, "We will see if you can fit in around Hayden and her brain." I heard what Melody said and I replied, "I work very hard at being smart. I work more than ten hours a day studying current subject matter and an additional three hours a day studying for the MCAT. Your comments about Teri and my brain are insulting and derogatory. I would say, "Hurtful" Please be supportive of me and Teri. I love Teri and she is smart – probably smarter than you might realize if you would take the time to listen to her and not judge her in relation to me." Melody looked at my mother and said, "I think I was just told off by a six-year-old."

Surviving Winter in the Wilderness

Our anticipated early winter hit hard and fast dumping twenty-three inches of snow in the first snowfall. It was obvious that many people in our community were ill-prepared for the onset of an early winter despite the daily news announcements that winter was coming quickly.

The medical center was literally overrun with patients afflicted with soft tissue injuries caused by low impact car accidents to slips and falls. I was home with my mother and grandmother doing some validity testing for my premonition skills when my mother asked me, "When the phone rings, who will be calling and why?" I replied, "My father will call on your cell phone. I believe the medical center is overrun with injured patients and he will ask us to work." The phone rang eleven minutes later. My father said, "I need all hands-on deck." My mother, me and grandparents left immediately for the medical center to provide assistance where needed.

We arrived to see the intake clerk inundated with patients waiting to be seen in emergency care. My grandmother joined the intake section and began processing patients. My grandfather prepared patient identification bracelets and helped move patients from the intake center to the emergency room. I volunteered at the medical center and typically I was the clinical gopher getting supplies and helping to move patients from one exam room to radiology or surgery. My parents purchased me a white lab coat with my name on the pocket. Underneath said, "Future OB/GYN." The medical center patients were usually happy to see me and I was pleased to be doing something other than sitting at home studying.

My mother grabbed me and said, "Come with me. I want you to learn about emergency triage today." We had forty-one patients in the intake holding area. My mother produced a series of tags colored red, yellow and green. Red meant the patient needed urgent care; usually the patient was bleeding or a significant medical condition existed like chest pains or a heart attack. If the tag was red, then I needed to contact a department once the patient was stabilized in the emergency room. The yellow indicted distress, but not serious injuries and the green was routine care for colds, flues and the like. Three hours later my mother and I completed triage and all the reds had been treated or sent into the emergency room for immediate care. After my first hour of observing my mother, she allowed me to meet with the patient, assess their medical need and then tag the patient. It was fun and the patients didn't even question my involvement. I wondered if it was my white lab coat.

I was very fortunate because I wanted to be a doctor and specifically an OB/GYN like my father. At six years old, I was very mature and communicated well with others at the medical center. I was permitted to wear scrubs and indirectly participate in C-section surgeries, normal deliveries and well-baby care. Once the patients understood that I was very bright and planned on being a doctor like my parents, they openly welcomed me into their care circle. My father and mother were so pleased with how I handled the emergency crunch that they planned into my weekly schedule two days a week where I could work at the medical center. I observed and sometimes assisted in more than thirty C-section births and over one hundred natural births by the time I was ready to take the MCAT. When time permitted, I sat in my parent's office and studied anatomy and physiology; medical conditions and various treatment modalities available from pharmacology to surgery and physical therapy. When I walked rounds with my parents, they would quiz me on a diagnosis and method of treatment. I looked forward to my time working at the medical center. The experience ingrained into my sole the desire to become a good medical doctor. I worked through the winter months and spring arrived along with my seventh birthday.

In a way, working with my parents was a negative in that my best friend, Teri and I seemed to drift apart and we spent little time together. When Teri did stop by, she was usually angry and asked, "How much time do I get to spend with you today? Five minutes?" I was frustrated because I needed Teri to be my friend, but I equally desired to improve my medical knowledge. The two goals seemed to be in conflict and irreconcilable. I was sitting at my work station at the medical center when my mother walked in and said she sensed I was frustrated or angry. She looked at me and said, "Talk to me Hayden." I explained my dilemma in reconciling my love of learning and my love for my best friend. My mother could see tears in my eyes and she said she understood how I was feeling. She commented, "What you are feeling is similar to what your father and I felt as we grew up together. We needed each other like you need Teri's friendship." I began to cry and said that Teri is so angry with me that she is avoiding me because I avoided her. My mother held me and when we landed that night, my mother and I walked over to Teri's house. Teri answered the door and I gave her a hug and kiss and said, "I love you Teri. I promise to spend more time with you because I miss you and the fun we share together." Teri cried and said, "Thank you Hayden. I have been so lonely without you to play with." My father was working late and Melody invited us to stay for dinner. She explained that staying a while would give me and Teri a chance to play together. My mother laughed when Teri and I walked into the room wearing old dresses that drug on the floor, old high heels and hats. Although I play differently, this was Teri's house and she could select what we did. I just liked being with my friend.

Teri asked me if I could join her swim club at our local community center. She explained that by joining, I know I will have you with me for four hours a week. I replied, "Teri that sounds like fun, but I can't swim very well." Teri smiled and replied, "I swim like a fish and I will teach you to swim." Teri's eyes brightened quickly knowing that even she could contribute to my education; or at least my well-being. My mother flew us to swimming twice a week and I made sure that Teri spent the night with me or me with her, at least once a week. I refused to lose my best friend. I learned that finding the time to be with Teri required me to jostle my own schedule. As much as I wanted to be with Teri, I had a goal of taking the MCAT not later than my tenth birthday. I prayed for an answer that could preserve my friendship with Teri while continuing to meet my study goals.

Melody and Teri stopped by our house to announce that Teri was beginning home schooling. Melody explained that she wasn't satisfied with St. John's Catholic School and Teri was bored and wanted to accelerate her academics like I do. This was my answer to my prayer. My mother purchased another chair for my study table and Teri would quietly join me studying in my bedroom. I appreciated that Teri respected my study time and she infrequently interrupted me which kept our arrangement working. Teri studied with me on the days we went swimming. That worked out well because we were in the throes of another wilderness winter where the outside temperature rarely exceeded the ten-degree mark. Over a few months I noticed Teri became more familiar with my study routine and she learned to develop her own learning goals. By age seven, we were two girls highly motivated to learn and have fun.

Just before Christmas I announced to my parents that I had modified my education goals. It was my intention to take the G.E.D. or General Equivalency Diploma after Christmas. I made application and the state rejected my application due to my age. My parents effectively argued my case to the state Superintendent of Schools that I was more than qualified and academically mature to move into college coursework. I was required to meet with an educational evaluation group of four college instructors. I was orally tested on my knowledge of chemistry, biology, physics, all levels of math through calculus, reading and reading comprehension, spelling and speech. I was evaluated and granted my exception to take the GED early. I scored in the 96th percentile and received my high school equivalency diploma.

I applied for full time studies at our state university. I was denied admission until I had completed the precollege admission's test. Once again, I was fortunate that the test would be given in two months. I worked on my medical studies while waiting to take the precollege admission's test. When the time came, I scored in the 97th percentile which was more than needed to matriculate at our university.

My parents graduated from undergraduate college by challenging all the courses necessary to enter medical school. I wasn't so fortunate. I was permitted to take pass/fail exams for math, writing, reading, history, cultural anthropology, macro and micro biology and chemistry. I was required to take the 300 and 400 level coursework in chemistry and biology and the general form of calculus. I had enrolled for the start of the winter semester, subject to my successful scores on the precollege test. I was almost seven years old when I started taking college classes. I received pass grades on all classes where I took the final exam for credit. The university refused my ability to do pass/fail on all classes. Due to my age, my mother had to be with me while I was on campus. My mother didn't mind since she had to fly me to college every day anyway. I completed the maximum 25 credits for my first semester and I finished my coursework during the second semester. I effectively graduated from college in one year with a 4.0 average.

My parents wanted to celebrate my graduation with a trip somewhere. It was summer and Teri was home and agreed to vacation with us for three weeks in Florida. My parents hired temporary physicians to cover for them and we were off to Florida. My father insisted we fly first class and that excited Teri since she had never flown that way. Teri and I sat together and ordered our drinks, food, desert and more desert and more drinks until we were nearly sick. The first-class cabin flight attendant said that we kept her busy. I looked at her and asked, "Do you have any more deserts?"

My father asked me and Teri where we wanted to go. Both Teri and I said, "Disney World" and then Universal Studios, and then the NASA Space Center. We arrived at Disney World and my parents allowed and look at exhibits. I had my cell phone in my pocket and my mother admonished me to keep my phone on and the ringer on loud. I took off holding Teri's hand as we ran to the first ride. I really had fun being with Teri and doing what most kids do. I have to admit that at night when Teri slept, my brain was reviewing materials I had studied for the MCAT. When vacation ended, I was personally exhausted. Having fun was more work than studying. The important thing was I had Teri with me and we had fun together. I hoped that our little vacation would fill the emptiness Teri felt when I was tied up with my own schooling and work responsibilities.

James A. Gauthier, J.D.

MCAT – How old are you?

I finished my vacation and verified when the MCAT was being given. I checked my calendar and it was scheduled for August that year. I had plenty of time to prepare which excited me. I would shut myself in my bedroom and I studied the type of subject matter that would be tested. I had excellent understanding of math, chemistry and biology, but I was lacking in some of the spatial reasoning activities. My mother had been shopping with my grandmother when she returned with a present for me. I replied, "It's not my birthday." My mother said, "Just open the package. I'm sure you will like it." I tore open the paper and my eyes lit up and my mother said I had a smile on my face from ear to ear. She had purchased a MCAT study manual that contained ten practice tests. I kissed my mother and said, "Call me in August. You know where I will be."

I shut myself in my bedroom and took the first practice MCAT test and scored 77 percent. That was an unacceptable outcome. I studied close to fifteen hours a day and discontinued volunteering at the medical center until I completed the MCAT example tests correctly. My mother would bring me iced tea and a sandwich, or soup in a cup and similar food so I could continue my studies. I had bowls of carrots, celery sticks, spray cheese and fruit to snack on throughout the day. My parent's only rule was that I had to join them for Sunday dinner which was fine with me.

By the end of July, I had successfully completed all ten MCAT pretests and felt I was ready to take the actual exam. The problem was the university wasn't ready for me. I was almost eight years old and my application to sit for the MCAT was denied. I filed a petition for review and reconsideration and requested a personal hearing before the medical school's admission board. I carefully documented my education, training, preparation and desire as a future doctor. My father said, "Don't be too upset if they reject you due to your age. You are brilliant, but probably too young to consider admission into the medical school. I replied, "You and mom were young and you were admitted and graduated at age fourteen. I am not too young and I will prove it to the admission's board."

I received a letter from the chairperson of the university medical board advising me that I could have my requested hearing, but a precondition was I get another IQ test to validate my last scores. I read the rest of the letter and unfortunately, the time appropriated for my hearing was after the MCAT cutoff date. I personally called the dean of the medical school and explained that I needed the hearing to qualify me to sit for the upcoming MCAT. I must have said what he wanted to hear because I received notification from the admission's board that a qualification hearing would be held in two weeks. My mother made arrangements for me to retake the two IQ tests in the interim. I was surprised that my averaged score was 154. I had increased by ten points. My mother said, "Good girl. I know you are our daughter. From here forward, you are not adopted – you are our natural child." I hugged my mother and replied, "I knew that already." My mother asked me, "What did you know?" I replied, "Scientifically my DNA matches my parents' DNA structure. Our hearts beat in a synchronized rhythm; I am smart just like my parents; my birth mother was an Archangel from God. Her DNA was male/female which is consistent with the biblical explanation that angels are hermaphrodites…Should I keep going?" My mother just smiled and replied, "No, I think you have identified enough."

I arrived at the interview with my mother and the board had five representatives in attendance. I was asked to sit at a desk across from the doctors that would be questioning me. The admission's chair made the comment that my application for review and reconsideration was very well written and quite persuasive. He looked me in my eyes and asked, "How much of the petition for review and reconsideration was written by your parents?" I replied, "None of it. I wrote everything and I meant what I wrote. If you want an excellent medical student, then you will allow me to sit for the MCAT exam."

I answered questions for nearly three hours about such things as anatomy, physiology, chemistry and philosophy. When the hearing was concluded, the chair suggested that I would hear from them in writing within thirty days. I replied, "The MCAT is scheduled for eighteen days from today. I need your approval today so I can get mentally prepared to take the MCAT. The doctors talked back and forth like I wasn't present in the room. The chair then turned to me and said, "Young lady, we will give you a chance to take the MCAT. However, if your score is below 78 percent, then you are going to have to wait until you are twelve to retake the exam. Is that understood?" I replied, "I fully understand and accept those testing terms."

Two days before the MCAT exam, I invited Teri to join me at the 'bear restaurant'. I needed my best friend to relax and clear my head before the exam. Teri and I played most of the games and had fun making hats, painting our faces like clowns and of course, eating too much cake and pie for our own good. Teri had started calling me Dr. Hayden. To level our playing field, I called Teri Dr. Teri. We both enjoyed our unearned titles. We were cutting out animal shapes for the animal tree when Teri asked me, "How is it that you are so smart. You look at something and learn immediately. I wish I were smart like you." I explained to Teri that I work on my education close to twelve to fifteen hours a day. What I do as fun would be work for most people. I like to learn new things and challenge myself. I work on goals and specific objectives to get me to my goals. I am what is referred to as a 'goal oriented personality'. I will gladly work with you in setting up your learning goals and objectives. The most important thing is, "Set your mind that you are going to accomplish the goal or objective and then do it. Don't make excuses or lie to yourself. The only person you cheat is yourself for only you are accountable for what you do or fail to do."

Teri asked me, "What objectives and goals are you talking about?" I explained to Teri that my end goal is to become a licensed, board certified OB/GYN. My objectives are the steps I need to complete in order to achieve my goal. In my situation, can you name an objective I need to accomplish in order to achieve my goal? Teri replied, "Don't you have to graduate from college?" I replied, "Yes I do. Good choice." I wrote Goal and objective 1. Get my undergraduate degree. Beside the notation I wrote "Accomplished and the date." Teri asked, "What is an undergraduate degree?" I replied, "It is your completion of the first four years of college. Without a college degree I cannot apply to medical school." I asked Teri for another objective. She replied, "You need to pass the MCAT." I replied, "Good". Can you think of anymore? Teri replied, "You need to get accepted to study in the medical school. I replied, "You are correct again. Once you accomplish your objective or bench mark then reevaluate your goals and objectives, possibly increasing the scope of your learning objectives. Teri hugged me and said, "Let's play some more games and get more pizza."

FOUR

Medical School- Getting Prepared

I arrived for the three-day examination with my mother. My mother gave me a hug and said, "Go show the university that we are ready for another medical doctor in our family." My mother helped me feel confident in my abilities. I received my MCAT results in a large envelope that included an application for admission to the medical school. I applied and had my parents countersign since I wasn't of legal age to sign much of anything except a letter to Teri or a shopping list.

I was scheduled to start classes first semester of 2015. I arrived at the medical school and was immediately informed that I wouldn't be permitted to study on campus due to my age. The medical school offered me an alternative of private instruction that would parallel the coursework I would be taking at the university. I asked to petition for review and reconsideration and was told, "home study or no study."

I was frustrated beyond belief. I wanted to be on campus and share in the campus life and associate with my peers. I felt like I was climbing a mountain of Jell-O and couldn't get to my goal no matter how much I tried. The dean of the medical school invited me and my parents to a meeting with my professors so they could explain how they intended to hold classes for me. I learned that I would be present during classroom lectures and question sessions. The only difference would be that I would be on a closed-circuit monitor in the classroom and I would have a similar dedicated closed-circuit monitor in my home. I could see and participate in all of my first-year classroom studies. The medical school sent out an IT person who set up the closed-circuit camera and monitor in my study room. We practiced using the system and I felt like I was somewhat in the classroom. At least I wasn't told to wait until I was twelve which was the universities' minimum age guideline.

I was scheduled for fall semester to take anatomy, biochemistry, cell biology, embryology, genetics, human behavior, immunology, neuroscience and physiology. The first-year curriculum was covered in a nine-month session with a two-week winter break and a one-month spring break. I had summer off to study, or pursue other interest. I was satisfied with the curriculum plan being offered to me at home and I anxiously completed my enrollment for my first-year studies. Classes started in seven weeks and I was given a list of books, workbooks, a computer monitor to interface with the medical school and all of the prepackaged animals that I would be dissecting and studying at home. Over my study area was a full-spectrum camera that could film me when I did lab experiments, dissections, or test taking.

I discussed what I needed on hand with my father and grandfather. My grandfather laughed and told me that I would need a shoe horn to get anything more in my bedroom. My father hired Gary Stern to build an addition onto my bedroom. Gary asked my father why my bedroom was too small. It is currently larger than our master bedroom. My father explained about the equipment and supplies I would need to participate in my first year of medical school classes. Gary replied, "I really thought everyone was kidding about Hayden and medical school. How old is she now?" I replied, "Hayden is eight years old." Gary replied, "Wow!" You should be on national news. My father quickly explained his past and his desire that our family's life, residency and accomplishments remain private. We shared with you and Melody, but no one else except the medical school. Gary promised to keep quiet about my accomplishments. In the back of my thoughts rested Jim's willingness to write the story of my miraculous birth. I remember kidding Jim when he said he would gladly write my story. I remarked, "At least it will be a short story given my age and experience at the time."

It took Gary and my grandfather seven weeks to complete the addition onto my bedroom. I should explain a little bit about my new study room. The addition is 25' by 30'. I have a built-in library for all of my medical books and literature. I have stacks of medical journals and tear sheets that wait for my attention. I have a full lab with dissection equipment, autoclave, 4000x scanning electron microscope, surgical table, surgical lighting, lab testing area, two sinks and an emergency wash station. I also have a propane gas feed, a helium feed and an oxygen feed. I have four Bunsen burners and a couple dozen flasks and bottles for doing my experiments. I also have a full bathroom and kitchen area. I have cadavers of various animals that I am required to dissect and study. This part of my study room is solely for academic study.

The next part of my new study room is my direct internet connection to the medical school. My medical school computer is a dedicated, closed circuit, monitor so I can participate in actual classes in real-time. I can ask questions and participate in classroom discussions as if I was actually in the room. Actually, I am in the room. I thought it was really funny when a new class first starts and students hear my voice through the classroom monitor and can't figure out who is talking or what is going on. When the students learn that an eight-year-old is taking the class, most students take the time to stand in front of the monitor to say hi to me. This same computer is used by the medical school for my proctored exams and the on-going barrage of literature, publications and email notices sent out by the school every day. I enjoyed my nicknames-'computer head and robot girl'.

My favorite part of the room is what I call my bedroom annex. I have a large, stuffed gorilla that I sit on to study or read. I have my lap computer and numerous games in this room. I text and Skype with my friend Teri from next door when I take a break from my studies. At one point I was limited to finding the time to contact Teri. Now I make the time since she is and will always remain my best friend. One section of the room is dedicated to brain games and challenges to determine if my collective intuitive skills have increased. My premonition skills appear somewhat static and I have yet to develop any telekinetic skills. I would love to be able to heal like my mother does, but I don't see that skill developing anytime soon.

Prior to entering medical school, I knew that I wanted to become an OB/GYN just like my father. Where we live in the wilderness, my father indicated we could use three OB/GYN doctors. I trained at least twice a week under my father and I had observed more than fifty deliveries, either by natural child birth or C-section. In addition, I observed surgical procedures, such as tubal ligations, cyst removal, ovary removal and endometrial tissue scraping and removal. The patients using our medical center were usually open and, after understanding my level of academic achievement, welcomed me into their care circle.

I also needed permission from the foundation that owned the medical center. I met with a representative and explained my education and my goal to become an OB/GYN like my father. I was very pleased to hear the representative say that he would welcome me to the medical center for intern activities and after graduation I could practice at the center. My father brought up the state licensing requirements that provide no medical licensing for any person under the age of sixteen years. He laughed and said that wilderness health care is a priority in the state. He made one phone call and received tentative approval for me to be licensed once I attained my training as an OB/GYN. The state licensing board followed up with a commitment letter to permit me to be licensed upon successful completion of my medical degree regardless of my age. I was so excited, one would have thought that Christmas was coming early for me; and it was!

Medical School – My First Year

The first year of medical school started off a little rough around the edges given the lack of experience for me and my different professors. Professor Davis apologizes to me all the time when he is asking or taking questions. I speak out, "I'm here too and I have a question or the answer." Soon the medical students listened for me and they would direct my professors to look at the monitor. A usual running joke would be my professor turning to my monitor and saying, "Oh, there you are." By the third week of medical school I was just another student in class; well almost in class anyway. I continually received comments like "Robot girl" because my head was rolled around in the classroom to assure I could see what was being discussed.

I also had a remote camera that I could position where needed to send the information being reviewed by my professor. For example, if I was dissecting an animal to study its nerve, bone or muscle structure, I could point my remote camera at my examination table and explain to the professor what I was doing and why. If the review was more detailed than a two or three-minute viewing, the professor would direct me to keep connected after class so he could review my work in more detail. If

A Gift from God

I was doing a dissection, I needed to explain my work, step by step, just like an autopsy.

Teri stopped by my house to see if I could play with her. My mother let her into my annex with the understanding that Teri wouldn't interrupt me. Teri quietly sat at my work table and watched me interact with my professor as I was dissecting an animal. Teri got sick watching my dissection and threw up in my sink. Teri whispered, "See you later Hayden." I learned that Teri threw up a second time outside waiting on her mother to pick her up. Dissections are not good for those with a weak stomach. As for me, I loved the excitement and challenges I faced in school.

Lab days were always a lot of fun for me. I could put my learning to the test. My remote camera would film what I was doing and I would explain as if I was doing an autopsy, or something. I had to verbally explain things because often the professor couldn't review my work in real time. A video was the next best thing. I quickly realized that I needed a white board for my study room. This type of board used marking pens that turned to powder and could be easily wiped off. I needed to perform my research calculations on the white board for the professor to review. Everything I did in class, or as homework, required monitoring at all times. Several medical students complained that I worked at home with two medical doctor parents that helped me with my work. My professor let them watch my live feed video and realized that no one was helping me with my assignments.

Test days worked out well under our closed-circuit system. At the appointed time, my professor's office would email me the mid-term or final exam. I had to place my remote camera on me to verify that I had no assistance with the assignment or test answers. I became comfortable being filmed throughout my day. I would complete all exams on line and return the completed exam by email to the professor's office. There was no way to cheat on my medical exams. When the rule said, "Clear your desk or table of everything except two number 2 pencils, they meant it. Cheating was generally followed by an expulsion letter which I felt was appropriate.

One morning I was expecting my latest lab assignment from my anatomy professor. I got out of bed and looked at the clock. It was three minutes to eight a.m. I walked into my study in my pajamas and immediately heard Professor Wilcox say, "Good morning Ms. Gehardi.

You decided not to dress today?" I looked down and I was in my pajamas. I excused myself and apologized to my professor when I returned dressed for class. My professor just laughed at me and said good morning once again. I had to remember that I was subject to monitoring at any time I was in the study room.

My cell-biology/chemistry professor suggested I attend a one-day lab event. He explained that direct participation would help me understand the subject matter of the lab and suggested that the use of complex ingredients required my personal attention at school. I talked with my mother and she agreed to fly me to the medical school and remain with me during the lab. My mother and I walked into the lab room and on the center table was a big cake with nine Bunsen burners lit around the cake. My professor introduced me to the rest of the class and they sang the 'Happy Birthday' song to me. I was so embarrassed, but meeting my fellow classmates was nice. Most of my classmates were a foot taller than me, but academically, I was their equal. I received lots of hugs and kisses from the students and even my professor gave me a hug. I had been so busy that I forgot about my birthday.

My parents invited Teri to join us at the 'Bear Restaurant' to celebrate my birthday. I had fun juxtaposing my fun time with Teri and my dedication to my medical studies. I eventually learned that slowing down sometimes doesn't mean stopping. Teri taught me quite a bit about friendship, loyalty and even love of my best friend. I learned as a young woman that life is too short to exist without friends.

Medical School – Second Year

I completed my first year of medical school with perfect scores. The dean of the medical school invited my family to the campus as a means of ushering in my familiarity with the medical school and campus life. I was prohibited from attending classes on campus until I was ten years old and then I still needed to be accompanied by a parent or guardian until I was twelve years old. I told the dean that I will have graduated from the medical school before I am twelve years old. The dean was very complimentary on how my first year at the medical school turned out. He affirmed that in his opinion I was probably the smartest medical student in the first-year studies. The dean took me and my parents on a tour of the medical school. I was envious when I saw the advanced equipment available to residents and the medical staff. I asked my father if we could add onto my bedroom so I could get a CT scanner. Well, I thought I was being funny.

The dean was curious about my knowledge of medicine and how I did so well my first year. He asked me if my parents assisted me in my studies. Both of my parents represented to the dean that I did my own work. He was curious about my study habits. I explained that I study from twelve to fifteen hours a day, six days a week. Sunday is reserved for my family. The dean suggested that I spend too much time studying. He hoped I did some activities outside of studies. I explained about my horses, swimming and my best friend Teri. The dean looked at my parents and commented that she sounds like she has a well-rounded schedule. My mother added, "Hayden didn't mention her volunteer work at the medical center. The dean asked what I did at the center. My dad replied, "She has assisted me with C-section births, traditional births and works in the neo-natal unit with post-delivery well-baby care. My mother explained that I shadow her as she sees patients. My mother was quick to explain that I never got near a patient unless they consented. The dean asked, "Do many patients consent?" My mother and father both replied, "All of them. They love Hayden." I mentioned to the dean that I even had my own white lab coat with my name and future OB/GYN underneath. My mother showed the dean a picture of me in my lab coat and stethoscope around my neck. The dean laughed and said, "By golly, you look like a doctor."

The dean explained that my second year would involve the study of systems, such as general principals and hematopoietic system; cardiovascular; respiratory, renal/musculoskeletal; gastrointestinal, central and peripheral nervous system and psychopathology; endocrinology and reproductive systems and extremes of life. The dean looked at me and said, "That's a mouthful of systems. Have you looked into systems in your studies?" I explained that I had spent a lot of time learning the systems of the body since age six and I am confident that my knowledge is already satisfactory enough to take my second-year exams and pass." The dean replied, "Hold up there. You are only nine years old. Don't rush because the state will not grant you a medical license until you are sixteen and that has never been done in this state." I explained that I was already preapproved for underage licensure by the state so long as I was working in a wilderness medical center. The dean just smiled and said, "You seem to know where you are going." I replied, "I hope to have my OB/GYN certification and a fellowship before I am fourteen or fifteen years old." The dean replied, "Good luck with that."

My father interrupted the dean and commented that I could probably deliver a baby C-section if given the opportunity. The dean asked what type of surgical training have I completed. I replied, "I have sliced up more pigskin that I would want to think about. My hand is steady and my scalpel cuts are near perfect in depth for human skin. I have observed numerous births from C-sections to natural child birth. I have walked rounds with my parents and I have participated in diagnostic evaluations of new patients. The dean smiled and said, "You are quite the little doctor." I replied, "Not yet, but I am working on it."

The dean asked my parents if I could take my second-year class exams just to see how much of the second-year courses I truly understood. My mother asked, "If she passes, will she still be required to take the course?" He replied, "No. She will get a pass on the course for each systems test that she actually passes with a 75 per cent or above." My mother looked at the dean and said, "The person you need to ask is standing right there." The dean looked at me and said, "Well Ms. Gehardi, are you interested in taking your second-year finals?" I replied, "Absolutely. May I have one week to freshen up on the systems. I didn't expect this opportunity to arise and I have premonition abilities." The dean suggested I take June and July off and have fun, go on vacation, see your friends, ride your horse; Just do something other than study. You can study in August and take each test starting the middle of August." I replied, "Thank you. Will I be taking the test over my dedicated monitor or at the medical school?" The dean replied, "I think you had better take the exams here, under staff supervision since what I am offering you is unheard of in our medical school." He went on to explain that I would be tested on two systems each day. He would not give me the order of the systems which was fine with me. I turned to my mother and asked, "Will you bring me to the university for the exams?" My mother replied, "Of course I will. We will book a nice hotel to stay in." The dean suggested we stay in one of the medical school dormitories. That would eliminate travel time. My mother replied, "That's alright. I remember medical school dormitories and the beds are not very comfortable. We will stay in a hotel and I can fly Haden to the medical school if you will give me authorization to land our helicopter on the helipad." He replied, "Done."

I left the medical school floating on Cloud 9. I was so excited to take my second-year courses and get them out of the way. I chatted all the way home. Mom commented, "You are being given a great opportunity. Enjoy some fun and then get ready to shine and complete your second year."

I did my own version of play and vacation. I reviewed all of the systems of the human body and within one week I was ready for the tests. I realized that I still had close to six weeks before I could take the exams. I don't like to waste precious time so I began to study the DSM IV, pharmacology and pharmaceuticals books while doing activities for me and Teri. To maintain my goals, I set up a schedule and informed Teri of my riding schedule, swimming and activity time that Teri could schedule things she liked to do. I will admit I had fun, but I was happy to get my studies on track and finish preparing for the system's exams.

I appeared at the dean's office and learned that I would be testing in the dean's conference room. The room was serviced with a broad-spectrum camera that could see most of the room. The dean commented, "The camera is not to film you cheating; rather it is there to validate your test taking for your protection." I replied, "That's fine because I am video monitored daily at home."

The first two systems I was tested on were cardiovascular and renal/musculoskeletal systems. The second day I was tested on respiratory and the nervous system followed by reproductive systems and hematopoietic system; and finally, the extremes of life and psychopathology. My mother would question me after each test and then would offer to help if I had questions.

On my last day of testing the dean indicated that my tests would be scored and I would be notified in writing of my scores for each test. My parents were quite surprised that my overall score was 92 percent out of 100 which wasn't too bad for a nine-year-old. I personally felt I did better than 92 percent, but that's life.

James A. Gauthier, J.D.

Medical School – Delays and More Delays

The dean was quite surprised at my test results. He notified me that I needed to attend a conference to evaluate me for a clerkship which was my third-year studies. The dean's letter outlined a list of the required clerkships required for my third year. The letter specified that I would need to complete family medicine (4 weeks); Internal medicine (2 weeks); neurology (2 weeks); Obstetrics and Gynecology (6 weeks); pediatrics (6 weeks); general surgery (6 weeks) and surgical specialties (6 weeks). I was excited to receive the letter until I read the last paragraph. It stated, "I have set up a conference with the medical school board to determine how you will proceed with your clerkship training." He set a date and asked that I be present along with a parent or guardian.

I wasn't sure what the dean tried to communicate to me. Was he informing me that I had to be on campus for the third year; or was he suggesting that due to my age, I couldn't work on my third year until I was older. I asked my mother and even she wasn't sure of what the dean was suggesting. I appeared at the scheduled meeting with both my parents. Dr. Andreson explained that third year studies involves a considerable amount of patient interaction and the board had significant concerns about nine-year-old examining patients. Professor Whitworth could see how disappointed I was and he suggested that the professor doing rounds and diagnostic evaluations wear a camera and microphone that could be sent to my study room. I could be there in real time, but not physically. I replied, "How can I learn from watching others. I am respectfully asking for direct patient contact just like my peers. I was told that a written finding would be mailed to me in two weeks.

The longest two weeks of my life had just happened. I waited patiently and checked the mail daily for the approval from the Board. Teri stopped by to play and I had to respectfully ask her for some private time. I was so nervous that I couldn't play with her. Nine days later, I received the following letter:

A Gift from God

Dear Ms. Gehardi:

"Congratulations on your completion of your second year of medical school. You have petitioned the medical school to consider you for on-site studies at the university hospital and medical center to meet your requirements for your third-year clerkship.

As members of the Board of Trustees for the medical school and hospital, we are charged with the orderly management of educational programs and we determine how students interface with our program goals. While we sincerely believe you are academically ready to complete your clerkship at nine years of age, you are not old enough to be placed in a position of providing direct or indirect patient care and the school's Errors and Omissions Insurance will not insure a student for medical malpractice less than fourteen years of age. In addition, the university has a long-standing requirement that any student under the age of ten may not take classes on campus. At age ten, the student may take classes if accompanied by a parent or guardian. Otherwise, a student must be at least twelve years of age before that student may take classes on campus without an adult escort.

The state will not provide a medical license for any person holding a medical degree until that person has reached the age of sixteen years. You are currently nine years old. Even if the medical school granted you leave to finish your third and fourth year now, you would be eleven years old and unable to get licensed for five years. It is the opinion of the Board of Trustees that you take some time away from direct medical studies until you reach twelve years of age. At that point, you may attend classes consistent with your clerkship and beyond."

We thank you for your understanding.

/s/ Chair of the Board of Trustees

James A. Gauthier, J.D.

I received the letter and decision of the Board of Trustees and I cried. I had worked so hard to achieve my medical degree and the medical school is going to delay completion of my medical degree and certification as an OB/GYN. My mother was at work, but she quickly experienced my personal angst and flew home to see what happened. My mother held me, but took the position that the decision had been made and she was uncertain how to make any positive changes to the decision. My mother said, "Let's talk with your father when he gets home."

I was usually a very calm, stable personality, but when my mother suggested I may have to give up on my education right now, I lost my control over my emotions and screamed at my mother, "I don't want to accept their decision. I have goals and I will meet my goals with or without your support." My mother replied, 'That's fine. What is your plan?" I replied, "What else! I am calling my lawyer to see if he has recommendations for me." My mother replied, "Go ahead. Jim might have some ideas that you haven't considered."

I called Jim and explained what the medical school was doing to trash my medical degree. Jim asked me to calm down and he made me breathe counting to ten before letting out my air. Jim made me do these ten times and then he commented that I sounded more under control of my anger. I snapped back at Jim and he quickly replied, "Hayden, you called me. I didn't call you. If you want my help, then treat me with the same respect that you expected from your medical school." I began to cry and told Jim that my dreams were being crushed because of my age. That is unfair and I think it should be age discrimination. Jim replied, "Hayden, let's not go there yet. If you threaten the medical school with a discrimination complaint, you can be assured that you will not get their support and your education will sit in limbo until the lawsuit is settled or tried." I asked Jim, "What can I do?" Jim replied, "Please describe to me what you will be doing in your third year that you called a clerkship."

I explained to Jim that my third year is called my 'Clerkship'. I will need to complete family medicine (4 weeks); Internal medicine (2 weeks); neurology (2 weeks); Obstetrics and Gynecology (6 weeks); pediatrics (6 weeks); general surgery (6 weeks) and surgical specialties (6 weeks). Each of these courses is hands-on working in tandem with licensed medical doctors. In a sense it is on-the-job training. Jim asked, "Hayden isn't that what you were doing with your mom and dad at the medical center?" I remember smiling and said, "Jim, you are right. Maybe I can do my clerkship through my parents at the medical center instead of the university hospital." Jim suggested he would write a letter to the medical school board requesting an accommodation to the typical course of study permitting me to do my clerkship under my parent's instruction. Jim said, "Let me do some quick research and I will call you back."

Jim called me the next day and I was a little angry and said, "It's about time. Why didn't you call me Jim?" I replied, "Cool your anger ets Hayden or I will hang up on you. I will do anything for you and I expect in return that you will help me and not berate me solely because you are upset with the medical school. I am not your enemy." I apologized to Jim again and politely asked if he learned anything that could help. Jim replied, "I researched the medical degree protocols; courses of study and the variations between medical schools. The only consistency between medical schools is that none are consistent. It appears that the medical schools have considerable latitude in setting graduation requirements. Some medical schools use a hands-on clerkship like your school and other schools simply require more third year testing with the patient contact all occurring during the fourth-year residency."

I asked Jim what he recommended we do. He replied, "Let me draft a letter from you and your parents to the medical school board of trustees. I will raise some points and make some recommendations. I will let you look over the letter before you send it to the medical school. I told Jim "Thank you so much." Jim wrote:

> To the Chair of the Board of Trustees
>
> Re: Hayden Elizabeth Gehardi, Student ID # HEG 388342Abl 11
>
> Subject: Request for alternative completion of third year Clerkship
>
> Dear Dr. Andreson:
>
> The purpose of this letter is to request approval of an alternate Clerkship program designed for student, Hayden E. Gehardi. As you know, Ms. Gehardi has successfully completed her first two years of medical

school at nine years of age. She was instructed by your office to stand down until she was twelve years of age. Standing down is unacceptable to us and especially to our daughter.

We are proposing that Hayden complete her third year Clerkship under our supervision. Hayden's father is a board-certified OB/GYN and her mother is a board-certified pediatrician and family care doctor. Together, we administer the Wilderness Outreach Health Care Medical Center. Our medical center is fully staffed with a cardiologist, an endocrinologist, pathologist, nephrologist and internal medicine, hospitalist, neurologist, pulmonologist OB/GYN and general surgery and emergency room surgeons, modern CT and MRI scanners. We also have well-baby care and a full scope well-family care including obesity and renal issues. We also have two full-time oncologists and our own lab and kidney dialysis center.

We recognize that our daughter is required to complete family medicine (4 weeks); Internal medicine (2 weeks); neurology (2 weeks); Obstetrics and Gynecology (6 weeks); pediatrics (6 weeks); general surgery (6 weeks) and surgical specialties (6 weeks) Our medical center has the facilities and professional medical staff necessary to work with Hayden in accomplishing her third year Clerkship offsite of the teaching hospital.

We would propose that Hayden wears a body camera while working at the medical center so her training and patient exposure is well-documented for review by the university. Hayden would be registered at the medical school, but take her training off campus. This is not something new. In 1983, the medical school had a student in the third year that was injured in a skiing accident. She was permitted to study outside of the hospital. In 1985 another student was badly injured in a car accident. He was a paraplegic, but otherwise healthy. To assist him in completing his degree, the medical school approved an outside third year clerkship. In 1990 a female medical student was permitted to do offsite third year clerkship studies because she was pregnant and travel was restricted. We would suggest to the board that Hayden is no more and no less disabled than the three students we cited herein. We would point out that there are a total of seventeen separate accommodations granted for students like those we mentioned.

We checked with the state and medical licensing department has no vested interest in where a student completes their third-year studies. The only limitation is that Hayden studies under the direction of a licensed physician and completes the subject matter attributed to the clerkship as required by the medical school.

The state has indicated in writing that Hayden may be considered for early licensure if she is going to practice at the Wilderness Health Medical Center. Providing health care in rural and wilderness areas of the state is a medical priority. The state licensing board suggested that Hayden would be permitted an early license so long as she has verification of her studies and the full backing of the foundation that operates the Wilderness Health Care Medical Center. I can assure you that we have their unlimited support.

Finally, if the medical school has any testing for third year clerkship studies, Hayden could take those tests just as she has completed her ongoing exams in her first and second year.

Hayden is an excellent student with a brilliant mind. She is motivated and dedicated towards becoming an OB/GYN. As such, Hayden will have about four more years of an O&G residency in order to receive her specialty license as an OB/GYN. If she completed her degree as planned, Hayden could be a licensed OB/GYN at age fourteen or fifteen. She is driven and only asks for the opportunity to keep moving through medical school.

/s/ Hayden E. Gehardi; /s/ Ian Gehardi, M.D.; /s/ Eli Gehardi, M.D.

I was so nervous waiting on a response from the medical school. My future and my dreams of accomplishment rested entirely upon the decision of the Board of Trustees. My friend, Teri tried to distract me by engaging in play. I had to apologize to Teri and explain why I was so uptight waiting on an answer. Seventeen days later I received the Board of Trustee's response. It read:

Dear Ms. Gehardi:

"Your request to conduct your third-year clerkship away from the university hospital must be denied. The situations cited in your letter were for students already in their clerkship when something happened to interfere with their studies. Under those exigent circumstances, the Board of Trustees felt compelled to offer an alternative to ending the student's medical school career.

Unlike the cited students, your only disability is age. We believe it is in your best interest to stand down as previously recommended by this board until you reach the age of twelve years. At that time, you may participate in on campus study programs without direct parental supervision.

As the medical school board, we believe we have no checks and balances in which to validate your training during your proposed off-campus clerkship program. The medical school is limited on resources to accommodate every student need. It is with our deepest regret that we must deny your petition. We know you will become an exceptional doctor, but take your time.

We look forward to having you on campus three years from now."

/s/ Chair

I was so upset that I called Jim to let him know what the medical school response was. I had to leave a message. I emailed the letter to Jim hoping he would see it and understand the urgency of my call. I paced around the house when my mother asked, "What did Jim say?" I replied, "Jim always answers his phone when I call. I have left him six messages and no return call. I became so agitated that I started calling Jim every five minutes and finally reached Jim nearly six hours later. I started to explain what happened and I broke into tears and said, "It isn't fair Jim." Jim asked me, "What isn't fair?" I replied, "I got a response from the board of trustees and they denied my request to study my third-year clerkship under my parent's supervision." I was told again to stand down until I am twelve years of age. I won't stand down! Do you have any more ideas?

Jim replied, "I read the letter you emailed to me. It would be my impression that they want to enforce their decision, but equally appear to want to keep you happy and in their system. Face it Hayden, you are beautiful and smarter that every doctor on that board. They need you for their school. Here is what I am proposing. I rudely interrupted Jim and asked, "What are you proposing?" Jim replied, "I am going to draft another letter and I will send it to the chair. If this letter doesn't work, then I am going to need time to look into the matter legally. There must be a vesting doctrine in your admission's handbook that says once you are admitted you have a right to continue in your studies to graduation. Anyway, let me draft this letter under my signature and we will see how they respond." I replied, "I have my medical school course catalog in front of me. I am going to email you the on-line catalog link." Jim replied, "Thanks. That will help speed up my research." I replied, "Good. How long will it take you to write this letter? Jim replied, "I will send you a draft by tomorrow morning."

I woke up early and checked my email. Jim's letter wasn't in my email at 7:00 a.m. I was frustrated, angry, hurt and felt hopeless. I sat down at the kitchen counter and started crying. My father put his arm around me and asked if he could help. I replied, "Jim promised me he would send his draft letter to me this morning. Here it is now, 8:00 a.m. and still no letter." My father asked when I checked my email last. I replied, "Five minutes ago."

I yelled, "Where are you Jim. You promised me that I would get the draft letter in the morning." Out of my frustration, I hit my cereal bowl and spilled milk and cereal all over the counter. My father handed me a wash cloth and suggested I finish my breakfast, but this time try putting something in my mouth. I cleaned up my mess and yelled, "This isn't fair. Where are you Jim?" I was upset and my mother asked if she could help with anything. I replied, "Yes, you can call Jim and ask him where my letter is. He promised to get it to me in the morning." My mother looked at the clock. It was 8:20 a.m. She suggested that it was 5:20 a.m. in Washington State so it may not yet be morning for Jim. I replied, "Sorry, I forgot the time zone." At 5:50 a.m. PDT, I received the draft letter from Jim like he promised. I felt so foolish and I apologized to my parents for my childish behavior.

Jim mailed me the following letter to consider:

Dear Dr. Andreson:

I have appeared pro hac vice and I represent Hayden Elizabeth Gehardi, a matriculated student at your medical school. Ms. Gehardi accepted matriculation under your school's student catalog and understood that once admitted she would be permitted to remain on her academic learning schedule to complete her medical degree.

I am in receipt of the Board's letter declining Ms. Gehardi's application for completion of her third year Clerkship off of the medical school and university hospital campus due to a disability tied to her age. The Board's decision based upon age materially breaches the implied contract that Ms. Gehardi entered into with the university when she accepted matriculation. I carefully reviewed the course handbook and nowhere does the handbook identify any course limitations on age of the student and treating a student differently due to age is a material violation of the ADA and the course handbook. The medical school accepted my client as a full-time matriculated student and she has a right to fulfill her education and timely complete her medical degree.

I am writing to afford the medical school, and the board of trustees, an opportunity to rectify this unfortunate case of discrimination and breach of enrollment conditions. The emotional distress caused by the Board's decision denying my client's right to finish her medical degree in a timely manner will be raised in litigation if that need arises. I believe the decision of the Board may actually meet the definition of outrage and entitle Ms. Gehardi substantial damages if that is the course the medical school chooses to take.

Ms. Gehardi and her parents have provided a reasonable accommodation plan for completion of Ms. Gehardi's third year Clerkship and possible fourth-year residency. I would ask that the Board reconsider its reasoning and approve the reasonable request for accommodation previously sent to the Board. I would like to thank you, and the Board for your careful reconsideration of Ms. Gehardi's request.

I would like to point out that I have already checked with the state and they have no objection to where Ms. Gehardi receives her Clerkship training. I also have two medical schools that are aware of Ms. Gehardi's issues and both have offered her matriculation as a third-year student at their medical school. I hope that does not become necessary for the reasons stated.

/s/ *James A. Gauthier, J.D.*

James A. Gauthier, J.D.

Jim reviewed his proposed letter with me and my parents. I was angry enough that Jim's letter was too polite and I wanted him to really threaten the board. Like always, Jim told me to breathe deeply and hold each breath for ten seconds. I did that ten times and it really does work. Jim's letter was approved by my parents and me and he sent it off certified mail to the Board. This time I really couldn't wait for the response. I called Jim daily asking if he received a response yet. I became very disappointed when Jim kept saying, "Nothing yet."

Jim called me on my cell eight days later. He read the response from the Board Chair:

> Dear Mr. Gauthier:
>
> The Board of Trustees is in receipt of your letter threatening litigation if the Board refuses what you termed reasonable accommodation for Ms. Gehardi's third year clerkship program. We have checked with our legal counsel and we hold an opinion about the ADA that is different than your interpretation. It is our conclusion that Ms. Gehardi is not disabled, as defined by the ADA.
>
> Ms. Gehardi's claim that the medical school has somehow materially breached the implied rights arising out of the course handbook is equally untenable. Nowhere in the student handbook is the medical school required to offer an alternate study program if a student is physically unable to participate in offered programs. The fact that Ms. Gehardi is underage and cannot participate in the clerkship at nine years of age is not the problem of the medical school.
>
> We do recognize that when Ms. Gehardi enrolled, and was offered placement in the medical school, that she had a reasonable expectation that she would be permitted to pursue her education through graduation. Although the medical school denies it has a legal or moral obligation, to use your word accommodate Ms. Gehardi, the Board

has approved her off-site studies for her third-year clerkship and tentatively her fourth-year residency.

I have enclosed a series of terms and conditions upon which Ms. Gehardi must comply with in order to receive her medical degree from this institution. If she meets these expectations, I will personally look forward to handing her a graduation certificate and confer her degree of medical doctor. I will point out that Ms. Gehardi's third year Clerkship will involve more work than students attending on campus solely for accreditation and not a punishment. Please make sure Ms. Gehardi understands her enrollment terms and conditions by signing and returning a copy of the attached. I personally wish her the best and remind her that she is required to register for each semester of her third and fourth year if she expects to graduate with her class.

/s/ *Chairperson*

Jim received the approval letter and quickly emailed it to me for review with my parents. My father commented, 'If Jim says it is okay, then sign it and we will email it back." I asked my father to please read the terms and conditions since he and my mother would be my professors for my third and possibly fourth year. My father read through the terms and conditions and said, "It looks good to me Hayden." My mother commented, "It all seems reasonable to me as well." I called Jim to get his final approval and he walked me through the terms and conditions just to make sure that I understood how I was to account for my time doing clerkship classes. Jim then said, "Go for it Hayden. You got what you asked for." I replied, "Jim, you mean I got everything you asked for." Jim laughed and said, "I am not going to argue with you Hayden. You always win our arguments." I laughed and said, "You let me win, but then again, happy client, happy life. Thank you, Jim, for helping me once again." Jim replied, "For you, anytime."

James A. Gauthier, J.D.

Medical School - My Third-Year Clerkship

I was visiting Teri and explained that I resolved my third-year Clerkship with the help of my attorney. Melody asked, "You have your own attorney Hayden?" I smiled and said, "He's all mine. When I have a problem of any kind, I call Jim and talk with him." Melody asked, "Where does your attorney live?" I explained that he lives between Seattle and Tacoma Washington. Melody asked, "How often do you call your attorney?" I replied, "At least once a month, sometimes more." Sometimes Jim calls me or my parents just to say hi. When I call Jim, we talk for at least an hour or two. One time we talked for nearly four hours." Melody asked, "Isn't that expensive?" I replied, "Not for me. Jim doesn't charge me anything. He is my personal friend and he insists I call him if I have anything to talk about." Melody said, "You are a lucky girl to have your own attorney." I replied, "He is the same attorney that did my parents' estate planning and he wrote the book, "Ian & Eli" which chronicles my parent's lives until age 25." Someday I want Jim to write my story about my miraculous birth. Jim told me it would have to be a 'short story' given my age and life experiences. I am sure Jim no longer thinks that way. I love having Jim as my friend and attorney. He helped me overcome the mountain of Jell-O I was facing trying to get my third-year clerkship approved.

I was doing some experiments in my lab when my mother stepped in and said, "Dr. Hayden, its bedtime. Are you at a place where you can stop and get some sleep? Remember you are going to work tomorrow?" I replied, "I know. I am almost too excited to sleep knowing that my education is back on track thanks to you, dad and of course Jim.

I started on my third-year clerkship by attending a staff meeting with the rest of the medical center's doctors. I was wearing my white lab coat and stethoscope and I fit in with the rest of the doctors; well almost fit in. I was five feet four and weighed 101 pounds soaking wet. I was already well-known to the medical center staff since I volunteered for nearly three months and shadowed my parents. My parents explained to all the staff that I would be completing my third-year studies at the medical center under the supervision of my parents and the department heads. My father explained that I was to be given the courtesies of a third-year medical student and please involve her in what you are doing with patient care. Hayden's third year schedule is broken down as follows:

Dr. Eli Gehardi will have Haden under her instruction and supervision for four weeks focusing on family medicine.

Dr. Ian Gehardi - I will have Hayden under my direct supervision and instruction for six weeks to complete her obstetrics and gynecology training.

Dr. Gary Phelps will provide neurology and internal medicine training for four weeks total.

Dr. Stephen Allan will work with Hayden on emergency room, general surgical studies for six weeks and 2 weeks of surgical specialties.

Dr. James Harris shall work with Hayden for two weeks of cardiology training.

I will then work with Hayden for an additional six weeks of OB/GYN related surgeries and deliveries.

Finally, Dr. Eli Gehardi will finish up Hayden's third year with six weeks of pediatric training.

For general information to the staff, Hayden is fully insured with errors and omission's insurance. Hayden is here to learn from each of you under your specialty and it is important that you have Hayden participate in what you are doing. For example, I intend to have Hayden in scrubs and assisting me and the surgical staff in delivering babies. Hayden is going to learn how to make surgical incisions and how to close up an incision with tape, staples or sutures. If Hayden is participating with a specific department, assist her in understanding your procedures and how you approach patient care. Hayden is here to learn from each of you. If any doctor I named is unwilling to accept the training role for Hayden, please see me after this meeting and other arrangements may be taken.

Dr. Allen asked, "Why is your daughter doing her Clerkship here, rather than at the medical school like the rest of us did back when we were in medical school?" My father explained, "Hayden is off campus studying due to her age and inability to complete her third year at the medical school. Hayden will be wearing a camera on her jacket that will document what she does each day. She is to journalize her experiences and formulate questions to be answered by her supervising physician. The camera is nothing new as everything we do in the medical center is documented with security camera footage. The video feed from Hayden's camera goes directly to a dedicated closed-circuit monitor at the medical school. Hayden must turn in her journals, video footage and identify what she learned during particular course of study under your direction.

Dr. Harris asked, "What is expected of me. My father replied, "Hayden needs to learn how to diagnose and treat heart conditions from congestive heart failure, atrial fibrillation, coronary heart disease, effect of blood fats, anticoagulation medication and of course heart surgery." Dr. Harris replied, "You are expecting me to have a nine-year-old assist in heart surgery? My father replied, "Yes. She should also be trained to look at echocardiograms and diagnosis heart disease and make sure she tells you the medical issue and then what she would do to ameliorate the condition by pharmacological means to surgery." Dr. Harris replied, "You mean everything I do as a cardiologist?" My mother replied, "Everything. Jim; please look at Hayden's on-the-job training in your perspective as a cardiologist. Would you want your physician to treat you with limited knowledge because her training physician refused to expose her to all aspects of the field?" Dr. Harris replied, "Fine." My Mother asked, "Any more questions?"

Dr. Allen indicated he had another question. He asked, "At what point can we, as the supervising physician permit your daughter to handle direct patient care? Does she require direct one- on-one supervision or can I allow her to deal directly with ER patients." My mother replied, "What Hayden does in your emergency room is subject to your medical and supervisory discretion. If you are of the opinion that she can do something in patient care without direct supervision, then allow her to do her job. It is always best to be a hands-on supervisor, but I can envision times when you will be engaged with one patient and another requires assistance, like sutures, bone breakages, etc. At a minimum, Hayden should do the initial triage work and do such things as sending the patient to radiology." Dr. Allen said, "Got it. Thanks."

My father went on to explain that in terms of direct patient care, it is up to the assigned physician to document the patient's approval before Hayden is permitted to participate in direct patient care. Previously every patient approved when Hayden volunteered and I see no reason why the same patient result won't repeat again. What I do not want to happen is an allegation that Hayden is practicing medicine without a medical license. She is an intern and please involve her in what you do. Thank you."

A Gift from God

My parents held a similar staff meeting for the nursing staff. My parents explained what a clerkship was and that I was going to be doing my on-the-job training in each major department of the medical center. At the end of the staff meeting my father asked if there were any questions about my role in the medical center. One of the supervising nurses asked if I would still be available to them as well. She liked my ability as a gopher and hoped I would still be their gopher. For those that may not know what a 'gopher' is, I was asked to gopher for this and gopher for that. Everyone got a laugh, but Nurse Daniels replied, "Seriously, what is Hayden's role in the hierarchy of the medical center. Can I direct her to do things like before?"

My father replied, "No, Hayden is to be treated as a third-year medical student and she is here to study medicine from a great staff of doctors. Hayden is no longer any department's gopher and I ask that you treat her with the respect she has earned."

Dr. Allen's nurse commented that emergency room was busy all the time and she didn't feel as though she could take time to work with me and still meet patient care." My father replied, "You work with Hayden like you work with Dr. Allen." The nurse replied, "I think that having a nine-year-old in emergency care is nothing more than ludicrous and an unfair joke on our patients." I heard my father say, "Let's talk after the meeting." My father insisted that I participate in the meeting as well as Dr. Allen. Nurse Jefferson thanked my parents for the opportunity to discuss my involvement in the emergency room. She then stated, "I cannot work for a nine-year-old. I don't care if she has ten medical degrees; having a nine-year-old practicing medicine should be outlawed. She is just going to be in my way as I handle emergency care with Dr. Allen." Dr. Allen responded, "That is how I felt, but now I am excited to work with Hayden. She may be small in stature, but she knows her stuff and I welcome her to the emergency room. Nurse Jefferson replied, "That's up to you, but I will simply ignore her and hope she keeps out of my way." My mother replied, "Thank you for your opinion. Nurse Jefferson was reassigned to the neonatal section and a new ER nurse was hired and in place the next day. She was excited to work with me and Dr. Allen.

James A. Gauthier, J.D.

Family Medicine

My parents surprised me by handing me a new lab coat with my name on it. Underneath my name read, 'Third Year Medical Student'. My parents bought me a new stethoscope and comfortable shoes. I could understand why after ten hours on my feet for most of the day at the medical center. I never realized the kind of pressure placed on my parents until I began working at the medical center as a full-time intern. Things moved quickly and I needed to learn to keep up with patient care. My first day ended with us landing at home at 8:18 pm. My mother asked if I was hungry. I was leaning against the wall and didn't realize that I had fallen asleep. My mother tried to carry me into my bedroom, and when that failed, she woke me up and said get your pajamas on and get into bed before you fall over. Tomorrow is another day. My father got home just before midnight. He ended up with a complicated C-section birth that took him much of the night. My father worked nineteen hours that day. *I wondered what I was getting myself into. Being a doctor was a lot of hours and demanding attention to detail. But then again, I was a young woman that loved challenges and appreciated detail.*

The next morning, I woke up, showered and dressed for my next day of work. My mother and I were seeing patients afflicted with colds, flu, runny noses, headaches, general nausea, etc. I received a patient and my mother indicated that I could do the diagnosis and then discuss the treatment for a nine-year-old girl suffering from a congested chest and sinus tract. I checked her ears and then I grabbed a tongue depressor to look at her throat to see if there was any type of infection. I asked the girl, "Look up at me." She tilted her head and then sneezed. She cleaned out her sinus on me. My mother watched to see how I would handle that situation. I quickly wiped my face and returned to what I was doing. I placed the tongue depressor a little too far back and it irritated the gag reflex and she threw up all over me. The girl's mother apologized and my mother indicated I needed to change clothes before seeing my next patient. My mother said, "Look in my closet." I asked, 'Which closet?" My mother replied, "In my office." I looked and my parents had purchased me seven lab coats and my mother had several outfits for me to change into. Sometimes, there is nothing more beneficial than a mother; especially one with premonition abilities.

My afternoon was dedicated to well-baby care and routine examinations. I sat and watched my mother do a well-baby check on a little three-year-old girl. My mother suggested I remember pediatric exams as WEEENT, or weigh, examine, ears, eyes, nose and throat. My mother then checked the girl for any signs of abuse and showed me how to do that outside the observation of the parent and patient. My mother explained that a significant part of my job as a pediatrician is to fully examine children for signs of abuse. I asked my mother how often she finds an abusive situation and she replied, "Not very often." We see more signs of physical abuse over sexual abuse. She explained that with children presenting with a broken bone or similar injury, that it is important that you check the child for other past injuries and check the patient file if the patient is a regular patient. You need to be a little suspicious when you find a parent jumping around different doctors and presenting their child with an abuse type injury." I asked my mother, "If I do find abuse, how do you handle it?" My mother explained, "I talk with the parent and objectively state my findings and put them on notice that they need to explain what happened in detail. If I am of the opinion that the child's injuries are abusive then we need to report the case to child welfare. It is important that you remain objective and limit your involvement or you will drive yourself crazy. Just remember, the presumption is that there has been no abuse and unless you are absolutely sure, you should chart your thoughts and move on."

The next patient was a two-year-old boy. My mother obtained permission for me to examine the boy for a well-baby checkup. My nurse removed the boy's clothes and laid a blanket over him. I did my required examination and then did my abuse check. I removed the blanket covering the little boy and I lifted his legs and checked his bottom. I laid him back down and I was about to check his penis when the boy peed all over me. My mother and the nurse laughed and said, "The purpose of that towel is to prevent that from happening." I may be smart, but I sure made a lot of dumb, foolish mistakes during my first week in pediatrics. I looked at my mother and she smiled and said, "Only three more weeks to go." I smiled and my mother said, "I think you need to visit the closet again. I am glad I packed four complete sets of clothes for you." The word spread about the little boy peeing on me and I was the object of the staff's jokes. When I refused to comment, the jokes stopped. I reminded myself that I was in training and things might happen. If getting peed on is as bad as it gets, then I will be happy.

My second week was much more enjoyable. I had learned a lot from my mother and I rarely made the same mistake twice. By the end of my second week, I was doing entire well-baby exams and diagnosing typical childhood illnesses like colds, flu, allergies and inflammations. I learned that even little girls experienced urinary tract infections.'

My mother permitted me to examine the next pediatric patient. My nurse had the eight-year-old boy change into an exam gown. I waked in and his mother asked, "Who or what are you? This isn't Halloween so what are you dressed up for?" My mother ran into the room and apologized that she didn't meet with the family first to get permission for me to examine their son. My circumstance was explained to the boy's mother and she reluctantly agreed to me doing her son's sport's physical over her son's objection. He didn't want a girl to see him naked. I looked him in the eye and said, "I can do your exam or you can wait here for an hour or so and Dr. Gehardi will be available to do your physical." When he realized that a 'girl' was going to examine him either way, he consented to my exam. I checked him for all the standard items and then explained that I needed to check him for a hernia. He asked, "What's that?" I explained and he replied, "No way." I smiled and said, "Just sit there. Dr. Gehardi will be here as soon as possible. Its lunch time and she may have left for lunch." His mother made him participate. I checked him for a hernia and believed he had a hernia. I touched him and he pushed me away and said, "That hurt." I notified my mother and she diagnosed a hernia as well. I felt so good about finding the hernia. The boy's hernia was actually bad enough that he needed surgery.

In my third week I examined an eleven-year-old girl that needed a sport's physical to join the cheerleading squad at her middle school. She noted that I was nine years old and was enamored with the fact that I was in medical school. I finally had to thank her and asked her to leave so I could see my next patient. My mother explained that patients often want to talk or ask questions of their pediatrician. You need to develop a nice way of answering questions while keeping on schedule. I replied, "That girl could talk about anything."

In my fourth week of training in pediatrics, I examined two boys with broken arms from soccer. I sent them for images of the breaks. I showed my mother the x-rays and she said, "Good call." She asked me, "Do the bones need to be set?" I looked again and replied, "No. The breaks are hairline and the bone is together." My mother said, "What do you do next?" I replied, "I create the mummy!" My mother laughed and suggested I limit the casting to the breaks. I was allowed to do both cast and it was fun.

My last pediatric patient had cut herself on broken glass. I cleaned the wound under my mother's supervision and then she took over and sutured the wound. I asked why I couldn't do the sutures and was quickly told, "Until I check your ability to suture anything, I will do the sewing." My mother could feel my disappointment and she brought in some pig skin used for medical training. Pig skin is the closest to human skin. My mother set me up in her office with the pig skin, a scalpel and some suture needles and thread. She showed me how to cross sew the sutures and I was left to practice for the rest of the day. By day's end, I could cut and sew like the best surgeons in my opinion. I showed my mother my cuts and sewing and she agreed that I am ready to suture the next wound that comes into pediatrics.

My final day of pediatric training arrived and I didn't get the opportunity to suture anyone. My mother asked me if I would like to spend the rest of the day in the emergency room. I was excited and received two opportunities to suture. I had a girl that cut herself on the palm of her hand and a boy that cut his foot. Dr. Allen congratulated me on a job well done and indicated that he was looking forward to working with me in the emergency room.

Under the terms and conditions of my externship, I was required to write up what I learned and where I felt I needed improvement. I was reviewed on the completeness of my training report and that was compared to my camera that couldn't lie. I received a note from the medical school dean that said, "Great job. Do you now know what that little towel is used for?" I had to think and then I remembered the little boy that peed on me. I replied, "Definitely, yes."

James A. Gauthier, J.D.

Obstetrics and Gynecology

I was excited to work with my father. My career goal was to become an OB/GYN and now I had the opportunity to actually work in the field as a medical intern. My father took some time at home to explain how his day is structured. He preferred to do gynecological exams in the morning and surgeries in the afternoon. I asked, "What about deliveries?" My father replied, "Deliveries are never on track and when those little babies want out, they become pretty impatient." My father also explained that this area of medicine is very sensitive and women and young girls are usually not pleased to see us. What we do in a gynecological exam is invasive and it is critically important that we calm the patient by telling her exactly what we are doing and why. Before we prescribe birth control pills, we need a current exam. I asked my father if I would be doing exams with him. He explained that he would do the initial exam and then allow me to repeat what he did so I had the experience and knowledge. When you do a gynecological exam, you need to turn off your camera. A camera would certainly offend patients undergoing our type of examination.

I arrived at work with my parents and joined my father in his office. He indicated that our first patient was a gynecological exam of a sixteen-year-old female that wanted birth control pills. She arrived with her mother and I listened to my father ask her questions. I memorized his questions and watched my nurse prep the patient for my father. We received permission for me to participate and I watched my father complete the examination. He then asked the patient if she would be offended if I repeated the exam. She gave her consent and I learned how to use the tools of the trade. I could see inside her vagina and clearly could see her cervix and healthy wall structure. She received her birth control pills. When they left, I told my father that she was a little young for birth control pills. My father replied, "I have patients that are eleven years old and on birth control. Do I like it? No, but that is a value's judgment and we are not here to deal with values, just health care. The eleven-year-old had an active menstrual cycle and she was apparently sexually active. It is better to put her on birth control over getting pregnant."

Our next pregnant patient arrived for her twenty-week examination. My father had ordered an ultrasound and he checked the mother and looked at the ultrasound. My father would point at things revealed by the ultrasound to help me understand what I was looking at. I concluded that the pregnancy was looking good and she will have a healthy baby boy. The woman yelled at me because she didn't want to know the sex of her baby. I was crushed and apologized. She replied, "I'm sorry too. I shouldn't have been so harsh, but if you are going to be a doctor, make damn sure your patient wants to know what you are about to tell them." I said, "Sorry" again.

Our next patient was a routine exam. I obtained her permission to participate when my father stepped into the examination room and said, "Hayden, put on your scrubs. We have an emergency C-section." I smiled at the nurse as I ran out to change. My mother and I shared an office. I grabbed my surgical scrubs, mask and hat and carried my shoe covers. I finished changing in the operatory and my father demonstrated how to wash my hands and arms. The nurses selected the smallest pair of surgical gloves that were still too big for my hands. My father told the surgical nurse to order small gloves that will fit my hand. To handle the immediate problem, my surgical nurse taped my gloves around my wrist and arm to keep the glove in place.

I stood next to my father and he showed me how the baby was turned sideways and the umbilical cord was wrapped around the baby's neck. My father touched the woman's abdomen and asked, "Where do I make my incision?? I marked the beginning and end of the incision line and said, "I would cut that section." My father agreed with me and I watched him cut open the woman's abdomen and recover a healthy baby boy. My father had me cut the umbilical cord and tie off the cord at the baby's naval. He handed the new born to the nurse that quickly covered the little boy's penis to avoid getting squirted. I know that through experience and that only happened to me once and that was one too many. My father closed up the incisions and we were done. In total it took my father twenty-four minutes from start to finish. I carefully watched how my father sutured the uterus, fascia and skin.

Our next patient was also a delivery. She wanted to be a totally natural birth. My father checked on her dilation and commented that the baby's head may be too big to pass through the birth canal. My father had made notes from her last ultrasound regarding the size of the baby's head. When the woman started to deliver, it was obvious that she was going to have a problem and my father did an episiotomy and she was able to deliver her child by natural childbirth. She needed sutures and I carefully watched my father sew the skin that was cut. I asked my father if I could do the next one. He just laughed at me.

I had six weeks with my father. True to his schedule most of the time we saw patients in the morning and did deliveries and surgeries in the afternoon. I had just returned from lunch when I received a call directing me to exam room 1D. I ran to the room and my father was waiting for me. A ten-year-old girl presented with a torn perineum. She explained that she was walking on a tree and slipped and fell on her vagina. She started bleeding and her mother brought her into the medical center. My father reassured the girl that she would be fine. He examined the perineum and pointed out to me a prior repair. My father asked, "Is this the only time your daughter has had an accident causing injury to the perineum?" The mother quickly replied, "Yes, this is the first time." My father mentioned to the mother that he could see at least one prior repair and asked if this resulted from abuse. The girl's mother denied abuse had occurred, but the girl spoke up and said, "My uncle raped me and my mother won't do anything about it." I asked, "Were you raped the other time too?" She replied, "Yes, by the same uncle. I was told to say how I was hurt so my uncle wouldn't get into trouble." My father took pictures of the torn perineum and indicated that we would need a referral to child welfare. My father sewed the perineum and ordered a rape kit. The mother refused and the child was kept until child services could investigate. The mother finally consented to the rape test because the alternative would be losing her daughter to the system; something that no doctor wants to happen. I learned that the little girl had been raped more than ten times by the same person. I felt sorry for her and gave her a hug and reassured her that she would be alright.

During my third week with my father, he had me look at the vagina of an eighteen-year-old. She had vaginal irritation, sores and puss in her vagina. I looked at my father and quietly said, "I think she has a STD." Her mother was with her and asked, "What is a STD?" I just about blurted out 'sexually transmitted disease' when I remembered to shut my mouth. I let my father explain that her daughter had what appeared to be a sexually transmitted disease. He explained that we would take some swabs of the infection for laboratory testing. The nurse obtained the names of her sexual partners and I was embarrassed because she named off nine boys from her school. My father received the lab results and called the girl in the next day and set her up on a STD treatment program and turned over the information to the regional health department for follow up with the boys she had sex with. I told my father, "That's never going to happen to me." He replied, "I hope not. Unfortunately, STDs remain hidden until it is so bad that it can cause a lot of damage including, but not limited to infertility."

I was seeing a fifteen-year-old girl for a general gynecological exam. She was there with her mother to get birth control pills. I asked the same questions my father usually asked and then I did the exam with my father. I looked inside her vagina and something seemed off to me. My father checked and agreed that something else was going on. My father directed me to get a pregnancy kit. As I was leaving to get the kit, I heard the mother scream, "Why do you need a pregnancy kit?" My father explained what he saw and asked the girl to pee on the stick. She asked, "Right here? I know I am not pregnant." I placed a towel underneath the girl and she peed while still lying in the stirrups. The test was negative for pregnancy. The mother replied, "Thank God!" The girl said, "I told you I wasn't pregnant." My father looked closer with a scope and found that she had a tumor type cyst that should be removed. I watched my father remove the cyst and cauterize the wound.

I received a call to get to another examination room and when I arrived, the woman was already in hard labor, was dilated and I could see the baby's head. I told her to stop pushing until my father could get there. Well, the baby didn't want to wait. I delivered the baby with the assistance of the nurse. When my father arrived, the nurse told him that I did a perfect natural birth delivery. He checked my patient and then quietly told me that I wasn't to be delivering babies by myself. I am only a student intern. I replied, "Sorry, but the baby was coming with or without me. I just did what you taught me and it worked out fine." My father said, "You are learning quickly."

I mentioned that I would like the opportunity to actually do a C-section birth. I could swear that I could do that in my sleep. I ended up in my father's office cutting and sewing more pig skin. My father showed me the cut depth for the scalpel and how to close up the incision. I wanted to know when you sew, tape and staple. When he was through, I was even more confused and decided I would learn as I went. I cut pig skin for three days to the point that I actually could get a perfect cut in my sleep. I was so bored working on pig skin and I begged my father to give me a chance.

We were packing to fly home when an ambulance brought in a woman in labor distress. I watched my father examine her while he asked me if I understood what he was looking for. I began to explain when he said, "Take over and show me what we look for and what your recommendation is." I felt her abdomen and could feel the baby's head to the side of her uterus. The baby had not moved down the birth canal and I concluded that we would need to do a C-section birth." In my opinion, the baby couldn't be physically turned because the head was lodged against the wall of the uterus. When I finished, the woman asked my father why a little girl was examining her. My father explained that I was an intern and would be an OB/GYN when I graduated from medical school. I was surprised that she consented to me assisting in the delivery. I was nervous on the inside, but on the outside my hands were steady and in control. I lowered the surgical table to my height. My nurse never objected which was nice. I marked where I would do the incision and my father lengthened the incision line by an inch. He explained that the head seems somewhat large and it is better to have a larger opening than to extend the incision during delivery. The mother was put under and I slowly cut her abdomen along my incision line. I pulled back the skin and then carefully cut the fascia and separated that exposing the uterus. I cut the uterus and carefully removed the connected tissue from the newborn exposing the child. I looked at my father and he encouraged me to keep going. I lifted the baby so carefully and the nurse was there to take the baby from me. My father asked, "Now what? I cut the umbilical cord and tied off the cord at the newborn's naval. My father said, "Good, now what?" I replied, "I need to clean up and account for all of my surgical sponges and tools. Once the count was verified by the surgical nurse, I was told to close up the woman. I used a cross stitch suture and closed the uterus, then I sutured the fascia and finally I sutured the skin and then taped over the suture lines. I looked up at my father and he smiled and said, "Textbook C-section delivery." I couldn't wait to tell my mother that I did my very first C-section birth by myself; well under my father's supervision.

By my sixth week practicing with my father, I delivered 12 babies by natural childbirth and 3 babies by C-section. I carefully documented my obstetrics and gynecology experience and turned in my reports, journals and self-criticism of things I needed to do in the future to improve my skills.

Winter Break

I had two weeks off of school/work and my parents insisted I take the time off and have some fun. Christmas was eleven days away and I was always excited for Christmas. My parents asked me what I wanted and I named two things. I want to finish medical school and I want to learn to fly our helicopter. My mother replied, "You are completing your medical training and doing exceptionally well. I am concerned about adding more information in that little brain." I did what every other child would do, "I turned to my father and said 'pleeeeeeeeeeease!' My father replied, "You need to be able to reach the rudder pedals to fly." I replied, "I know, but can I at least try?" My father handed me the helicopter pilot training manual and said, "Read this and then we will talk."

I read and memorized the manual in two days. I was so excited to join my father in my first attempt to fly. I climbed into the helicopter like I was ten feet tall. I was ready to master the helicopter when I had to admit to myself that my feet didn't reach the pedals and I needed at least eight more inches of leg. I suggested I wear platform shoes, but both parents nixed that idea quickly.

My father took me flying and quizzed me on the different operational parts of our helicopter. He asked me to explain in detail how the inertial forces relate to flying. I explained, "The main rotor, collective and the cyclic or stick and rudder pedals control the aircraft's up and down, forward and backwards movement. The collective allows for the pitch of the helicopter, such as lifting off and landing. The cyclic or stick is what someone usually sees the pilot holding onto. The Cyclic with the rotor pedals move the helicopter in the direction you want to go. The tail rotor is a countermeasure for the helicopter rotor blades. Without the tail rotor, the helicopter would fly in right sided circles, lose altitude and ultimately crash. The tail rotor uses the inertial force of the main rotor blades to move the helicopter forward or even backward."

My father replied, "Good job" and allowed me to use the cyclic and had me direct him on how to press the rotor pedals for the direction I wanted to fly. My father explained to me and my mother that I have a good grasp of how the helicopter works, but I wasn't tall enough to fly. I put flying as one of many goals for me to accomplish when I was a little taller.

My Christmas break was the perfect time to be with Teri and enjoy Christmas activities together. I had been so busy for three months that I wasn't aware that a new neighbor arrived in our community. Like Teri's parents, the Lyle family also lived in their motor home until their house was built. I knocked on Teri's door and was surprised that Melody answered and said, "Teri isn't home right now." I heard Gary say hi to me and I asked, "Where is Teri? I was hoping to do something with her. I am off work and school for two weeks." Melody replied, "Teri is over at the Lyle's motor home playing with their children." I asked, "They have children?" Melody replied, "Yes. A ten-year-old son named Dennis and a nine-year-old daughter named Janine. I have met both children and they are very nice." I asked Melody if she thought I would be intruding if I went over to the Lyle's motor home. She replied, "I wouldn't think so, but I can't say for sure. I would go over there so you can meet your neighbors and see Teri."

I got my grandfather to drive me the quarter mile to the Lyle's motor home. It was two degrees outside and too cold to walk and even fly. I knocked on the door and said, "Hi. My name is Hayden." Dennis replied, "Oh, the brain." I asked him, "Who said I was a brain?" He replied, "No one". I knew better. The 'Brain' name had to have come from Melody or Teri; however, I hoped it was neither of them. I turned and walked away while Dennis shouted, "There goes the brain." I could hear Teri and Janine laughing in the background. I got into our car and slammed the door. My grandfather was pulling out of the Lyle's driveway when Teri ran out screaming at me to wait. My grandfather stopped the car and Teri apologized and began to cry. She kept saying, "Hayden, I am sorry and please forgive me." I told Teri that I forgave her and then asked my grandfather to take me home. Teri yelled, "Hayden, please stay." I didn't look back. I was hurt and it was my best friend that hurt me the most.

My mother greeted me and asked if I needed to talk. My mother could sense that I had a bad moment and she wanted to discuss it with me. I told my mother that it is nothing. Who needs friends anyway? I excused myself and left for the solitude of my bedroom. I hurt inside and I couldn't let it go no matter how much I tried. Teri tried calling me about a hundred times while I was off from work and school. I ignored her calls and focused on my goals and objectives. Apparently maintaining a close friendship was no longer available to me. I knew that

Teri must have been saying things about how smart I was or mocking me. Regardless of the reason, what she did to me hurt and hurt deeply. I couldn't wait to get back to work and my education.

Neurology and Internal Medicine

I felt good being back at work and school. I was assigned to Dr. Phelps, a board-certified neurologist and also held certification for internal medicine. I hate to say it, but neurology is so boring that I often day dreamed due to the lack of excitement. I learned how to test for nerve damage and pretty much consumed the topic in three days. I had almost no direct patient contact until I started on my last week. I learned how to read and understand test results following a full metabolic panel or similar blood tests. I learned about sugars, blood fats called triglycerides and cholesterol, anemia, obesity and some exposure to diabetes and kidney function. I was so happy to finish with Dr. Phelps. At the end, I asked him if he really liked what he did. He replied, "It's a living and I don't need to do surgery." I did my typical write ups and sent the information into the medical school.

I received a certified letter from the medical school informing me that I had been disenrolled for failure to pay my tuition and register for the next semester. I read the notice and was inflamed with anger. I personally mailed in my registration package and my tuition check. I called the medical school and they said I would not be enrolled for this semester due to nonpayment. I could enroll for the next semester. I had our bank pull the check I mailed with my registration. The bank had the endorsed cancelled check so the medical school had to have received my registration for that semester. When they confirmed that they didn't have my registration, I wrote back, "YOU WILL HEAR FROM MY LAWYER!!!!!!!! I was mad. I called Jim and he told me to breathe again. I shouted at Jim and said, "This isn't funny Jim. I can't lose a semester of study when I didn't do anything wrong. Jim promised to write the dean another letter on my behalf.

James A. Gauthier, J.D.

Dear Dr. Andresen:

Hayden E. Gehardi has brought to my attention a problem with her enrollment for the current semester. Ms. Gehardi mailed her registration and fee payment to the medical school in the same envelope. Her parent's bank statement shows that the tuition check was endorsed by the medical school and cleared their bank two weeks prior to the current term. I believe it is a fair presumption that if the medical school received my client's tuition payment that it also received her registration. In light of the fact that the tuition check was negotiated prior to the registration cutoff, I see no reason why Ms. Gehardi isn't allowed to re-register, assuming the medical school still hasn't located her registration.

I am tendering another copy of Ms. Gehardi's registration and kindly request that you reconsider your position on her current enrollment. The acceptance of her tuition is tantamount to accepting her for enrollment in the current semester.

I look forward to a favorable response at your earliest convenience. In the interim, I have directed Ms. Gehardi to resume her Clerkship program as was previously arranged.

/s/ *James A. Gauthier, J.D*

    I thanked Jim for his help and returned to my education pending the response from the medical school. I tried so hard to avoid pushing Jim, but I had to know the response as soon as Jim heard. Jim called me five days later and confirmed that I was registered for this current semester. I thanked my special friend once again. I never thought a medical school student would need a full-time attorney on call. I am thankful that Jim is my attorney. I owe him a big hug when I next see him.
    I began my semester with Dr. Allen, the medical center's emergency room physician. I was excited because I would have a substantial amount

of exposure to cuts, wounds, broken bones and even surgery. I appeared in the emergency room ready to work when Dr. Allen suggested I sit in his office until he had time to talk with me about the emergency room protocols and what would be expected of me and my limitations towards patient care. I sat in the office for nearly three hours when Stephen finally stopped long enough to talk with me. The first thing he said was, "My name is Dr. Stephen Allen or Dr. Allen; not Stephen." I apologized and he tersely said, please remember that and we will get along just fine."

Dr. Allen explained that as an intern, my patient exposure would be limited to triage, setting broken bones, suturing small cuts and possibly assisting in emergency surgeries. He then commented that he heard that I had completed three C-section deliveries under my father's supervision, and then stated that I wouldn't have that much freedom under him as my supervisor.

I shadowed Dr. Allen for my first week, observing how patient care was prioritized by the nursing staff at admitting, and how the patients were directed within the ER. I was amazed at the number of people that used the emergency room for minor cuts and burns, strains and sprains, otherwise known as soft tissue injuries. Each time I got too close to Dr. Allen he would suggest I ask fewer questions and spend more quality time observing what he did as the emergency room physician. At the end of one week, I had done nothing but follow Dr. Allen around and act as his gofer and I wasn't very pleased.

I asked for a private meeting with Dr. Allen. He replied, "I suppose I have to meet with you since your parents run this medical center." I replied, "I am not bringing my parents into this. I want to work out my education with you being an active participant and not shoving me into corners like you did all last week." Dr. Allen replied, "Look, I accept you are in your third year of medical school, but you are nine years old and no one would ever consent to you carving on their body or anything else." I looked him in the eye and said, "I am going to prove you wrong if you will let me do my job." Dr. Allen commented that he liked my bravado and he would see if I could contribute anything to the ER. I also pointed out that I was almost ten years old.

A father presented with his fourteen-year-old son and reported that his son broke his leg playing soccer. Dr. Allen told me to handle it and he would listen in on what I said and did. My first obligation was to obtain the patient's consent to treat them. I gave my three-minute explanation about being an intern and the father had no objection, even as to my age. He told me, "If you are smart enough to be in medical school then you should be able to begin practicing with patients." Stewart, his son said, "She's cute; I want her to be my doctor." I replied, "I will help you, but I am not a doctor yet. I am a third-year intern."

Because of the location of the pain was near the patella, or knee cap, I examined Stewart for a ligament tear before sending him to x-ray. I checked for extension and flexion of the joint and he experienced pain. I looked at Dr. Allen and said, "I don't think it is a broken bone; instead it appears he has an ACL injury. The father asked me, "What is an ACL injury?" I explained, "ACL means Anterior Cruciate Ligament. Stewart's knee is held together by four primary ligaments. I pointed out the medial collateral, lateral collateral, anterior cruciate and posterior cruciate ligaments and explained that I needed to send Stewart for x-rays and if the ACL is torn, he may become a referral to one of our orthopedic surgeons to fix the ligament tear." Stewart asked, "How soon can I return to playing soccer doc." I replied, "You are out for the count. If you have ACL surgery you will need some physical therapy and hopefully you will be physically eligible to play soccer next year." I stepped outside the examination room and for the first time Dr. Allen smiled at me and commented, "You do know what you are doing. I would have done nothing different. Good job." When the x-rays were returned, Dr. Allen sent him to the orthopedic surgery center and our job was done.

I liked working in the ER because there were a wide variety of patients; something unique to the ER since most medical fields are specialized like obstetrics and gynecology.

I was in my third week in the ER when a young mother presented with her son. She was screaming for immediate help and Dr. Allen sent me to admitting to evaluate the patient. The mother explained that she was boiling water to make her son macaroni and cheese. Her son pulled on the pan to see if his lunch was ready and the boiling water hit his face, arms and upper body. I called for the burn center, but the doctor was engaged in a surgical procedure and couldn't leave. I had the boy sent to the ER and I watched Dr. Allen flush the second degree burns with sterile saline water, then a topical burn ointment followed by wrapping the boy in wet burn sheets. Dr. Allen said, "He is stabilized. The burn center will contact us and take over case management."

I had a twelve-year-old boy present with a cut hand. He and his friends were breaking glass bottles for fun and he fell on a shard and cut his hand open. He presented with a hand wrapped in a dish towel. I looked to Dr. Allen for permission to treat the patient. He replied, "Your parents say you have a really good suture so go ahead if the family will allow you to treat the cut. I explained my typical background and the boy replied, "I'm not having a little girl work on me. I want a real doctor." His mother said, "Sorry." I replied, "Sorry isn't necessary. I understand there will be those times when patients will not trust someone as young as me." I alerted Dr. Allen and he talked to the mother and son and explained, "You can have our intern help you, or you can return to the waiting room until I am available." The boy asked, "How long do I have to wait?" Dr. Allen described the ER protocols and the more serious injuries or conditions are treated ahead of minor injuries like your cut. He then asked, "What is your preference?" The mother said, "I will accept the intern and my son will shut his mouth while she is providing care." I examined and cleaned the wound. I estimated sixteen stitches. I could do everything except inject a patient with anything. Dr. Allen injected the boy's wound and I finished irrigating the wound and sutured it. It took twenty-three stitches and my sewing job received another gold star from Dr. Allen.

I was near the end of my fourth week with Dr. Allen when a pregnant woman presented. She was already in active delivery with runaway contractions. I called my father and he said, "I am in the middle of a C-section. You are going to have to handle the birth if Dr. Allen will allow you that opportunity. I spoke with Dr. Allen and he somewhat laughed and said, "We don't have a lot of time to discuss it. The baby is on its way." I told Dr. Allen that I had participated in close to forty natural births and I could handle this." I received the mother's permission, I think if for no other reason that she wanted her baby delivered by someone. I checked the baby for position and dilation and followed the birth. It took nearly an hour to pass the baby. I picked up the baby and told the mother that she had a healthy baby girl. My nurse took over and I was done for another week.

I think my most interesting patient in the ER was Mr. Botts. He presented in the ER with confused thoughts, muscular and motor control issues, and lack of attentiveness. His wife explained that he is meticulous and detailed in everything he does. He was a CPA or certified public accountant for forty-two years. Last week he was in a car accident, but appeared fine to her until he began acting differently. She couldn't identify any medical injury, but settled on the fact that it was like he wasn't there anymore. Dr. Allen listened as I asked a few questions. I learned that her husband was putting a new battery in their golf cart. Changing the battery typically took her husband five minutes. He was outside changing the battery for almost three hours. When his wife asked him if he was alright, he said he was fine. The wife then looked at Dr. Allen and said, "What do you think?" Dr. Allen asked if I could do a neurological assessment first and then he would discuss what may be off in your husband. I had learned from my time with Dr. Phelps how to do a neurological assessment. I checked his eyes, hands, walking and motor skills; I asked open ended questions requiring an answer more detailed than yes or no. When I finished my assessment, I concluded that the patient either had a serious concussion or a brain bleed. Dr. Allen concurred and we sent him off for an MRI. The scan verified that the man had a ruptured blood vessel in his brain that was filling up inside his skull and depressing the different lobes of the brain. We made an immediate referral for surgery. Dr. Allen asked me if I knew what kind of surgery. I replied, "First they need to drain the blood from the brain. You do that by drilling a hole in the skull. Second you see if the blood vessel can be cauterized and if not, then opening up the skull will become necessary." Dr. Allen gave me another gold star.

I think I enjoyed my training in the ER. I sutured six wounds; I delivered two babies; I treated one burn case and a neurological impairment. I must have visited with more than one hundred patients presenting in the ER for colds, flu, and minor complications. I wrote up my experiences in detail and thanked Dr. Allen for treating me like a professional.

Cardiology

My last department before break was cardiology. Dr. Harris was a heart surgeon and treated patients suffering from heart attacks to leaking heart valves. I lightly assisted in three heart surgeries, but I wasn't permitted to do much of anything except watch Dr. Harris. I ordered echocardiograms and learned how to read the results. I learned quite a bit about cholesterol and triglycerides and impact on the heart and arteries. I had a better understanding as to the relationship of heart disease and diabetes, but mostly, my two weeks in cardiology were somewhat boring after the six weeks in the ER.

Spring Break at Last

I was excited to get two weeks off of school and work. The weather was cooperating with my schedule and this year spring came a little earlier than usual. The temperature was a balmy fifty-two degrees and the snow was quickly melting off the roadways and roof tops. I began to notice buds on our fruit trees and leaves beginning to form on the deciduous trees that surrounded our wilderness home.

My real excitement was seeing my friend, Teri that lived next door. My grandfather dropped me off and Teri welcomed me into their home. I felt uncomfortable around Teri for some reason. I felt like she was waiting to lunge at my throat and tear me to pieces because I spend all my time studying. I tried talking with Teri and received one-word answers. I explained that I was going to the horse barn to ride and invited Teri to ride with me. Teri asked me, "Why should I? You and I are no longer friends. Your head is bigger than your heart and I have found normal friends like me." I was crushed. At nine years old, my best friend just dumped me. I began to cry and left Teri's house in tears.

I did what I always do. I escaped into my bedroom and began studying anything that would keep my mind off Teri. My mother and grandmother flew me to the horse barn so I could ride midnight and get the stress off my back. I no sooner started riding and Teri showed up with Melody, Dennis and Janene. I heard Dennis say, "Are you sure we can ride in the barn. The brain is in the barn taking up all of the space and air." I became angry and dismounted my horse and ignored Dennis and Teri. I walked over to my mother and said, "I am going to put midnight away and we can go." My mother replied, "No, you get on your horse and ride like you planned. You are too smart to let those comments detract you from your goal, which for today was to have fun. I saddled Midnight again and I was riding by myself when I met Cynthia Tewes on the horse trail. She asked if I was new at the barn because she had never seen me before; however, she had seen Midnight. I began to explain when Cynthia said, "Do you like hot chocolate and banana bread?" I replied, "I love both." Cynthia said, "Let's tie off our horses and have something to eat and drink. It is a little chilly today."

Cynthia and I sat with my mother at the picnic table enjoying our food and drink. I learned that Cynthia had been boarding for four months and she liked the barn. As we talked, Cynthia's mother drove in and joined us. She brought more hot chocolate, donuts and cookies. I learned that Cynthia was nine years old and studying at a high school level. She was home schooled by her mother and she liked to learn. Cynthia's mother asked me what grade I was in. When I explained that I was a third-year medical student, she said, "BS". My mother confirmed that I was truly in my third year of medical school. Cynthia's mother is a urologist and internal medicine doctor. My mother asked if she would be interested in working for the Wilderness Health Outreach Medical Center since our medical center didn't have a urologist. There was an interest and time was set aside to give her a tour of the medical center. My mother asked me if I would like to give a tour to Cynthia. I replied, "Sure; that would be fun."

My mother and I flew Sandy Tewes and her daughter Cynthia to the medical center. Sandy commented, 'I didn't expect this at all." Cynthia asked me, "Do you fly in the helicopter all the time?" I replied, "Most of the time because it is faster and usually safer than driving, especially on icy roads in the endless winters around here."

I gave Cynthia a tour of the Medical Center and she was impressed that I actually worked there. As we walked through the center I would get comments like, "I thought you were off for two weeks and so on." It actually felt comfortable being back in my work setting. For me, work had always been a method of fun.

We finished the tour and ate lunch in the cafeteria before flying to our house for coffee, hot chocolate and desert. Teri saw the helicopter land and she ran over to my house and knocked on the door. I answered and explained to Teri that I was visiting with my new friend and I might find time to call her later if I could. I watched Teri's eyes begin to fill with tears and I felt she deserved the treatment because of the way she treated

A Gift from God

me. I was talking with Cynthia when it hit me. I am not the person that I had become with respect to Teri. I was bigger than being called the "Brain". I knew that Teri was most likely motivated to treat me in the manner she did because of Dennis and Janine. I grew up about ten years when I looked at Cynthia and said, "You know, I have a really good friend next door. She is my age and really nice. Do you mind if I invite Teri over to visit with us?" She replied, "I would like to meet your friend." I called Teri from my bedroom and I apologized and asked her to come over and meet Cynthia. My phone call healed a lot of emotional wounds and sutured tightly my ongoing friendship with Teri.

The following morning Teri arrived and my mother flew us to the horse barn where Teri and I spent the day riding with Cynthia. We each packed a large picnic lunch and for that day I returned to being a young girl having fun with my girlfriends.

I turned ten years old during spring break. Cynthia invited me and Teri over to her house for a sleepover and go to the most recent Disney movie playing at our local theater. We were dropped off by Cynthia's mother and told to go nowhere outside of the theater. The three of us sat in the back of the theater so we could talk and watch the movie at the same time. While we talked, three boys showed up and sat directly in back of us. They would touch our hair to get our attention. Cynthia knew two of the boys and agreed that they could sit with us. We sat boy-girl, boy-girl, boy-girl which I found a little discomforting. I had just turned ten and the boys were nine and ten years old. I sat next to Gary and he tried to hold my hand. I pulled it back and said, "I do not want to hold your hand." Gary asked me if I liked kissing boys. I replied, "I have only kissed my father and grandfather – never a boy yet and I am not starting tonight so please leave me alone. Gary tried to tickle me and I slapped him silly and said, "Don't you ever touch me again without my permission." I looked at Teri and Cynthia and asked to move to a different section away from the boys. Teri and Cynthia remained and I sat off by myself to avoid Gary.

The movie was almost over when a boy named Scott walked in and said, "Hey, aren't you my doctor?" I replied, "I am a medical student in my third year. I am not a doctor yet." He replied, "You probably do not remember me, but you diagnosed me having a hernia. I had it treated and I am doing fine because of your care. I didn't mean to disturb your movie, but I had to say thank you." I replied, "You are welcome. You may sit and watch with me if you would like." He slid his hand over to mine and held my hand and I decided to let him. That was it. The movie ended and he walked out front with me and waited with me while I waited on Teri and Cynthia. I kissed his cheek and said thank you for being a gentleman." Teri saw me kiss the boy and they teased me for the rest of the night. Sadly, I never saw Scott again, but that is the life of a medical student. Besides, I am too young for boys and too busy to fit boys into my life. Teri, Cynthia and I had a wonderful time being girls and talking about boys. For a few moments in my life, I was like my friends and it was refreshing.

Obstetrics and Gynecology – Part II

I was happy to return to work. I was to spend another six weeks with my father and then six weeks with my mother doing pediatric medicine. At this point in my third year, I had handled emergency room cuts, scrapes and breaks, concussions, neurologic assessments, delivered three C-section babies and nearly sixty natural childbirths, of course all under the watchful eye of my father and the other clinicians.

I flew into work with my parents like we do every morning, except today was to turn out a little different. My father said, "Hayden, when we get to work I want to have a meeting with you and my nursing staff." I asked my father, "What about?" He replied, "Several of the nurses believe that you do not belong with patients at your age. The nurses can't cite a single incident where you committed error on the job, and to me it seems like some petty jealousy. Regardless, I feel the need to clear the air, especially with Nurse Radeen who is the nursing supervisor in the obstetrics and gynecology section of the hospital." I looked at my father, rolled my eyes and said, "I know all about Nurse Radeen. She refuses me contact with a patient and the new born infants except when you are present. I asked her one day if she had a problem working with me. She replied, "Your damn right I do. You think you are something special and above the nursing staff. I refuse to work with you Hayden. You are just a little girl playing doctor and I don't like it."

My father met with the nursing staff and discussed my role at the medical center. He explained that I might be nine years old; I quietly reminded my father that I was ten. He continued, "Hayden is a third-year medical school student meeting her Clerkship training obligations at the medical center. I looked at Nurse Radeen, expecting a negative response from her. When my father stopped talking, Nurse Radeen stated that she refused to take orders from an eight, I mean ten-year-old and she didn't give a damn what my education was, or what I wanted to be when I grew up. My father surprised me by saying, "Thank you. You are terminated for insubordination towards Hayden and me." My father then appointed the next senior nurse as the supervisor unless she believed the same as Nurse Radeen. Nurse Thompson replied, "I have no problem working with Hayden." My father said, "Let's get to work then." The mutiny was over as quickly as it began. When everyone left my father's office, he explained that Nurse Radeen will not be the only person with an attitude towards me. He said, "Keep your perspective and your eye on your goal and you will do well."

My father informed me that my last six weeks would focus more on gynecology and gynecological disorders. He handed me literature on pelvic inflammatory disease and the impact on infertility; chlamydia, and endometriosis. These common, but serious disorders lead to infertility if not diagnosed and treated in a timely manner. I was to study gynecological disorders and he would quiz me at the end of the week. I looked at the stack of medical journals on the topic and I sat down to begin reading the material when my father said, "You are a medical student. Read on your own time. I need you with me in the clinic seeing patients. I was so busy at work that I had to do my reading and studying when I got home.

My second week of studies focused on female cancer, such as breast cancer, endometrial and ovarian; cervical; cancer of the vulva and vaginal cancer. I finished my studies and successfully answered my father's questions. I thought my two-week cram course was over, but my father instructed me to study the presenting symptomology for each type of disorder and cancer and then be prepared to discuss the method of treatment. He required me to revisit pharmacology and other known treatment modes from the least invasive to surgery. I thought I understood female disorders until my father pointed out my shortfalls. I took a third week to keep studying treatment modalities and what the tell-tale signs were for disorders, such as pelvic pain, burning, ruptured ovarian cysts and uterine fibroids.

I was sitting in my bedroom study when my father walked in and asked me how I was doing. I explained what I had accomplished and he acknowledged that he was pushing me harder than the medical school would require because I was going to become an exceptional OB/GYN. His reassurance that I was doing an outstanding job meant more to me than anything. When he left my study, I buckled down to my studies and stopped feeling sorry for myself. I thought to myself, *if I am going to become a medical doctor then I had better start acting like one.*

I arrived with my parents and discovered the waiting area was overrun with patients. The flu and pneumonia were running rampant through the wilderness community and it looked like most of the community was waiting for us to get to work. I asked my father, "Do you want me doing triage or report to our section?" My mother asked that I be released to do triage since there were 42 patients waiting. I quickly talked with each patient and tagged them with the appropriate red, yellow and green tag. Once everyone was tagged, I reported to my father. I explained that when I was doing triage, I have a female patient experiencing difficulty with her menstrual cycle. I quietly told my father that she is quite rude, but then again, she is in pain. There is a second patient that explained to me that she had substantial pain and discomfort when she engaged in intercourse. I asked her for more detail and she described a burning sensation when she urinated. I mentioned a urinary tract infection, but she would need to wait for a full pelvic exam. I have one more patient coming in. She is having blood in her urine and significant pain. She described a few sores on her labia and vulva. We have six pregnant women to be seen today.' My father thanked me for my complete report and said, "Let's get that first patient in."

Our OB/GYN protocol provided for seeing patients with appointments first and then those walk-ins to the medical center. However, if a woman presented with symptoms like puss and blood in her urine, her priority is elevated to immediate care when possible.

The first patient was the woman with puss and blood in her urine and inside her vagina. The nurse prepped the patient and my father did an exam, but didn't say anything. He got permission for me to do the exam as well. I looked and noted dark hemorrhaging along her vaginal wall and cervix. She had what appeared to be an ovarian cyst to me and possibly an infection, but I couldn't determine the origin. My father explained that the dark walls of the vagina suggested an on-going problem; and possibly cancer. I was asked to take some swabs and send them to the lab for analysis. We allowed the woman to go home and we would call her. The results came back as ovarian cancer. At that point we sent her to our oncology department.

My next patient that day was the young woman that had been so rude to me. When my father asked for her consent to examine her, she replied, "Hell No. That little brat most likely hasn't even started her menstrual cycle. What can she do for me except leave me alone?" My father did the examination and explained what he found. He asked her if I could at least look inside her vagina to see what he saw. She finally allowed me one look. I turned to my father and quietly said, "ectopic pregnancy". My father said, "Good call." My father removed the ovary and terminated the ectopic pregnancy. I was allowed to assist in the surgery.

Our next patient was a scheduled pregnancy follow up. I did the exam and ordered the ultrasound. Routine pregnancies were a real no brainer. I was getting ready to see our next patient when my father was contacted by the emergency room. A pregnant thirty-eight-year-old woman was in a serious car accident and wasn't expected to survive. My father delivered the baby by C-section, but didn't want me to assist. He later told me that you will see enough death in your career. I didn't want you exposed. I replied, "If I am going to be a doctor, then I need to deal with the living and the dying. Please don't shield me. I am not four years old anymore." My father agreed with me and helped me to feel part of the team and not an occasional observer.

I explained to my father that we had a walk-in needing to see us. I met with the girl and her mother and learned that the pregnant girl is thirteen years old and according to the mother, she wants to keep the baby. Her mother is in agreement. My father gave his consent for me to do the pregnancy examination while he watched. The pregnant girl watched me closely asking me repeatedly if I knew what I was doing. I tried to reassure her. I used the Doppler and could determine the baby's heart rate and I concluded that she was seven weeks along. The girl replied, "You don't know what in the hell you are doing. I just had sex with my boyfriend last week. I asked, "Have you engaged in intercourse with anyone else; let's say seven weeks ago?" The girl laid on the exam table and said, "No, Bobby was four weeks ago. Ah, Steve was about five weeks ago. Oh, and then there was Curtis; it must have been Curtis but I don't love him anymore so it can't be his baby." I replied, "You will need a paternity test for all of the people you have engaged in intercourse. One of them got you pregnant." I recommended regular checkups until the baby is born. I could hear her mother yelling at her on the way out of the medical center.

I was amazed at the number of young girls seeking birth control. These are outback girls; not city girls. My father explained that our job is to determine if the patient is healthy and then prescribed birth control pills. We are not in the judgment business; except for you. You are never to have sex with anyone until you are thirty years old. I got a laugh out of that one and mentioned that seeing girls that are pregnant, having STDs or similar problems is a good motivator to avoid unprotected sex.

I was talking with my father when he said, "I think we finished another day. We have no more appointments on the schedule and I checked the ER and they are fine. Would you like to go home early? It is Friday and you get the weekend off." Before going home, I checked with my mother to see if she needed any help. She was fine and my father flew me home. I immediately called Cynthia to see if she would like to ride over the weekend. She indicated she could Saturday, but she had other plans for Sunday. I called Teri to see if she was interested in riding. She replied, "Not with you. My cousin, Jake is coming and we are going riding together." I had to wonder again what I did to Teri for her to treat me that way.

I met Cynthia at the stables and we rode trails most of the morning. We stopped for lunch and had a nice laugh because I brought Cynthia's favorite sandwiches and she brought mine. The hot chocolate felt nice and warm for a brisk spring day. We finished lunch and were getting ready to ride again when Teri showed up with Dennis and Janine. Teri wouldn't even look at me. I hurt inside, but remembered what my mother said, "Whose problem is it?" I figured it was Teri's problem and I enjoyed the rest of my day with Cynthia. I decided to invite Cynthia to spend the night at my house and she accepted.

We arrived by helicopter and Cynthia was thrilled with the ride. When we walked into my bedroom and study, Cynthia's eyes lit up and she was excited to see all my literature books and lab equipment. I found out that Cynthia was taking an advanced placement course in biology and chemistry. We spent the rest of the day playing like I like to play. I reviewed some lab experiments that were of interest to Cynthia. We set up the experiment and that led to us completing experiments for the next eight hours. We cleaned up the lab and went to bed. Cynthia commented on how clean and organized I was. I replied, "I have been that way since I could walk." I talked with Cynthia about medical school and my experiences as an intern at the medical center. When we finished, Cynthia was excited to go to medical school. She commented, "Wouldn't it be nice if we had a medical practice together." I replied, "You can join me at the medical center." Cynthia replied, "Did my mother call your mother yet?" I asked, "What about?" Cynthia replied, "My mother would like to accept the urology position at the medical center." I checked with my mother and she smiled and said, "Yes, I offered the job and she accepted. I think you will be seeing a lot more of Cynthia in the coming months."

I was sitting on my porch Sunday morning when I saw Teri walk out to their mailbox. I waived, but she ignored me and went back inside. I called Teri and I heard her tell Melody that she wasn't there. I spoke up and said, "I know she is there. I watched her walk into the house." Melody said, "I'm sorry Hayden but Teri isn't interested in playing with you. Her cousin will be here any time. He is the cousin that is a near genius. I hung up and ten minutes later I heard a knock on our door. I opened the door and Jake said, "Hi Teri. I am your cousin Jake." *I thought 'near genius'. He can't even find the right house."*

I introduced myself to Jake and he replied, "Oh, you are the stuck up little bitch with the big brain." I looked at Jake and asked, "What did you call me?" Jake quickly apologized and commented that you seem nice. I replied, "I am nice and I do not have a big brain." Jake asked me how old I was. I replied that I was ten. He said, "I am almost eleven." He asked me what grade I was in and I replied, "It's none of your business." Jake replied, "You are really cute." I replied, "Thanks, but I am not looking for a boyfriend or a date. He said, "Neither am I." He looked at me and said, "I already heard that you are in medical school so why the rude treatment?" I replied, "I am tired of being treated rudely just because I work hard at my studies." Jake replied, "I will never treat you that way. I like you and you are really nice and down to earth."

Teri ran over to my house and said, "Jake, you are supposed to be visiting me, not her." Jake replied, "I am going to stay here for a while and talk with Hayden. Why don't you stay too?" Teri folded her arms, pouted and sat on the porch with us. She interrupted our discussions about six times asking if Jake was ready to leave. When talking with Jake, I learned that he lives on a ranch and he rode horses all the time. I invited him to our barn to ride. He said no at first, but when he learned that we fly there in our helicopter, he said, "Good-bye" to Teri. My mother flew us to the barn and Teri showed up about an hour later. When we returned to the helicopter a note was left on my side windshield. It said, "Hayden I hate you."

My mother sensed my frustration and once again came to my rescue. She explained about the difficulties of interrelating with friends that lack any common bond except the friendship. Teri isn't mad at you specifically. I truly believe she is mad because you exist in a world over which she has little input and feedback. You may call it jealousy or just a lack of her understanding what you are going through. Teri will rethink who she is in relation to you this summer when you get some time off work and school. Until then, focus on your schooling and let Teri think about your friendship."

My mother's pep talks always helped. I didn't want her protecting me, but in the same vein I liked her support and counsel. I decided the best way to respond to Teri's note was to send her a note right back. I emailed to her computer, "TERI, I STILL LOVE YOU AND I FORGIVE YOU. PLEASE FORGIVE ME FOR WHATEVER I MAY HAVE DONE TO YOU AND OUR FRIENDSHIP." Teri briefly answered and explained that Dennis and Janine kept pushing her away from me. She would like to end her friendship with them, but she would have no friends to be with. I replied, "I will always be your friend. Just let me in and try to understand what I am going through."

I shook off my disappointment about Teri and returned to work focused on my fourth week of OB/GYN training. My father was permitting me to do more exams once the patient approved. My diagnostic conclusions were about eighty percent accurate so I knew that I had a long way to go. My father kept reminding me that he had an additional four years of medical training, post medical school, to receive his certification as an OB/GYN. He put his arm around me and said, "Hayden, you are doing very well and quite frankly better than I anticipated. I am receiving the same reports from the other physicians that have worked with you on your Clerkship."

I asked my father if I would get any more opportunities to do another C-section with him. He sent me to the supply room to get another pig skin to practice on. During breaks in patient care, my father would watch my hand as I carefully made my incision on the pig skin perfectly. Once I made my incision, and obtained approval, my father would say, "Good, now close." I went through the process of accounting for my surgical tools, sponges, gauze, etc. before closing the incision. My father pounded into my head, "You never, and I repeat never close up a patient until the charge nurse has fully accounted for every piece of gauze, bandage, and surgical tools used in the procedure." I practiced stapling small sections of pig skin and must have sewn and taped a mile of pig skin; at least it seemed like a mile. I asked, "Do you think I am ready for another C-section?" My father replied, "I think so."

My opportunity to do another C-section delivery came three days later. I diagnosed the turned baby and I couldn't physically turn it so its head would pass through the birth canal. I informed my father that we have need for a C-section delivery and he replied, "Why do you think a C-section is necessary?" I explained my findings and recommendation. He checked the patient and agreed. It took twenty minutes to obtain the mother's consent to allow me to do the delivery, again under the direct supervision of my father. This time he said, "I am going to let you solo. I will only comment if you have overlooked something important." The patient has approved your camera and I want you to explain to me exactly what you are doing and why so whoever watches or listens to your video recording will understand the steps you are taking to complete a C-section delivery." I asked, "Like an autopsy?" My father replied, "No, like the birth of a healthy baby." *I felt so stupid.*

Prior to today, I had delivered babies with my father, or closely under his supervision. Today I was going to get tested on my ability to complete a C-section delivery. In my mind I walked through the delivery steps. (1) Check baby and determine if there is a chance for a normal delivery; (2) explain the C-section surgery to the mother; (3) Mark my lateral incision line across the abdomen; (4) Cut the skin and pull it back; (5) Cut the fascia underneath the skin and pull it back; (6) Cut the uterus and remove the baby taking care to remove tissue that may get in the way. (7) Hold and upend the baby until it breathes and cries; (8) Cut and tie the umbilical cord and give the baby to nurse; (9) Stich the uterus referred to as closing the uterus; (10) Stitch the fascia; and (11) Stitch the skin. My father asked if I was reviewing the steps. I replied, "I am." He replied, "Good. I do that every time. I am just a little faster than you. I listed off all eleven steps verbally and the birth mother commented that I sounded like I knew what I was going to do. She then looked at my father and asked, "You will be right here with her – right?" My father replied, "I am her supervisor and I will not leave your side throughout the procedure."

I received the go ahead and the nurse asked me if I was nervous. I replied, "Not anymore." I marked my incision line and informed the anesthesiologist that I was ready. I slowly did my incisions and carefully removed some tissue and the baby's head popped out of the incision hole. I carefully cleared away the obstructing tissue as I worked the baby out of the mother. I laid the baby on the delivery table, cut and tied the umbilical cord and the nurse immediately wiped down the little girl. I cleaned up the incision as my nurse accounted for our surgical products and tools and then reversed my steps first suturing the uterus then the fascia and finally small stitches for the skin. I wiped off the sutures and my father said, "Text book C-section delivery once again." I may only be ten years old, but I feel much older and wiser. I love being or becoming a doctor.

The mother that I delivered her baby by C-section had her husband buy me an X-Box Game Station. I had to read to see what an 'X-Box' was. My nurse asked, "You don't know what an X-Box is? What planet have you been living on?" I replied, "I have never heard of an X-Box game." She replied, "Maybe you have never played on an X-Box Play Station, but you must have seen the game advertised on television." I replied, "We don't own a television and I have rarely played electronic games and the only time I see a television is when I am visiting my friend, Teri." Just then my eyes started to water as I thought about Teri and how she had hurt me so many times when I can't recall doing anything to her except being too busy to always find time to be with her. My nurse asked, "Hayden, are you alright?" I replied, "Yes, I am fine. Please donate this X-Box game to charity. I am sure someone will put the gift to good use."

My final week with my father was all gynecology patients. I examined patients for pills, infections, urinary tract infections, pelvic inflammatory disease and normal pregnancy check-ups. I developed a skill in watching and interpreting ultrasounds and I was always pleased to let the expecting parents listen to their baby's heartbeat. It is that point of hearing a heartbeat that the true bonding takes place between parent and child.

On my final day with my father, I joined him in the surgery center. He was going to remove endometrial tissue that was affecting a young woman's ability to get pregnant. I watched with interest as my father removed the endometrial fibers allowing for a freer movement of the egg from the fallopian tubes and promoted more sperm to have a chance to reach the egg and fertilize it. The procedure was called a laparoscopy and permits surgery through a small hole with the use of a light and camera. It is much less invasive over a full surgery.

I returned to my office and my father asked me why I was sitting down. He said, "You have six more patients that are backed up because of our surgery." I walked into the examination room and my parents had a cake celebrating my successful training with my father. My mother looked at me and said, "Have a good weekend because Monday you are going to run your little tail off." That's just what I liked to hear.

Pediatric Medicine Part II

My last six weeks of my clerkship placed me back with my mother handling pediatric medicine, or what I referred to as the runny nose or upset tummy section of the medical center. Nothing very exciting happened and I learned to listen and be supportive of my patients. I enjoyed the occasional broken bone or wound, but I would never wish an injury onto a child.

My mother stopped by and let me know that I would be doing the school physicals for swimming, track and field, cheerleading and drill team. I was surprised that the block of physicals I had were all girls ranging in age from eight to fifteen. I anticipated problems due to my age, but I received no resistance from parents or my patients. A typical school sport's physical involved checking ears, eyes, nose, throat, lungs, weight, height, gait, flexibility, diabetes, types I and II, and hernia. I had completed four physicals under my mother's direct supervision when she turned me lose. I was placed in an exam room and the nursing staff cycled the girls through every fifteen minutes. If the girl met the physical guidelines then I filled out their approval form and my mother signed it. I thought to myself *necessary, but boring.*

I spent my first week in pediatrics handling school physicals, runny noses and the flu. I thought about the upcoming five weeks and started looking for a means to a little more excitement. In my second week, my mother had me read several journals on pediatric care, including methods to diagnose such ailments as childhood leukemia and lymphoma; tonsil inflammation; appendicitis swollen glands, urinary tract infections, sinus related issues, allergies and sexually transmitted diseases. I completed the review and asked my mother how frequently any of the illnesses I studied were actually treated at our medical center. My mother replied, "Not often, but you must be prepared to make the correct diagnosis and recommend the proper treatment." I thought I was headed back to seeing patients; however, my mother had a different idea. I was handed several journals which informed pediatricians and general practitioners of the tell-tale signs of abuse and neglect. Once again, I finished my review of the literature and asked how many abuse cases my mother saw last year. She replied, "Two, and neither child lived in the wilderness. They were traveling when presented with an illness and signs of physical abuse. My mother said, "Let's go to work."

My first patient ruined my day. A ten-year-old female patient presented with multiple bruising all over her body. I examined the girl and found no signs of sexual abuse and the girl denied being physically abused. I listened to her describe how she felt; how her back hurt and how she was tired most of the time. I did a more thorough exam and found she had substantial pain near her kidneys and she had blood in her urine. I ordered a lab and decided she needed to be hospitalized until we knew what was going on in her body. My mother examined her and agreed that the symptoms suggested kidney failure or cancer. The girl crashed in the hospital and was immediately placed on dialysis until the lab results were back. I had to follow up because once she was admitted as an in-patient, the hospitalist and specialist would see her. It was determined that she had a urinary tract infection that remained untreated and that affected her kidneys. Fortunately for her, the condition was treatable and normal kidney function would return.

I finished with my morning schedule of physicals and routine care when my mother handed me journals on pediatric type I and type II diabetes mellitus and I needed to test and evaluate a child's actual or propensity towards developing diabetes. Our medical center lacked an endocrinologist resulting in placing the burden of diagnosis and treatment of diabetes on the pediatric doctors. I learned about how diabetes relates to other ailments such as heart failure, peripheral nerve disease, kidney failure, renal failure and even death. I believe the most important observation from the literature is that everyone is subject to diabetes. The literature suggests obesity is a cause, which it is a substantial cause, but there is approximately thirty-eight percent of diabetics are of normal weight or even underweight requiring qualification of the causes. Regardless of whether a child was born with juvenile diabetes type I or they develop type II later in life, it is a horrible disease that leads to more amputations than any other disease.

I finished my review of pediatric medical conditions and the preferred method of treatment and asked my mother if she had more for me to read. I sounded so bored when asking my mother my question. She replied, "Get used to reading. I read every medical journal article on conditions that may affect my area of pediatric and family medicine. As a general practitioner, I must always be prepared to accurately diagnose a medical condition, even when the likelihood of ever seeing certain types of patients is almost zero. Not understanding the subject matter may lead to treating the symptom without understanding the cause. If you overlook the cause, you may lose your patient. Unfortunately, reading is a critical part of patient care." I replied, "I know that. I want to experience being the primary care giver and learn with as much hands-on learning as I can possibly get." My mother replied, "Your residency next year will afford you the opportunity to specialize. For now, you are in school and learning so please keep up with your reading."

The following day my mother permitted me to see patients once again. The medical center developed a disclosure form that patients could sign approving me to provide primary care to their child. I received a considerable amount of questions and concerns about my age, but my reputation was developing and return patients openly requested me as their care provider. My mother reviewed our appointment schedule for the day and assigned me to half of her patients. On routine matters like runny noses, the flu, suturing a wound, physicals and well-baby care were all within my area of expertise. Everything else required direct supervision.

I anxiously awaited my first patient. The nurse explained that my patient had untreated constipation. The twelve-year-old boy hadn't had a bowel movement in more than a week and his mother was concerned. I did my exam and referred the boy to x-ray so I could see if he had an impacted bowel or something more serious. When the x-ray was returned to me, I could plainly see the impacted bowel. I discussed the condition and the mother said she had tried stool softeners and suppositories without success. She explained that her son couldn't fasten his pants in the morning due to the pain. I reviewed the x-ray with my mother and she confirmed the patient had an impacted bowel. My mother smiled at me and asked, "You do know how we treat an impacted bowel?" I replied, by rolling my eyes and said, "I do." My mother told me to take the patient to the wash room where I had to do an enema. It took nearly an hour to clean out the blocked intestines. I had a follow up x-ray and confirmed that the impacted bowel was resolved. I recommended stool softeners for the next week.

My next patient was a little unusual. He was apparently zipping up his jeans when he caught the foreskin of his penis in his zipper. His mother was able to free the skin, but he wouldn't stop bleeding so she brought him in on an emergency basis. My nurse prepared him and I walked in and he moved so quickly that he fell off the examination table. He took one look at me and said, "No way is she looking at my dick. I want to go home." I gave my usual response and suggested the boy go back to the waiting room until Dr. Gehardi can see him. His mother asked, "Can you estimate how long that will take?" I replied, "Maybe an hour or two. She is very busy. I am a third-year intern and I can help your son if he will grow up a little and understand that I am here in a medical capacity. I then looked at the boy and explained that I may be a ten-year-old intern, but I had seen more penises than he would ever see so let's get you treated." The boy asked, "What are you going to do to me?" I replied, "I am going to clean the wound, cauterize it if I can't stop the bleeding. Given the location of the cut, I can't put a bandage on your penis or you won't be able to urinate." He asked, "What does 'urinate' mean?" I replied, "Going pee." I cleaned out his wound and cauterized the wound and prescribed a mild ointment. I filled out the prescription and my mother signed it and checked my work.

I was excited because I was actively providing patient care at ten years old. I finished my patient list and checked with my mother to see if she needed help. She was fine and suggested I take the rest of the day and read the pile of journal articles related to pediatric care. That was not what I was looking for. My mother pointed to her office and suggested I study there. I asked, "May I leave the wing and study in the cafeteria?" My mother replied, "Anywhere is fine. Just keep your pager and phone with you just in case you are needed for patient care."

I was sitting in the cafeteria reading, when not being bothered by everyone stopping to say hi to me. I was about to leave the cafeteria to a quieter venue when Marcus sat down and said, "Hi". He introduced himself and asked, "Are you a doctor?" I replied, "Not yet. I showed him my lab coat that said, 'Third Year Medical Student." *I wondered if the boy could read. My name and status were in plain view on my lab coat.* I realized that Marcus wasn't going to take a hint so I stopped reading to talk with him. I learned that he was almost eleven and the son of our town's selectman. He was dropped off by his mother every Friday for his dad's weekend. Marcus explained that his parents were divorced and his mother used the medical center as a safe drop point. He explained that he sat in the cafeteria until his father picked him up. *I thought, too bad for Marcus. I was pleased that my parents would never separate and I found comfort in that point.*

Marcus had a lot of questions for me about medical school and how hard was it for me to get where I am today. I replied, "It takes a lot of hard work studying most of the day and night. I spend about twelve to fifteen hours a day, mostly reading, but now my time is consumed in direct patient care. I asked Marcus if he would like a tour of the medical center. I walked him around to the various departments I worked in. I stopped by an examination room and Marcus asked me how I could examine a patient so high in the air. He asked, "Do you have a stool or ladder you carry around?" I laughed and said, "Watch this." *I pushed the elevation button and the examination table lowered to a height I could work at.* I replied, "Miracles of modern medicine."

I liked Marcus and introduced him to my mother who politely welcomed him to the center and then excused herself because she was knee deep in patients. I asked my mother if she needed help. She smiled and said, "No, enjoy a little time off and finish your tour of our medical facility." I thought Marcus was cute and I enjoyed talking with him. He kept looking at me and said, "You sure look like a doctor. Does that thing work? I allowed Marcus to listen to my heart through the stethoscope and he thought that was fun. I let him listen to his heart and he asked me if his heart sounded healthy? I replied, "It sounds just fine."

I walked Marcus to the delivery center to introduce him to my father, but the desk nurse said my father was just starting a C-section and he had a natural birth pending in Room C. I started walking away when I heard a scream from Room C. The attending nurse yelled for me to come back. I excused myself and ran to Room C where I learned the patient's baby was dropping and on the way out. The woman was in severe pain with contractions that were more than three minutes apart. I apologized to Marcus as I closed the door and checked the woman for dilation. She wasn't ready, but very close. I asked for her chart and noticed notes from my father concerning the head size. He underlined the anticipated need to do an episiotomy to allow for the natural birth. I asked the nurse to check on my father's availability and he was still in the middle of a difficult C-section delivery of triplets. I wished I could have been in there with my father, but my hands were full with his other patient. I washed up and got on my gloves and explained to the woman who I was and the fact that I had delivered over twenty babies by natural child birth. I explained the head size and the need for an episiotomy which I explained to her. I used a topical anesthetic and did the episiotomy myself. It was a good thing because the baby dropped and she pushed and the baby boy was delivered. I cut the umbilical cord and tied off the cord at the naval and then handed the baby to the nurse so I could suture the skin. I waited for my father to check her and my sutures. My father examined the mother and congratulated me on a job well done. When we were out of earshot of the patient my father asked me how I deadened the skin to do the episiotomy. I replied, "I used a topical lidocaine and it worked well. I had no choice." My father gave me a hug and said I would become a good OB/GYN when my training was concluded in five more years.

I left the room and Marcus had patiently waited for me. He asked, "What took so long in there?" I replied, "I had to do a delivery which included an episiotomy." He asked, "What is that?" I explained and Marcus got sick just thinking about what I did. I recommended he find a future profession that didn't include blood. Marcus looked at his watch and said, "I need to get back to the cafeteria. My father will be picking me up there." I walked back with Marcus and I bought him a hot chocolate while we waited for his father. Marcus stood up and said, "That's my father. May I see you here next Friday?" I replied, "Maybe."

When he left, I decided that I liked Marcus. I talked about him all weekend until my mother asked for a different Hayden channel. She remarked, "I am sure he was nice, but you are not ready for a relationship with a boy while you are, or should be studying the materials I gave to you."

I returned to pediatric care and saw more runny noses and upset tummies. I had three well-baby check-ups and four sports physicals. How boring after delivering a baby and doing my first episiotomy. I checked with the nurse and I had no more patients. I checked with my mother and she had it covered and my father was finished for the day. I asked if I could work in emergency until we were ready to fly home. My father said, "Go for it."

I entered the ER and asked Dr. Allen if I could be useful. Dr. Allen welcomed me back into the ER. The nurse indicated that she had two lacerations needing sutures, a broken arm and a patient complaining about severe indigestion. I prioritized and took the laceration patients first. A young girl fell and hit her head on a step. She had a deep cut across her forehead about one-inch long. I cleaned the wound and had Dr. Allen inject lidocaine to deaden the area. I very carefully sutured the cut since it would be visible on the little girl for the rest of her life. I made the tightest sutures I could do and Dr. Allen checked my work and said, "Beautiful job. I doubt the young lady will have much of a scar, if any.

My next patient was a cut foot. I cleaned the wound and asked Dr. Allen to deaden the area. He looked at me and said, "Now is a good time for you to learn how to do injections." I was shocked that he would allow me to do that. I explained how and where I would inject the wound and he concurred. I numbed the area with a topical anesthetic and then said, "A little stick here. I injected the anesthetic in three places and within minutes the boy's foot was numb. I carefully sutured his wound with fourteen stitches and he was out of there.

I checked a young girl who presented with a broken right arm. I sent her to x-ray and read the radiologist's notes. He wrote, "Similar break right radius healed. Similar break left radius healed. Current break right radius. I looked at the x-ray again and asked the mother if this was her daughter's first broken bone. She acted defensive and said, "Of course it is. Why?" I showed the mother the evidence of two prior breaks in the same area as today's break. The mother denied that her daughter had any broken bones previously. I replied, "I understand, but the x-ray shows something different." I asked the little girl how she hurt her arm. She started to talk when the mother grabbed her and yanked her off my exam table and said, "We are leaving and I am going to report you and this medical center to the AMA. It is ridiculous that a ten-year-old is practicing medicine. If you do anything to me or my daughter, I will put you out of business for malpractice."

I was dumbfounded, somewhat shaken up and wasn't sure how to proceed. It was clear to me that the little girl was physically abused. At four years old, very few children sustain three breaks on the same bone. My mother reviewed the file and x-ray and said, "I will call child services. We need to help stop further injuries to the little girl."

My mother said, "Shake it off and keep going. I want you to see the next patient for me. I have already spoken with the father and he will allow you to handle his daughter's examination. I welcomed a seven-year-old girl into my examination room. While the nurse prepped the patient, I washed up and then asked the father what was the problem. He explained that he rarely bathed his daughter, but last night he was with her and he gave her a bath and noticed substantial chaffing and irritation around his daughter's pubic area. He said, "Angela is always touching herself and rubbing or scratching herself leaving her almost raw from her fingernails. I examined the girl and calmly checked for abuse. I asked the girl how long she had experienced the itching and chaffing. She replied, "Almost two weeks." I asked if she had any idea why it started. She could only say, "I started itching and I scratched and it is getting worse and it is painful. I was at a loss. I took a swab of the irritated area and sent it to the lab, but I was without an explanation or how to treat the condition.

My mother arrived about ten minutes later and examined the girl. It turned out that she had an infection on her skin of unknown origin. My mother prescribed some antibiotic ointment and asked for a follow up in ten days. She returned and the condition had abated.

I looked around and there were no more patients. I looked at the clock and it was 7:15 p.m. *I thought no wonder there were no more patients- our day should have ended around 6 p.m.* My mother just smiled when I yawned and she said, "Welcome to the practice of medicine." I fell asleep on the way home. Fortunately, it was Friday once again and I had the weekend off work, or so I thought. In the morning I checked my communications with the medical school. I received the following letter from the medical school dean.

"Dear Ms. Gehardi:

Pursuant to your third-year clerkship outline, you should be at a point where you are concluding your externship. A fundamental part of your third-year studies includes your personal, objective assessment of your strengths and weaknesses in each specialty area of study, including, but not limited to (a) Obstetrics and Gynecology; (b) Family medicine; (c) Pediatrics; (d) Emergency Room; (e) Cardiology; and (f) Neurology.

In preparing your objective assessment, please keep in mind that your paper will be reviewed by the medical school's teaching staff to determine if your third-year externship meets the minimum acceptable standards for third year course study. The terms and conditions of your externship were accepted by you and I look forward to your assessment.

Please turn in your personal assessment not later than twenty days from the date of this letter if you intend to timely pursue your fourth-year residency.

In addition to your personal assessment, your supervising physician in each course is required to submit an assessment of your strengths and weaknesses. These assessments are also due within the twenty-day period.

The Board has scheduled you for a question and answer (Q&A) on Friday, May 11th at the medical school conference center. You must be accompanied by one of your parents while in attendance on medical school grounds.

I look forward to seeing you and hearing about your externship.

/s/ Dean"

I printed a copy of the letter and walked into the kitchen in my pajamas and showed the letter to my mother. She looked at me and asked, "Why are you standing here when you have work to do?" She laughed and suggested I get started after breakfast.

I returned to my study and broke down my assessment by the same categories that governed my third-year clerkship. I consumed my entire weekend doing my required personal assessment. In order to be objective, I wrote on my white board 'strengths' and in another column 'weaknesses'. As I prepared my list, I decided to add a third column 'accomplishments'.

Under the strengths column, I wrote, "learns quickly, adaptable, energetic, flexible, focused, skilled, helpful, open to learning, accepting criticism, excellent patient relations, recognizes limitations due to training, accepts challenges and is compassionate.

Under weaknesses I wrote, "need to follow instructions of my supervising physician; recognize and accept when I cannot legally perform a medical procedure even though I am confident I can do the procedure, develop the ability to comfort a patient, especially when disclosing a serious medical issue like STDs, cancer, etc., learn when to disclose certain information like the sex of the baby, need to relax and take time to enjoy life.

Under accomplishments, I wrote, "I can deliver a baby by natural birth and by C-section, I learned how to read ultrasound images, diagnose illnesses from ectopic pregnancy to ovarian cysts removal, how to irrigate and close wounds of all types, set and cast broken bones and read or interpret x-rays, MRI and CT scans, understand blood panel findings, perform neurological assessments, doing physical exams, and knowing when to seek guidance when in doubt.

I spent my entire weekend writing my assessment and asked my parents to look over my assessment before submitting it to the medical school. Both of my parents indicated that I keep my assessment focused on specific skills learned over the year, avoiding too much detail. The medical panel will ask you specific questions so brevity is better than an assessment that is so long that no one will read it.

On Monday morning, I had to request an assessment from my each of my supervising physicians. I could only hope for the best assessment, while expecting something less. I worried all week about the assessments being prepared by my assigned physicians. I would walk through the center and see one of my supervising physicians and I would detour and avoid contact. I became a nervous wreck, and by Thursday my mother left me home for a long weekend. My mother asked, "Why is the assessment issue so burdensome on your thoughts that you can't work?" I replied, "I can do my very best and know my strengths and weaknesses. I can't tell any of my supervising physicians what to write or if they will say something that negatively impacts my third year. I am not in control of this situation and it unnerves me. I guess you can call me a control freak because I am out of control waiting to see what they write about me."

I relaxed and read the latest medical journals covering obstetrics and gynecology. I decided to call Teri and see if she would like to get together and do something like riding. Melody indicated that Teri was with Dennis and Janine on a hike and wouldn't be back until Sunday night. I called Cynthia and she was home. We talked, but I learned that she was restricted to the house for being rude to her mother. I had no friends to be with and I needed to distract my thoughts.

I decided that morning that I wanted to look nice. I wore a gray pleated skirt with mauve leggings and a white blouse. My father commented that I looked beautiful and asked why. I replied, "I just want to look nice. I don't need my pants, scrubs or anything else for the day." My mother chided in saying, "She is hoping a boy she met in the cafeteria will be there again." My father put his arm around me and said, "I hope your friend is there. If he is, I would like to meet him this time if I am not in surgery."

My parents and I walked into the medical center together. They ordered coffee and I ordered a hot chocolate, the first of many that day. My mother's parting words were, "Please do not leave the cafeteria area without letting me or your father know what you are doing." I replied, "I'm going nowhere" and I looked for a table away from the crowd so I could read and possibly talk with Marcus if he showed up.

I sat and stared at my medical journal, but I wasn't into studying at the moment. While I sat alone, I was bombarded with staff members asking me why I was sitting alone. I was joined by most of the staff over the morning which kept my mind off of the assessments, but I was looking for conversation with Marcus. I decided to order the lunch special of soup, salad and a roll while I kept watch to see if Marcus would show. I felt a little silly since I was going to be eleven shortly and definitely not of an age to have a boyfriend; but I did like talking with Marcus and I looked forward to talking with him again.

I was drinking my cup of soup when a young boy ran for a paper plane he threw across the room. The boy hit me and my tomato soup spilled down my front. I was upset because I dressed nicely for this special day. I was wiping off the soup when Marcus asked if he could sit down with me. I was so embarrassed, but Marcus took his finger and ran it across my tomato soup soaked arm and then licked his finger. He laughed and said, "The soup is really good today, maybe I will wear a cup too." Marcus made me laugh and explained how I was to use a spoon or drink slowly next time. I excused myself and said, "I'll be right back. I need to change my clothes." I was grateful that my mother kept at least two pair of my pants and two blouses on hand. I changed and returned to the cafeteria and Marcus was gone. He wrote on a napkin, "My dad showed up early. Please call me." Marcus wrote his number on the napkin. I was truly disappointed and thought this was the worst week of my life.

To get my mind off of assessments, and now Marcus, I put on my lab coat and joined my father. He had me handle gynecological exams for the afternoon. I was a little irritable with patient questions, like "How can you see or do anything when your head isn't much higher than the examination table?" I would show them the miracles of modern medicine by pressing the up and down button on the exam table. I could lower the table to my height which helped me greatly in my clerkship. I finished the exams and checked if my father had any more work for me. He replied, "No, check with your mother." I checked and she was fine. I walked into the ER and Dr. Allen welcomed me and asked if I was there to see patients. I replied, "I have nothing else to do." He replied, "Good. Please check the patient in Room 1F. The boy was cutting wood and cut his hand in the process. I irrigated the wound, deadened the area around the wound and placed eleven sutures across his hand. Dr. Allen checked my work and smiled.

I asked Dr. Allen if he had anything else I could do. He replied, "All the time. Room 1B has a young man that was hit by a car on his bicycle. Check him over and let me know your findings before sending him to x-ray, if needed." I walked into room 1B and my patient was Marcus. I couldn't believe he was my patient. I asked him what happened and he explained that he rode his bike onto a crosswalk and didn't see the car taking the right-hand turn. The car knocked my bike over and I landed on my shoulder and head." I suggested that next time he hang around the cafeteria a little longer. I would rather see him there than in the ER. Marcus looked at me and said, "You really are a doctor. I thought you were actually pulling a joke on me." I replied, "I am a student intern completing my third year of medical school. I will be in my residency next year and then I will receive my medical degree. I checked Marcus and it appeared to me that his right shoulder pain was the result of a dislocated shoulder. Dr. Allen concurred and asked me if I knew how to reset the shoulder. I replied, "Yes I do." I tried, but I was either not strong enough or I wasn't doing it right. Dr. Allen asked me to repeat what I did. He said, "Stop right there. See how his arm is positioned, you want your patient to turn his arm this way." Dr. Allen turned Marcus' arm and he screamed out in pain. Dr. Allen then said, "Try to set the shoulder again. I looked at Marcus and said, "You might not like what I am about to do." He asked, "What are you…That hurt!" I asked Marcus to move his arm and I checked him for shoulder rotation and he said, "It no longer hurts. Thanks doc." I replied, "You're welcome, but like I said before, I am not a doctor yet." Marcus replied, "As far as I am concerned, you are my doctor."

    I walked back to the waiting room and met Marcus' father. I looked at the clock and I knew that I had a couple more hours before we would leave for home. I asked Marcus if he could go to the cafeteria for a cup of hot chocolate. He asked his father and received permission to visit for the next hour while his father ran a couple errands. I called to let Dr. Allen know where I was just in case an emergency arose and I might be needed." I spent the next hour visiting with Marcus. I learned that he lived about ten miles from the medical center and was going into seventh grade. Marcus liked much of what I liked and my being in medical school didn't affect our friendship. Marcus asked me what I would be doing over the weekend. I replied, "Probably work or study. I don't retain friends too long because of my work and study schedule." Marcus asked me if I would like to do something and I suggested the 'Bear Restaurant'. Marcus was thrilled to fly to the restaurant with my parents.

    I enjoyed being with Marcus. We ate too much and had fun painting our faces, making balloon hats with the clown and singing with the other kids in attendance. Marcus and I had a lot of fun together, but I realized that the only time we were having fun was when we were actively doing something. If we stopped, and just talked, I quickly discovered that

Marcus' childhood was one hundred eighty degrees opposite of mine. We shared little in common making anything more than small talk difficult at best. When I got home, I asked to talk with my mother. I explained how much fun I had with Marcus and she replied, "But?" I teared up and explained that I have nothing in common with Marcus, Teri, Dennis or Janine. I am very smart, but I am alone. My mother reassured me that I would find a friend that is compatible with my knowledge and suggested I call Cynthia to see if she could ride.

I called Cynthia and learned that she was already at the barn. She was excited that I was going to ride. She said, "I can't wait for you to meet my cousin Jeremy. He is ten and riding with me. I will let Jeremy introduce himself when you get here. I asked my mother if she would take me to the barn. I need to be with a friend and Cynthia is already at the barn riding with her cousin. We arrived by helicopter and Jeremy was impressed with my 'ride'. I laughed and said, "The helicopter is the safest way to travel." I hugged Cynthia and said 'Hi' and then introduced myself to Jeremy. He talked with me as I saddled Midnight. I checked with my mother and she allowed Jeremy to ride her horse. I offered to help Jeremy with the saddle and bridle and he accepted. I later learned from Cynthia that Jeremy had been riding horses since infancy. The bottom line was that he didn't need my help.

I liked Jeremy. Like Cynthia, he was studying ahead of grade level and was a highly motivated student. He mentioned taking the GED as early as he could and move into completion of his undergraduate degree. Jeremy was going to become a lawyer like his father. He offered his services when he was a lawyer. I politely thanked him, but explained that I had my own personal lawyer. Jeremy asked, "Why would a ten-year-old need a lawyer?" I explained about medical school and how my lawyer was able to get the medical school to approve my third-year clerkship as an extern working at my parents' medical center. Jeremy said, "I have heard of interns but not externs. What's the difference?" I explained that I was studying off campus so I am an extern instead of an intern that works within the medical school system." He asked why I wasn't an intern." I replied, "My age keeps me from taking direct classes."

We rode trails for about an hour when we stopped for some hot chocolate and sandwiches. Cynthia apologized that she only had enough for two, but they could share what she brought. I replied, "Go ahead and eat. I am not that hungry." Jeremy looked up and said, "Isn't that your mother's helicopter." I thought his question was a little dumb and replied, "Duh!" My mother stopped and picked up sub sandwiches for all of us plus a gallon of chocolate milk. We could heat the chocolate milk in the microwave in the barn if we wanted it hot. Cynthia said, "Your mother is so nice to bring us all this food." I replied, "My whole family is just as nice to be around." I asked Cynthia if she could spend the night when her cousin went home. She replied, "Jeremy is going to live with us through the summer." Cynthia then turned to my mother and said, "My mother loves working at the medical center. She asked me to thank you from her too." My mother replied, "We need to thank your mother. We needed a good urologist and she is great to have on our medical team."

Cynthia, Jeremy and I went riding the trails again and had a lot of fun just being together. We returned to the barn and Teri was there with Dennis and Janine. I said 'Hi' to Teri and her friends, but received no response from Teri. Instead, she turned to Dennis and Janine and said, "Let's do something else. I don't feel like riding my horse today. I heard Teri tell her mother, "We are not going to ride today. Let's go home now please." Melody replied, "I just sat down with Eli and I am not leaving until I am ready to leave. You wanted to ride so please go ride." My mother said, "Ride with Hayden. I'm sure she won't mind." Teri walked over towards me when Cynthia said, "Let's go riding again." I felt torn between my friend that liked me and my friend that apparently no longer liked me. I left with Cynthia and Jeremy ignoring Teri and her friends.

March arrived along with tree and flower buds, warmer and drier sunny days. I would look out at our deciduous trees and was excited for my birthday which usually preceded the formation of leaves on the trees. My birthday also preceded Easter, this year by almost a month. I asked my mother if I could have a small birthday party and invite Jeremy and Cynthia. My mother replied, "Just them? What about Teri and possibly Dennis and Janine?" I replied, "Not them. They treat me badly like last week when we were at the barn. Teri acts smug and refuses to even acknowledge me." My mother replied, "That's fine. Go ahead and set up the party." Spring break for the schools was in eleven days so I planned my little party during spring break week.

My party day came and Teri knew that my birthday was near, but she didn't acknowledge me or my age. I felt justified in not inviting Teri to the party. Cynthia and Jeremy arrived with Cynthia's mother. She visited with my parents while we had fun playing a few games my mother had purchased. We were eating cake and ice cream when Teri knocked on our door and asked for me. I was a little angry with Teri and I actually shook inside wondering what I would say to Teri. I opened the door and said, "What do you want Teri? I am busy with my new friends and my birthday party." Teri handed me a present and said, "I'm so sorry for my behavior towards you. Will you please forgive me once again? Please Hayden, "I am so sorry." Teri emptied my sails and my attitude came to an abrupt stop. I hugged Teri and said, "I love you and can you stay and join my party?" Teri called Melody and received approval. I introduced Teri to Jeremy and again to Cynthia. The emotional burden I carried with me was now gone and my friendship with Teri was once again on the right track. I ended up with a sleepover for everyone. Teri and Cynthia slept in my room and Jeremy slept in the guest room. The following morning my mother was overrun by hungry ten-year olds.

I said good-bye to my friends. Cynthia's mother picked up Cynthia and Jeremy and Melody stopped by for coffee and picked up Teri. Melody observed me and Teri playing with Mitzie and she relaxed and enjoyed a cup of coffee with my mother. When the others left, I asked Teri why she treats me so poorly around Dennis and Janine. She replied, "It's called peer pressure. You are too busy to be my friend and they are the only kids in our area besides you. Dennis tells me that he and Janine will not like me, or play with me, if I am your friend too. Dennis calls you stupid and Janine says you are just a show off smarty pants that is too brainy to have any real friends. I cry myself to sleep every time I treat you badly. I am so sorry." I hugged Teri and asked her what she would like to do. She replied, "Can we just sit and talk, maybe put on some make up, or maybe try some of your games." I replied, "Anything to keep my mind off of my assessments." Teri asked, "What is an assessment?" I explained an assessment is like a report card that you get at school. Each of the doctors I worked with over the past year need to write out an assessment and I am concerned about what they might say. That is why I am so nervous. Teri replied, "Then let's do something that takes your mind off of your school stuff." We made Jell-O pudding and popcorn and ate it all. I enjoyed having my friend back once again. This time Teri promised that she will not treat me badly again.

Third Year Clerkship Assessment

My third-year assessment was timely submitted to the medical school along with sealed envelopes enclosing my assessments from my supervising physicians. I was set for a formal Q&A in front of six medical doctors from the university medical center. I learned that they would be questioning me about my personal assessment and then commenting on the training assessments. I was shaking on the inside, but outside I was able to keep my calm composure as I prepared to answer questions. The dean who chaired the evaluation session explained that before they began to ask questions, I was being asked to comment on my third-year studies. Dr. Erikson stated, "I would like to hear specifics about your placement in the obstetrics and gynecology field of study. What specifically did you accomplish as an extern in that department?"

I replied, "I was fortunate that my supervising physician was my father. While working in his department, I spent a considerable amount of time studying medical issues related to obstetrics and gynecology. I learned how to do exams, develop patient trust, and diagnose cancer, an ectopic pregnancy, and surgery to remove endometrial tissue, diseases such as STDs and how to deliver babies.

Dr. Erikson asked, "How about your specific experience in deliveries. How many deliveries did you watch your father perform during the academic year?" I replied, "More than fifty natural births and more than fifteen C-section births." He asked, "Did you feel you learned by watching your father do the deliveries?" I replied, "Of course, but I learned a lot more when I delivered a total of five babies by natural childbirth by myself and I did three C-section deliveries by myself; that is under my father's direct observation and supervision." He asked, "Do you represent to this panel that you, a ten-year-old, did deliveries by yourself?" I replied, "No, I was nine at the time and I was never alone with all but two patients."

He asked, "What happened with respect to the two patients?" I replied, "One woman was in the stand-by birthing center when her baby began to arrive. I checked and my father was doing a C-section on triplets and there was no one else to deliver the baby except me. I delivered a healthy baby. The other patient was in the ER when her baby was coming.

I had to drop what I was doing and deliver that child because Dr. Allen was tied up."

He asked, "Tell me about delivering a baby C-section. He looked at my father and asked, "Did your daughter actually deliver three babies by C-section at ten years old?" My father replied, "She was nine at the time. I had her cutting and sewing pig skin and she was ready. I supervised her, but she needed no direction from me." He asked me, "Describe the steps you took to do a C-section delivery. I replied, "(1) Check the position of the baby and determine if there is a chance for a normal delivery; (2) explain the C-section surgery to the mother and obtain approval for the C-section and for me doing the delivery; (3) Mark my lateral incision line across the abdomen; (4) Carefully cut the skin and pull it back; (5) Cut the fascia underneath the skin and pull it back; (6) Cut the uterus and remove the baby taking care to carefully remove tissue that may get in the way without cutting the baby. (7) Carefully lift and extract the child, hold and upend the baby until it breathes and cries and let the mother know if it is a boy or girl if she didn't already know, (8) Cut and tie off the umbilical cord and hand the baby to the nurse; (9) Stich the uterus referred to as closing the uterus; (10) Stitch the fascia; (11) Stitch the skin and (12) Congratulate the parents on their newborn." He replied, "Excellent text book answer put into actual practice. Young lady, do you know that your peers in the medical school have not had the opportunity to actually deliver a baby? I replied, "No, because I am not present for the clerkship program at the hospital."

He said, "One more question. What happens when you are doing a natural child birth and the head is too large for the vaginal delivery?" I replied, "The ultrasound would have given me an indication that the child's head may exceed the vaginal opening. In that instance, I would need to cut the perineum to enlarge the vaginal opening." He asked, "How would you handle that?" I replied, "Just like I did in an actual delivery. The baby's head was crowning, but it was obvious to me that the baby's head would be too large and would most likely tear the perineum. This was the delivery next to where my father was engaged in a C-section delivery. I wasn't approved to do injections yet so I used a topical anesthetic and deadened the perineum and cut the skin just in time for the baby to push through and out. I cut the umbilical cord and tied it off, then I sutured the perineum and my father inspected my work once he was finished in surgery. My father told me that I wasn't to be doing deliveries solo, but in this instance the baby wanted out and it was going to harm the mother if I didn't react. He said, "One more question, what is the procedure called when you cut the perineum?" I replied, "An episiotomy". He replied, "Thank you. Excellent job."

He asked my father, "It sounds like you developed a lot of confidence in Ms. Gehardi's abilities as an intern in your department. How do you feel she did overall, rating her from 1 being the lowest and 10 being the highest?" My father replied, "I would give Hayden an 11 because she was outstanding. I would represent to this panel that Hayden knows as much about deliveries as I did when I obtained my fellowship. She has a lot more learning about illnesses incurred by woman, but she accurately diagnosed an ectopic pregnancy in one patient, an ovarian cyst in another, cancer and even STDs. Eleven may not be high enough in my opinion." He replied, "Ms. Gehardi is fortunate to have had such experiences while in her third year. She is so far beyond her peers at the medical school and I am pleased that her training, at least in our field turned out so well."

The professor then asked me what my future goal(s) were in medicine. I replied, "I have not wavered in my desire to become a board-certified OB/GYN and practice medicine with my parents at the wilderness medical center." He replied, "Good luck."

Professor Wilson introduced himself and his specialty was pediatric medicine. He asked me to describe my experience in the pediatric section of the medical center. I replied, "I worked under my mother who is a board-certified pediatrician and family practitioner. While working with my mother, I learned how to do pediatric exams, school physicals, check for abuse and diagnose childhood illnesses. I correctly diagnosed cancer in one child and I can't even describe the number of runny noses, sore throats, plugged ears, and the like. I dealt with one boy that had an impacted bowel. I spent two hours doing an enema to resolve the problem. I learned the less obvious lessons of pediatric medicine. I had a female patient with severe congestion. I had her tilt her head back and she sneezed covering me with her sinus discharge. I wiped my face and carried on. I had her tilt her head back, but this time I was careful and watched for a sneeze. I got my tongue depressor too far back and triggered her gag reflex and she threw up all over me. One final lesion I learned and never repeated the error was when I was examining a little boy. I was finishing his checkup and I was going to examine his penis and bottom. I removed the towel and looked at his penis and he peed all over me. I learned why my nurse put a towel over the little boy's penis. Other than this, I sutured cuts, set two broken bones and casted the arms, diagnosed a case of physical abuse where the mother grabbed her child and exited the facility. He replied, "That was pretty thorough. I don't have any questions. Thank you Ms. Gehardi."

Dr. Stevens introduced himself as an emergency room specialist and hospitalist. He asked me if I did training in the ER. I replied, "Of course. I did ten weeks with Dr. Allen." He asked, "What did you do, shadow the ER physician in charge?" I replied, "The first week I shadowed Dr. Allen. After that I was meeting patients in the ER, under his supervision. I learned how to inject patients with an anesthetic, how to suture hands and feet. I sutured one little girl with tiny sutures and Dr. Allen felt that she would have little or no scar as she grew up. I set a dislocated shoulder, delivered a baby and sewed more skin than a seamstress. Well, that may be an exaggeration by a little bit." He asked if I would be interested in becoming an ER physician. I replied, "I really liked the fast action in the ER, but my desire is to be an OB/GYN and I plan to have that training completed before my fifteenth birthday." He commented that my assessment from Dr. Allen made it sound like I walked on water. He said, "Good job. I have no other questions."

Dr. Reamy asked me about Cardiology. I indicated that I spent two weeks in cardiology and I studied mostly about atrial fib, congestive heart failure, the effect of blood fats, stress and when and when not to use blood thinners. I observed one heart surgery, but that was about it. Dr. Reamy commented, "Your assessment was outstanding."

Dr. Walters introduced himself as a neurologist and wanted to know my experiences working in that department. I yawned and Dr. Walters asked me if that was my response. I apologized and said, "Sorry, my yawn had nothing to do with neurology. I then explained that I learned to do a neurological assessment. I didn't have any real patient experience while in the department, but when I worked in the ER I correctly diagnosed a subdural hematoma that resulted from a car accident. His wife described what she saw. She explained, "He could change out the battery in our electric golf cart in five minutes. A day ago, my husband took close to three hours to change the battery and he thought he was doing well. A CT scan revealed the brain bleed and he was sent into surgery. That was about all of my experience." Dr. Walters said, "I should mention that your review was outstanding."

I finished with the panel discussion and then I was scheduled to meet with the medical school board to discuss my fourth-year residency. We played musical doctors. The first group left and the board took their places. The dean congratulated me on an outstanding third year of studies and said that the board was there to discuss my fourth-year residency. The dean explained that the same limitations applied due to my age and the board was considering my application to do my residency off-site. The Chair asked me, "What area of medicine do you wish to specialize in Ms. Gehardi?" I replied, "Obstetrics and Gynecology." He mentioned, "You do realize that to get your certification will take approximately another four years of study?" I replied, "I will be eleven when I graduate from medical school. I understand I will have four more years which will place me at fifteen when I am board certified. I already have approval to practice before I am sixteen so long as I practice at the wilderness medical center since there are simply not enough OB/GYNs in the wilderness areas of our state."

The dean mentioned that I had already completed my placement requirements in my third year and I was cleared by the medical school to complete my residency with my parents. My residency would be in obstetrics and gynecology, but I could work in any department requiring assistance. He indicated that he would be sending me a confirmation letter outlining the requirements for my fourth-year residency. I left so excited and couldn't wait to thank my supervising physicians. I asked my parents to stop at the local drug store so we could have an ice cream cone at the old fashion fountain and then eat dinner at the bear restaurant.

One week later and I received the following letter from the Dean.

> Dear Ms. Gehardi:
>
> Congratulations on your successful completion of your third-year clerkship. Your personal and professional assessments reflect positively upon you as a future medical professional.
>
> The purpose of this letter is to outline your requirements as a fourth-year student completing your residency off

campus at the Wilderness Health Outreach Medical Center. You will be assigned to your parents who will be responsible to write up an assessment of your residency prior to graduation ceremonies. As a resident, you will not be required to stay in a dormitory, but you shall be responsible for attending at least fifty hours of work/instruction weekly. You and your parents may determine how those fifty hours is met given your age and the child labor laws.

You shall complete an assessment that highlights your strengths and weaknesses and a plan to improve any weakness on a monthly basis emailed to the medical school.

You shall not be required to use a camera except when directed by the medical school.

You shall identify yourself as a resident student and obtain patient consent prior to you providing direct patient care.

You are required to have a minimum of 1,600 hours of patient care/training during your fourth year. Each monthly assessment shall include the number of hours worked and the breakdown between hands-on training and studies.

Finally, like last year, you will be responsible for timely registering and paying tuition for the last two semesters.

If you concur with this instruction then please sign a copy of this letter and e-mail it back to me not later than May 30th.

/s/ Dean

I looked over the letter and it wasn't anything new. I signed the letter and presented it to my parents for their endorsement. This time I returned my registration form and check by certified mail. I heard nothing further and I anxiously awaited my fourth year that wouldn't start until September 4th. I had approximately four months off school with nothing to study; or so I thought. My father handed me twenty-two Obstetrics and Gynecology journals and suggested I read up on diseases and diagnostic skills and procedures. He said, "When you have those read, then let me know because I have a lot more for you to read. I will quiz you on the topics so be ready at any time to answer questions. I recalculated my summer break and felt that I could handle my reading two days a week and take the rest of the week off, unless I was needed at the medical center.

A Time for Friends and Reflection

I anxiously sent a text message to Cynthia, Jeremy and Teri alerting them that I had almost four months off to do fun things with them. I received no responses from any of my so-called friends. I tried to call Marcus, but even he didn't answer. I had missed my birthday because of the assessment meeting and I hoped that I would have friends to celebrate my tenth birthday with me. I teared up and remembered how sad I was when my mother failed to return with a puppy for me. Back then, I had a premonition that my parents had purchased a puppy, but now I couldn't see into the afternoon, much less into a future event. My mother heard me sniffling and crying in my room. Like always, she comforted me and asked what was wrong. I explained that I had no friends to talk with. No one is at home and I might as well go to work. My mother replied, "I think that is probably a good idea. Let's go and maybe your friends will be available tomorrow." I replied, "I doubt it. None of my friends understand me and what pressure I am under to succeed in my medical training. It is probably best that I don't have friends. At least you and dad had each other. I have no one."

James A. Gauthier, J.D.

My Tenth Birthday

We landed at the medical center and I put on my lab coat and wrapped my stethoscope around my neck. I asked my mother if she needed any help. She checked her schedule and she was fine. She suggested I check with my father since I would be specializing in his field. I walked to the OB/GYN section and the nurse explained that my father was in the middle of a surgery and he asked that I wait in the waiting room for him. I offered to assist, but the nurse said your father left specific instructions that you wait here until he is finished. Not even my father wanted me around him at present. I sat down and covered my face. I was hurting inside and felt like I had been kicked by Tempest. About five minutes later the lights turned off and on and everyone walked out of surgery and yelled, 'surprise'. My parents had purchased a full sheet cake and ice cream. Teri, Cynthia and Jeremy were there along with Marcus and any staff that could get away. The cake read, "Happy 10th Birthday and Hayden Gehardi, Resident Intern." I was so happy that I started to cry. I am a tough girl when it comes to medicine, but with friendships, I am still a little girl at heart and often become emotional. I hugged everyone and said, "Thank you so much for remembering my tenth birthday."

My mother handed me a large package to open. I looked inside and I had eight more white lab coats with my name and the words, "Resident Intern" I received a new stethoscope, shoes and polo shirts with the name 'Wilderness Health Outreach Medical Center'. My mother said, "Put on your new lab coat almost doctor Hayden." I excitedly replaced my lab coat and wrapped my new stethoscope around my neck and said, "I am ready to go-just please not today."

I was talking with my friends when my father handed me several presents as well. I opened the heaviest and I received the book, "The Essentials of a Modern Obstetrics and Gynecology Practice". The next package contained the last twenty-four issues of 'Obstetrics and Gynecology' with a note saying, "Please have all of this read by your fall term." Teri asked, "Don't you get any good presents?" I replied, "Teri, I love my presents."

The nurses gave me a combined present. I actually received surgical gloves that fit my hands and a new pair of scrubs. Teri and Cynthia both asked how I could be so excited over rubber gloves. I replied, "It is embarrassing to have the nurse tape on my surgical gloves because they would slide off my hand. Although the medical center had purchased me surgical gloves in the extra small size, I noticed that the gloves I received were packaged with the words, "I wore this pair of gloves on my first solo delivery." It made a nice remembrance of my third year."

My grandparents purchased four surgical scrubs in my size with my name embedded on the front pocket. I walked around and said, "Thank you all so much." I had happy tears when I heard from my friends that even they brought me a present. Cynthia explained that they had no idea what I would want so they wrote me a letter:

"My Friend Hayden"

A friend is someone who accepts your apology when you have hurt them.

You are my friend Hayden because you graciously forgave me unconditionally when I was rude to you and ditched you for other friends.

You are my friend because you accept me for who I am and not who I become when my heart hurts because you are too busy to be with me.

You are my friend and I don't care how smart you are.

You are my friend because you are you and that is good enough for me.

James A. Gauthier, J.D.

Teri

Cynthia wrote:

Hayden is my friend because she accepts me and when time permits, she shares her life with me on horseback or experimenting in your bedroom laboratory.

You are my friend because you are not judgmental of me and you never compare me to you and your brilliant mind.

You are my friend because you help me smile and motivate me to achieve.

You are my friend because we both like to drink hot chocolate while sitting on our horses laughing. I cherish your laugh and our friendship.

Cynthia

Jeremy wrote:

Hayden, I don't know you very well, but I believe I can fill in the missing pieces of who you are by how you treat me and our friends. I want our friendship to last for you brighten my day and remind me that I can achieve like you if I work hard and apply myself. I like you because you have opened your heart when your thoughts are somewhere else.

Jeremy

Finally, Marcus wrote:

I laughed when I met you and your tomato soup dress. I knew you were embarrassed and uncomfortable, but you smiled and took the time to meet me before changing your clothes. Friends accept each other for who they are without limitation. I hope to know you better in the future because I like your friendship.

Marcus

On the bottom of the card, Teri wrote:

Friday, we are all going to the bear restaurant to be kids so put on your kid hat and hang up your stethoscope for one night and let's have fun. The letter was signed by my friends with happy faces.

I liked my presents and couldn't wait to go to the bear restaurant. My parents flew us there and let us stay for four hours while they shopped for my birthday. My friends and I painted each other's faces, made balloon hats and characters and sat in the circle to clap and sing with Rolo the clown. I knew better, but that special birthday my friends and I ate three pizzas and we each had five deserts and a birthday cake. The hostess asked for my name, age and what school I attended. I replied, "Hayden. I am ten years old and I don't attend school here. I am just visiting my friends." I did not want to talk about medical school, or draw attention to myself, as my family is, or tries to be very private in the conduct of our lives.

We got home and I learned that my mother planned a sleepover for my friends. Teri and Cynthia slept in my room and Jeremy and Marcus slept in the guest bedroom. The following morning, we were going swimming and then back to the bear restaurant and that would conclude my birthday celebration. As girlfriends, we chatted most of the night and even told scary stories. I was almost asleep when I heard Jeremy and Marcus arguing. I got out of bed and opened their bedroom door and asked, "Why are you guys shouting and arguing with each other. This is supposed to be a fun weekend for me." I heard Marcus say, "I'm sorry Hayden, but Jeremy started the fight." Jeremy replied, "I did not–you did when you said that Hayden likes you more than me. I am her boyfriend and you are just a friend. Tell Marcus how you feel Hayden." I replied, "We are ten years old. I don't want or need a boyfriend. I want both of you equally as my friend and that is it so stop arguing and get to sleep please."

Morning came and I stood in my window and let the sun shine on my face. Cynthia said, "Hayden, close the curtain, the sun is bright." I replied, "I know. I love waking up to the sunshine. It starts my day right." Cynthia asked, "Were Jeremy and Marcus arguing last night? I thought I heard them yelling at each other." I replied, "They both want something that neither can have. I don't think there will be anymore arguments."

I was sitting with my friends while my mother made breakfast. She said, "Breakfast is almost ready. Please come and sit at the table." The first thing I heard from Jeremy was, "Hayden, where are you sitting? I would like to sit with you." Marcus responded, "No way. I want to sit with Hayden." I ended up sitting on one side of the table between Jeremy and Marcus. It was the only way to stop the arguing. I heard Teri ask, "What is Cynthia and me, chopped meat?" *I began thinking that work would be a welcome relief.*

The boys didn't let up when we hit the pool. All three girls were cute and wearing bikini swim suits. I became angry with the boys because they started pushing and shoving again because both wanted to swim with me. I got mad and asked both boys to stop please or I am getting out of the pool. Finally, I had some peace to be with all my friends. When I got out of the pool, Jeremy apologized and kissed my cheek. Marcus also apologized. He kissed me on my lips and I pushed back and said, "That's enough kissing. Let's get ready to go home. My mother will be here shortly." While waiting, Jeremy asked if he could be my boyfriend. I replied, "No". He asked me if I liked Marcus more than him. I replied, "No again." He then asked, "Why can't I be your boyfriend?" I replied, "I am ten and do not need or want a boyfriend. I said that before so please quit asking me the same question because you will get the same answer."

What is a Miracle Anyway?

The Stern family is Catholic. They attend church at St. John's almost every Sunday. On this particular Sunday, Father Earhart was giving a sermon on miracles performed by Jesus when he walked the earth with his apostles. He talked about God's seven Archangels namely Jegudiel, Gabriel, Selaphiel, Michael, Uriel, Raphael and Barachief and how the angels were created by God to serve God and carry out God's will. He specifically mentioned Archangel Michael as being a messenger angel for God. Melody was so excited to hear the topic of angels that she stayed after church to talk with Father Earhart about me and my miraculous birth.

Melody explained that she had no first-hand proof, but my parents believe I was a gift from God delivered to my parents by the Archangel Michael. Melody mentioned what she could remember and Father Earhart asked how he may be received by my family if he stopped by for a visit. Melody replied, "I'm not sure. They like their privacy and I should not have said what I did. I broke my promise to keep their family issues private." Melody called my mother and exposed what she said to the priest. I could hear her apologizing to my mother for opening her big mouth. I heard my mother reply, "Maybe it will pass over. I am not interested in discussing anything with the priest. In our lives, that only complicates our otherwise complicated lives and usually causes us harm or grief. When you see Father Earhart, please explain that we want our privacy and wish to be left alone."

My parents discussed the disclosure of my birth with the local parish priest, Father Earhart. My father took the position that the priest was probably more curious than anything. It has been more than three weeks since Melody made the disclosure and nothing has happened. Let's not worry about something that most likely will not occur.

My parents and I were having breakfast when we received a knock on our door. Father Earhart introduced himself as the pastor of St. John's Church. My father replied, "I know who you are. It is our medical center that sponsors your annual Easter egg hunt and coloring contest. He replied, "That's why I knew your name. I checked our church registry, but your family is not listed as members of our church." My father replied, "We are not Catholic."

Father Earhart introduced a second man, Raymond Gussardi, who he explained is a researcher interested in finding miracles of God's work and documenting the miracles for the Vatican. He explained that nothing said in our interview will be published in any public journal, but the information would be stored in the Vatican library under Miracles of God if he found that a miracle had actually occurred. My father replied, "Sorry, but we are not interested in sharing anything about our daughter's birth." My father then asked, "How do I know that you are a Vatican representative and not some journalist hoping to make some money on our life?" The man removed a business card identifying him as a Vatican Historian. My father replied, "Anyone can have business cards printed to say anything." He then showed his Vatican identification and even shared several pictures of him meeting with the Pope. My parents agreed to share my miracle with him so long as it was kept private.

My father explained, "I am sure you have noticed that Eli is Hayden's mother and my near identical twin. I am Hayden's father. Eli and I are life partners. We have loved each other since our birth and we jointly adopted Hayden. If our relationship troubles you, I can stop right here." Father Earhart asked that my father continue to describe my birth. My father replied, "The day was Good Friday in 2007. I was planning on shutting down the medical center for Easter. The weather was a mixture of freezing rain and snow. My mother was working the admission's desk at the medical center when she was startled by the sudden appearance of a very pretty young woman dressed in a wet white nightgown with hair down to her back and very pregnant. My mother opened the door and asked her if she had an appointment. The young woman replied, "Yes I do. I am here to deliver this child." My mother asked her where her coat and shoes were because it was freezing outside. My mother grabbed a warm blanket and the young woman thanked her, but said, "I am not cold. I am here to deliver this child. My mother asked for any identification. The young woman had a well-worn card that had the name "Michaele" There was a second name, but the card was so poor that it couldn't be made out. It also had an address and a picture that didn't resemble the young woman. My mother asked for her full name, address and the name of the birth father. She replied, "That is not important. I am here to deliver this child." My mother contacted me and I set up the operatory for a delivery.

One of my orderlies arrived with the pregnant woman. My mother whispered to me, "She might be on something. She keeps saying she is here to deliver this child. I couldn't get any information from her except her desire to deliver this child."

The young woman was brought into the delivery center where I asked the nurse to remove her wet nightgown and put on a surgical gown. I examined the girl and determined that the baby was lying sideways and would not pass by natural childbirth. I explained about a C-section delivery to the young woman and she just smiled and said, "I am ready to deliver this child." My surgical nurse tried to get some information from her, but she kept saying, "I am here to deliver this child." My nurse asked her if she was a surrogate and she said, "Yes", but when asked for whom, the young woman replied, "I am ready to deliver this child."

I set up for a C-section birth and Dr. Morrisi prepared the anesthesia for the delivery. He placed the mask on the patient and asked her to start counting backwards from ten. As she counted, Dr. Morrisi began slowly administering the anesthetic and the young woman's heart stopped. I delivered the child, but we lost the mother. I asked Dr. Morrisi what happened and he explained that she didn't have enough anesthetic to kill her. She just died. I verified that she had no heart or brain function. I obtained DNA from the birth mother and then directed an orderly to take the deceased patient to the morgue. I was certain that the medical examiner would want to do an autopsy and determine what happened. I called the Sheriff and he said the address on the identification card was a vacant lot and he had no missing persons that would fit the young woman that he fingerprinted and photographed.

I routinely take DNA samples if questions may arise about the familial relationship of a new born. I had samples from the birth mother and the newborn baby girl. I sent the DNA samples to the lab for a rush order and the lab reported back that the birth mother's DNA was contaminated and the lab would need another sample. I asked the lab about the contamination and the lab tech explained that the DNA sample was both male and female and there was no relationship between the birth mother and the newborn baby girl. The latter confirmed to me that the woman had to be a surrogate; however, I had in the back of my thoughts that the young woman may have been an angel delivering the child. I didn't know what to think as my mind raced trying to understand why my patient died.

Father Earhart asked, "What caused you to think the young woman may be an angel?" My father replied, "It was her appearance, absolute innocence in her face and smile, her indicating that she was a surrogate and she was there to deliver this child – not her child. It was a gut feeling that she was different."

I asked an orderly to bring the young woman back to my surgery center so I could get additional DNA samples that were not contaminated. My orderly reported back to me, "She's not there. She isn't in the morgue where I left her." I called the Sheriff, but neither he nor the coroner had the body. I directed my staff to look for her body because it could not have left the building. After three hours of an exhaustive search, the only thing we found was her surgical gown. We never found the body and the coroner ordered the DNA samples sealed until the body was found."

My father was asked, "Do you still have some of the birth mother's DNA. My father said he had three vials of blood and some hair. My father was asked if he could share some of the DNA with them. He replied, "I will need the coroner's approval."

My mother then explained that she was drawn to the nursery. She couldn't explain why, but she had to see the newborn girl. She said, "I immediately bonded with the little girl and my premonition saw me and Ian as her parents. Six months later and we adopted Hayden and we believe that the adoption concluded the angel's delivery. I am sure you realize that I cannot bear children for Ian so adoption would be our only method of having children."

Mr. Gussardi interrupted my mother and said, "So far, I fail to see anything miraculous about your daughter's birth. Is there more information you would like to share for my investigation?" My mother replied, "We have a lot of information if you will be patient; I will explain everything for you." Mr. Gussardi said, "Thank you."

My mother explained that I looked just like her and my father as babies. She showed pictures of them and me and we looked enough alike to be twins or triplets. My mother explained that I had many of her characteristics such as premonitions, etc. He asked, "What else?" My mother explained about our heartbeats being identical in rhythm. He doubted what my mother said until he saw that what my mother said was the truth. He asked, "How could someone else's baby have an identical heartbeat with adoptive parents?" I replied, "It is because I am part of my mother and father. As best I can tell, God took a part of each of my parents and created me. An angel delivered me to my parents that could not have children and here I am."

He looked at my father and asked, "Anything else you wish to share?" My father replied, "I had our DNA submitted to a local lab for determination of relationships. Eli's and my DNA is an identical match. Hayden's DNA was almost identical at 99.892 percent. Her DNA is part of our DNA and she is our biological child. Our blood types are the same and Hayden has a 154 IQ where Eli and I have a 160 IQ."

My mother asked, "How could a complete stranger's child not be a gift from God when she was delivered to us and as we have explained, she is part of us?

Mr. Gussardi requested a vial of blood for analysis at the Vatican. My father obtained approval to release one vial. He then asked, "Any final thoughts before I return to the Vatican?" I replied, "Something my parents didn't indicate to you. The card that the young woman presented had the name 'Michaele'. Our neighbor pointed out that if you drop the 'e' on the end of the name, then you have 'Michael' who is one of God's messenger Archangels." Mr. Gussardi replied, "How interesting."

Mr. Gussardi asked me if I had anything more to discuss. I replied, "Not really." He asked for my age and I replied, "Ten". He asked me what grade I was in or just completed. I looked at my parents and said, "I am entering into my residency which is my final year of medical school."

My family heard nothing further from Mr. Gussardi. My mother contacted the Vatican and spoke with Mr. Gussardi. He apologized and explained that my information was placed in the book of Miracles and the information would never leave the Vatican.

It's Summer Time

I woke up to the morning sun and said, "Good night" to the evening moon that I could lightly see across the horizon. Today was the beginning of my summer break before starting my residency. I was reading my steeplechase information and noted that qualifications for six-foot fences would be starting in one month. I checked the qualification requirements and learned that I had to have three out of five qualifying runs in order to compete at the six-foot fence professional level. I was mentally and physically ready to compete. My trainer at the ranch kept Tempest in top condition for these events. I had to rely on a professional trainer because of my work/school schedule. I asked Jeremy and Cynthia to join me today so I could blend friendship time with my qualification rides.

I was third in line and I watched the first rider knock down two laterals as he finished his run. Second rider made it through the entire course without effort. He was nice enough to warn me that the southwest corner of the field was soft so keep out of it. I thanked him and then hugged Tempest asking again that he soar like the wind and protect me through the course. I heard go and Tempest cleared every six-foot fence and water hazard with ease. I was asked by Jeremy what it was like jumping a six-foot fence. I replied, "It is like sitting in a rocket that is ready to launch over and over." I was pleased that my first run was flawless and my butt remained in the saddle.

I patiently waited for my second run on the course while talking with Cynthia and Jeremy. I tried to explain how it feels when Tempest does his jump, but I truly believe the only way to understand is to experience it and they were not yet ready for that experience. I excused myself and walked Tempest to the stand-by area. When my number was called, I mounted Tempest and gateman said, "Go". I mistakenly turned to look at Jeremy because he wanted to take my picture. As I turned to look at Jeremy, Tempest leaped out of the starting box and I fell backwards and landed on my leg. I had immediate pain and saw my horse running the course without me. I pulled my whistle and Tempest ran and stood by me. My mother led Tempest off the field and a stretcher carried me to the medical area for examination.

My mother asked me if my right fibula was hurting. I replied, "I think I broke my right fibula. I can feel the pain right here. Several people heard me say I broke my leg and they politely wished me well. I looked to my mother and she placed her hands on my Fibula and within a minute I had no more pain. She kept her hands on my leg for five minutes when one of the judges walked over and asked if I was planning to forfeit my last three rides. I replied, "No. I will be fine and ready to ride on the next call." He asked, "How? I understand you have a broken leg." My mother replied, "I am a medical doctor and I just checked my daughter's leg and it is fine. I stood by Tempest and hugged him and apologized for not paying attention. I turned and asked Cynthia and Jeremy to not talk with me when I am preparing to ride. Both of my friends acted like they were zipping their mouths shut. My number was called and I returned to the ready box. The judge asked me if I was prepared to ride and I replied, "Ready and able."

My next run was near perfect and the fastest time for the day. I hugged and thanked Tempest and promised him a stock of carrots if we make it through the next two runs. My number was called and I heard my mother tell Jeremy and Cynthia to keep quiet until I am on the course. I finished again with a perfect run and had one more to go.

My final run for qualification would be critical because there were nine riders left for an eight-rider season. I held Tempest and said, "I love you Tempest. Let's jump high enough to see the sun and remain in the air long enough to greet the moon tonight." I hugged Tempest and said, "Let's fly high and long please." The judge asked me, "What did you say to your horse?" My mother answered, "She asked her horse to jump high enough to see the sun and to remain in the air long enough to greet the moon tonight." He replied, "That's the first I have heard that line. Let's see if it works." Tempest cleared all of the six-foot fences by a minimum of two feet and he cleared the water hazards by four feet. Our ride was flawless and I soared high and placed second overall. I qualified for the summer competition at the six-foot fence level.

Cynthia asked me if I always talk to my horse like that. I replied, "I do because Tempest needs to believe in himself as he clears the hurdles with me on his back. Tempest knows that he is responsible for protecting me and for completing the course. I will now give Tempest his carrots, but the treat Tempest likes more than a carrot is me hugging him and hanging from his neck. He also likes to play and I will stand underneath him and he will look upside down to find me. Tempest is smart and a great jumper." Cynthia asked if she could sit on Tempest one time. I explained to Tempest that he had a novice rider and he slowly walked around the stand-by area. Cynthia said, "When Tempest moves, I can feel his powerful leg muscles." I replied, "I wish I could give you the experience of jumping a six-foot fence." Cynthia's mother had a twenty-five-foot measuring tape in the car. She measured Tempest to the top of his legs and then added another ten feet. Cynthia looked up and there was another six feet above her seated position. I said, "That is where your butt is on a jump. Your head is another two to three feet higher." Cynthia replied, "Never. Please get me off this monster."

I pulled my jumping saddle and walked to the side pasture so Tempest could graze and rest. I was approached by a couple who asked if they could take a picture of Tempest and me. I replied, "I guess so, unless it is for commercial purposes." He replied, "No. I want my barn manager to look at your horse. He is a beautiful jumper. Would you consider selling Tempest for $50,000? I kid you not, when Tempest heard the offer, he turned, snorted at the man and walked away pulling me by his harness. The man caught up with me and asked again, "Will you consider selling Tempest?" My mother came running and asked what he needed. "He replied, "Is this your daughter?" My mother replied, "Yes, why or what do you need from her?" He replied, "I made an offer of $50,000 to purchase Tempest." My mother looked at him and said, "We wouldn't sell Tempest for $500,000." He thanked my mother and said, "I will see you next weekend for season I. My rider will be riding Moonlight. We will see whose horse is the better jumper. My rider has been riding fences for twenty-six years. He has won the season seventeen times to date." I replied, "I look forward to ending his career wins next week. See you there."

Jeremy, Cynthia and I walked Tempest back to his field. I gave him the last of his carrots, checked for food and water and watched Tempest take off like a lightening streak across the field where he quickly rolled onto his back and acted silly once again. I know that the grass was cooling after getting off the hot saddle.

My friends and I boarded the helicopter and I said, "Mom, I am starving." Mom suggested we go to the bear restaurant for a late lunch. I thanked my mother and for the next few hours, I was a little girl enjoying a little friendship. We were getting ready to leave the restaurant with our painted faces; balloon hats and we were carrying two pieces of pie each. I stepped out of the restaurant door just in time to see a truck broadside a car. The truck had a single driver and the car had a woman and four children. I screamed, "Call 911 Cynthia and tell the operator where we are." I screamed for my mother who was still inside paying.

I couldn't wait and I approached the car to do an immediate triage assessment for when the medics arrived. My mother checked the female driver and she was unconscious. One child hit his head on the ceiling light and cut a large gash in his skull. Another child's arm was bent in such a manner that I knew the Ulna was broken. I could see immediate swelling. Cynthia and Jeremy approached and I told them to get back and stay out of the way. I placed a clean cloth on the boy's head and had him hold it with pressure. He was eight and old enough to do as he was instructed. The last child I checked was a three- year old girl that was lying upside down on her head. She wasn't in an approved car seat and I feared she may have broken her neck. I did a quick assessment and she wasn't breathing. I called my mother, but she was caring for the mother that had broken ribs and potential internal bleeding. My mother could feel the breaks. The woman's temple was throbbing suggesting a brain injury where her head whiplashed to the right and then to the left breaking the side window. My mother told me to do what was needed to save the little girl. If she isn't breathing, carefully move her to clear her airway and do CPR until the medics arrive. I carefully rotated the girl freeing her neck. I laid her on the seat and did CPR for five minutes when she began breathing again. I fashioned a neck brace with a magazine and tied her head to the magazine to immobilize her head and neck. I asked her brother to keep her still and not let her up. My kids were temporarily taken care of and I went to check on the truck driver. I opened the truck door and he was also unconscious. Two beer cans fell onto the ground and his truck cabin reeked of beer and marijuana. I checked his eyes and they were dilated and he was bleeding out of his left ear. I felt around his neck, but I couldn't feel any breaks. I decided he was best left there for the medics. It took the medics eleven minutes to get onto the scene. The police arrived and the chief of police ordered everyone back. He looked at me and said, "That means you too young lady." He looked over and saw my mother and said, "Excuse me, but the fire department and paramedics will be here in five minutes so please stay back." My mother yelled, "Hayden, I need you now." I ran to the car and the little girl in my makeshift neck brace was throwing up. I checked her eyes and they were fully dilated. I checked her head trauma and found an indention in her skull the size of a quarter suggesting brain damage, or at least a serious concussion. I stayed with the kids as the police chief kept yelling at me to get back. Finally, my mother stood up and said, "I am Dr. Eli Gehardi. She is my daughter, and despite her age, she is now in her fourth year of medical school and knows what she is doing. Please stand back and let us handle this emergency." The police chief asked, "You are the folks with the helicopter that I said to put a red cross on the port side widow." My mother replied, "Yes and there is my helicopter." When the paramedics get here, I have to transport two very serious head injuries so please keep the people back. As I cared for the kids, my mother reversed the helicopter seats into gurney platforms and readied the helicopter for an emergency take off.

  I grabbed my phone and called into the ER and talked with Dr. Allen. I explained our triage findings and he prepared the ER for immediate care and called in a neurovascular surgeon from the city. He also flew by helicopter and would be there within ten minutes of our arrival. The paramedics arrived and moved the mother and three- year old girl to the helicopter. We got them buckled in and took off. Later that night, Dr. Allister called my mother and explained that our triage saved the little girl's life by immobilizing her head and clearing the impact area. My mother replied, "Thank my daughter. She did the triage and immediate care."

My mother said, "They are in good hands now. Let's get back to the restaurant and pick up your friends." I replied, "Mom, Dr. Allen is all alone in the ER and he has five patients coming in fast and injured. I need to stay and assist in the ER. Please pick up my friends and meet me back here." Dr. Allen said, "Thank you Hayden for staying. Get dressed and I will let you know where you are needed."

I returned to the ER and Dr. Allen had the eight-year old boy waiting for me. His brother was also on the table with the broken leg. I sent the little boy to x-ray and then I irrigated, deadened and sutured the boys head. He got a little upset when I shaved some of his hair off, but I couldn't sew over his hair. Dr. Allen checked him and said, "Nice job as always. Hayden, you can have a job in the ER anytime you want."

I waited for the x-ray. I made sure the bone was set and I casted the break. I wrote my name on his cast and drew a heart. I saw the little girl being held by a nurse on the sidelines. I thought she was fine because she was in her car seat. Apparently, the nurse didn't look closely, but I did. I saw blood inside her stocking running down her leg. I quickly directed the nurse to remove the little girl's clothing and diaper for a checkup. The nurse asked, 'Who are you to be telling me what to do?" I replied, "I am a fourth-year medical student resident at this medical center now move it please." I found a piece of the side glass blew back into the car seat and was sticking in the girl's side. The nurse replied, "I will get the doctor." I replied, "He is busy. I will handle this." I irrigated the wound and cleaned out three small pieces of glass. I sutured the cut and put a smile face band aid over the wound. When I finished, the nurse asked again, "Who or what did you say you are?" I replied, "I am a fourth- year resident in medical school. I am doing my residency at this medical center." I looked up and my mother was walking in to the ER. Nurse Adams immediately asked my mother, "Do you know who this little girl is. She is trying to play doctor here and refused to wait for Dr. Allen." My mother replied, "Nurse Adams, please meet Hayden Gehardi. She is my daughter and she is a fourth-year medical student and resident practicing medicine at this center. You will give her the same respect as you give Dr. Allen." She immediately apologized and quietly said, "You could have said your parents run this hospital." I replied, "Why should I, and for your future understanding, this is a medical center."

I removed my bloody lab coat and tossed it in the wash bucket and greeted my friends. We sat in the cafeteria talking for three hours until my parents were ready to leave the medical center for home. I invited Jeremy and Cynthia to spend the night once again. My mother picked up some goodies and we ate pie and popcorn until we dropped off to sleep. In the morning I was surprised to hear that my friends didn't even realize that we didn't own a television. Jeremy said, "I watch television all the time, but I never even thought about it here." Cynthia replied, "I didn't either."

The following morning my mother flew Jeremy and Cynthia home. I was a little tired so I said good-bye at my house and promised to call both of them soon. I didn't know it, but Teri was watching my house to see who was leaving in the helicopter. When she saw I wasn't in the helicopter, she ran over to my house and knocked on my door. I was tired and a little irritated because I had just laid down for a quick nap before reading O&G articles to prepare for my residency. I politely invited Teri in and we had a heart to heart talk about being friends. Teri explained that I was still her best friend, but she felt I didn't put a lot of effort into our friendship. I replied, "Teri, I will never be friends with you in the same manner that you are friends with Dennis or Janine. It is not because I don't love you; it is because I am on a fast track through medical school. I have to balance my time with my friends and my residency obligations. If I have to defer more to one over the other, I am sorry, but my residency obligations will always take precedence over fun." Teri replied, "Hayden, you are my friend, but you don't know how to have fun. Your fun is locked in your study reading medical literature. What fun is that for either of us?" I walked Teri into my study and showed her the two-twenty-inch tall stacks of medical journals that I have to read before I start my O&G residency in a couple months. I enjoy our time riding, being silly at the bear restaurant, and even sleeping over and telling stories. I dislike playing dress up as much as you dislike doing reading and experiments in my lab. We are two different girls with one common bond. We love each other like sisters. We fight, hug and even kiss once in a while, but that is all I can offer. I cannot be with you daily and if that is your expectation, then I am sorry and play with Dennis and Janine." Teri replied, "I am trying to understand. Oh, by the way, my mother asked me to give this article to your mother." I read the article and it was about the triage work we did at the accident scene. I turned to Teri and said, "This article is a good example of what I am trying to communicate. I was at the bear restaurant after my steeplechase qualification ride. Jeremy and Cynthia were with me, but when this accident occurred in front of me, I had to push my friends back and out of the way because my mother and I did immediate triage work to save some lives." Teri asked, "What is Triage?" I explained, "It is a process of prioritizing patient care from least in need to urgent care. I did assessment and CPR on a little girl and I saved her life. That is my world Teri. My friends unfortunately must stand aside when my life demands my attention elsewhere, such as my studies. I hope you understand." Teri replied, "I think so. You like being with friends, but your school and work must take priority over having fun.

Are you asking me for a Date?

I was sitting at home on Friday reading my O&G medical journals focusing on female ailments and how to diagnose conditions by degree. For example, endometriosis can be light to heavy tissue. It is important to determine if surgery is required to improve fertility. The literature suggests that pregnancy should occur within six months of laparoscopic surgery removing endometrial tissue because it will grow back. I need to know the intention of the patient and pregnancy to determine if immediate surgery is needed, or if it can be postponed.

I found that there was a whole lot of O&G that I knew nothing about. I'm sure that is why certification and a fellowship take at least four years of additional study following medical school. I was studying when I heard a knock on my door. I replied, "It's open." My father sat by me and gave me a hug and complemented me on my skill development and devotion to becoming an OB/GYN. He wanted to know if I had any questions. I asked, "I still have three and one-half months before I start my official residency. Is it possible that I start my residency Monday through Thursday each week leaving Friday, Saturday and Sunday to have some time to be with my friends? I know it is jumping the gun, but it seems silly for me to wait to start when I am ready and currently bored out of my mind reading instead of being at your side." My father replied, "I will check with the boss and see what she says."

My mother showed up about twenty minutes later and said, "Supper in twenty." I replied, "Thanks." My mother kept me guessing until dinner. At dinner, I asked, "Did you both discuss my request to begin my residency Monday through Thursday reserving Friday through Sunday off; that is unless I am needed to work the additional days." My mother replied, "You are going to be in the O&G section working under your father. It is up to him." My father smiled and said, "Of course. We will give it a try and see if it works out alright. Your residency requires you to put in fifty to sixty hours a week. If you work ten hours a day, then you will need to factor in study and reading time to fill your hours." I replied, "That's fine with me. I would like to spend some time with friends this summer. Once they start school, then I will work Monday through Friday and take the weekends off." My father again said, "We will try it and see if it works out."

I started Monday and worked through Thursday. Friday morning, I arrived for breakfast wearing my gray pleated skirt with my mauve stockings and a light cream blouse. My father replied, "You look beautiful today. Why are you dressed up?" I replied, "I am off work and decided to dress up." My mother smiled and asked, "Are you going somewhere all dressed up like that?" I replied, "I just thought I would take some reading materials and sit in the cafeteria reading. It will be a nice break from sitting in my study all day alone." My mother smiled more and asked, "Is that young man, Marcus, going to meet you in the cafeteria?" *I had forgotten that I introduced Marcus to my mother previously.* I replied, "Yes, I think so; I hope so; I don't know what I am doing. I just enjoyed talking with Marcus and he indicated that he would be in the cafeteria at 1:30 pm today. This time I am not going to have spilled tomato soup down my front." My father replied, "You are going to work to see a boy? Let's go."

I walked into the cafeteria and ordered an orange juice in a cup with a straw. I wasn't going to have orange juice spilled all over me. Around lunch, I ordered a ham and cheese sandwich on dry bread so I didn't spill on my clothes. I wanted to look nice when Marcus arrived. I finished my sandwich and looked at the clock. It was 1:20 and still no Marcus. I returned to studying when I heard Marcus yell, "Hayden, I'm here. I will grab something to eat and be right there." Marcus grabbed a hamburger and I watched him put mustard, ketchup and mayonnaise on the bun. I thought it looked good, but not today. I was clean and presentable. Marcus sat across from me and I said, "That smells so good. Did you put onions on it?" Marcus replied, "No way. How could I eat onions and then expect to talk with you?" Marcus opened up his hamburger to show me no onions. He closed up the burger and leaned over the table to give me a bite when a man bumped Marcus' chair causing his hamburger to smash into my shirt. I began laughing and that was the start of our conversation. Marcus ordered two more hamburgers, but this time I didn't worry about getting my blouse dirty. After lunch, I excused myself and grabbed a polo shirt from my locker and we just talked about everything and nothing. I liked Marcus, but I was mixed up inside me. I knew about human development, hormones and attractions. I understood the science, but I was at a loss of words when it came to a boyfriend type relationship. *I thought no worry. I am too young for a boyfriend and Marcus is too young for a girlfriend. We can be just friends.*

Marcus and I finished and we walked around the medical center. Outside the temperature was a warm seventy-six degrees. The deciduous trees were in full bloom providing shade for us to sit and talk on a park bench outside of the emergency room. Marcus explained to me that he was going into seventh grade in the fall. I replied, "I am not familiar with public school grades since I never went to a formal school. Marcus mentioned a year-end school dance for the sixth grade and asked me if I would be his dance date. I replied, "I don't know if I could attend. I would need to discuss it with my parents. I asked more questions and learned that the dance would have six chaperones plus three teachers, a nurse and the principal in attendance. It will just be dancing and having something to drink, so what do you say Hayden. May I take you as my dance date?" I replied, "I must ask my parents, but more importantly, I don't know how to dance. I have played music, but I have never danced. I am afraid I would look foolish."

Marcus asked me to stand up. I stood in front of him and he took my left hand in his and then put his right hand in mine up in the air. He tried to teach me how to dance in the cafeteria and I was so embarrassed that I said, "Let's find my mother and I will talk with her." My mother was in her office and I asked Marcus to wait outside. I entered and explained to my mother than Marcus has asked me to go to his sixth-grade dance at his school. It is well chaperoned with parents, teachers and the principal. His parents will pick me up and drop me off after the dance." My mother smiled again and asked, "Is this dance something you would like to do with Marcus?" I replied, "Yes and No." Yes, because it would most likely be fun and I would be around other kids my age, but bad because I don't know how to dance." My mother asked, "When is your dance to take place?" I replied, "Marcus said next Friday." My mother replied, "That doesn't give too much time to get a nice dress and shoes and learn how to dance." I asked, "Can you teach me?" My mother replied, "I could, but your grandfather taught dance and music a while ago. I bet he would love to teach you how to dance." I asked, "Would he know how kids dance today?" My mother replied, "I don't know. Ask your grandfather tonight or call him right now if you want." I turned my back to Marcus and called my grandfather. He replied, "You show me how the kids dance and I will teach you." I called Cynthia and she knew how to dance. She stayed over Friday through Sunday and she taught me how to dance."

Marcus' father picked me up in a fancy limousine. I was wearing a blue pastel party dress, stockings, black shoes with a low heel and a white sweater. My grandmother fixed my hair and helped me put on a little makeup. My mother reminded my grandmother, "Just a little makeup." I looked in the mirror and I was very pretty – that is pretty scared. I had never been on a real date, especially with a boy. Tonight was going to be another breakthrough in my personal education.

I watched the car door open and Marcus was dressed in a dark blue blazer, white shirt and blue tie, tan pants and black shoes. He looked different too. I could see he was as nervous as me. He took my arm and walked me to the car and waited to get in until I was seated. He was quite the gentleman. I found out that Marcus' father was also a chaperone for the dance. When we arrived at the school, a photographer took pictures of singles and couples as we entered the school gymnasium. The room was all decorated with flowering trees and flowers. The music played on stage by a man flipping records all the time. The music started and Marcus took my hand and asked me if I cared to dance. I replied, "Thank you" and we walked to the center of the gymnasium. I was so embarrassed because there were only two couples dancing. After the first dance, many more students began dancing and it was a lot of fun.

Marcus walked me to the punch bowl and I looked at my new dress and said, "No thank you. I don't want to wear the punch bowl." We laughed and danced again. I was watching Marcus dance with a girl in his class when Jeremy showed up and asked, "Why are you here? You don't go to school here." I replied, "I was asked by Marcus to be his dance date." Jeremy was mad and said, "I asked you about dating and you said that you were too young to date and too busy to date, but here you are with Marcus. I feel like smashing his face in." I asked Jeremy why he felt that way. He replied, "Because I like you too. You are the cutest girl at this dance." I replied, "You don't need to be angry. How about asking me to dance with you?" Jeremy smiled and walked me onto the dance floor where we danced through three songs. I asked for a quick break because I needed to use the bathroom. Jeremy followed me and so did Marcus. From inside the bathroom I heard both of them arguing over me. I returned and said, "If you both don't stop arguing, I am calling my parents and leaving. You are embarrassing me and you. I will dance with both of you tonight."

Marcus and Jeremy competed for my attention and it strangely felt good, but I didn't like the attention it brought from the school principal. Mr. Evans stopped the arguing by threatening to kick both Jeremy and Marcus out of the dance. They would be held in his office until their parents arrived. They agreed to stop. Mr. Evans then asked, "Who are you. You don't go to this school, do you?" I replied, "No, I am home schooled." That was sufficient as he walked away. With two dance partners, I received no rest as I danced through every song played. I was so happy to be home that night in the quiet solitude of my bedroom and study.

I woke up with the sunshine through my window as I welcomed another day. I was up for ten minutes when the phone rang. Jeremy asked if he could take me horseback riding. He had a picnic lunch for us. I replied, "Is Cynthia invited?" Jeremy said, "Not this time. It is just you and me on this ride." I replied, "I need to talk with my mother. I will call you back. I walked towards the kitchen and the phone rang again. It was Marcus asking me if I would like to go swimming with him. I replied, "I need to check with my mother. I will call you back." I walked into the kitchen, hugged my mother and said, "I have boy problems." My mother replied, "I was afraid of that. What is going on that has created a problem for you?" I explained about horseback riding and swimming and I don't want to choose one over the other. Both boys are my friends. My mother's wisdom shined. She suggested I ride horses with both boys and then swim with both boys. That way you get the fun and you don't need to choose one friend over the other." Wrong!

I arrived and Jeremy and Marcus were both at the riding stable. They were saddled and both offered to saddle Midnight. I replied, "Thanks, but no thanks. I saddle my own horse." Jeremy offered to help me mount Midnight and so did Marcus. I walked Midnight to the mounting block and handled it myself. We started riding and they fought over who was lead and who followed me. When we stopped for lunch, both boys brought enough sandwiches for ten people. Marcus brought six kinds of sandwiches since he didn't know what I liked. Jeremy knew I liked ham and cheese and all of his sandwiches were ham and cheese. We had three thermoses of hot chocolate and enough candy and sweet pastries to last for a month. Jeremy would hand me a pastry followed by Marcus. I would point out that my mouth is only so big and I don't eat that much either. The boys drove me crazy. I decided I liked to ride with Teri and Cynthia more than with the boys.

My mother arrived four hours later to pick me up. I got off Midnight and both boys were right there to help me down. I got mad and asked them to back off and leave me alone. They fought over who would remove Midnight's saddle and while they argued, I removed the saddle and started brushing Midnight. Within seconds, both boys were brushing out Midnight and ignoring their own horses. I put Midnight and my tack away and ran to the helicopter saying, "Please get me out of here." I told my mother about the boys and she laughed all the way home. That night both Marcus and Jeremy called to take me on another date. I apologized and explained I was starting my residency and wouldn't have time to date for another year. *So, I lied a little. It was worth it. They left me alone.*

FIVE

My Residency

My father talked about my residency on the way to the medical center. He explained that I had it easy during my first year. What was new and exciting then will be everyday work this year. He said that I would be doing most of the gynecological exams for birth control; early pregnancy and pregnancy follow up. In the afternoons I will be asked to deliver one to two babies by natural child birth and at least once a month, I will be doing a C-section under my father's supervision. When not busy, I needed to complete my reading of the medical journals and be ready to answer questions as we walked from patient to patient. He reminded me that I am a resident, not a doctor yet. If I find anything of concern when doing an exam, I am to refer the issue to him for consultation before taking action.

I asked my father if I would be exposed to laparoscopic surgery and he indicated that I would be doing surgeries and learning how to remove endometrial tissue, cysts, etc. He finally explained, "You will be treated by me as another physician. You will make sure your patients sign a consent to treat under you, and if not, then return them to the waiting area until I can see them.

My father also explained that practicing medicine, especially O&G is a fast-moving practice and I need to remain flexible and deal with situations as they come. I replied, "You can trust me."

My very first day was exciting, but stressful. I was working with a woman who was slowly dilating. It was her first pregnancy and I was patient and checked up on her every five minutes. I checked the ultrasound and concluded the baby's head would clear the birth canal.

I checked her again and I could see the baby's head crowning and I stood by. I checked my watch and my father's surgical nurse ran into my delivery room and said, "Your father needs you to assist immediately. I checked my patient and my nurse said, "Hayden, the baby is coming." My father's nurse screamed at me to hurry. I tore off my surgical gown and mask and ran to the door when my nurse yelled, the baby's head is almost out. I put on my surgical gown and mask and told the nurse to tell my father I can't leave yet. I am delivering a baby. I had the baby out in two minutes when my father's nurse yelled, "Hayden, now please!" I directed my nurse to keep the baby comfortable and I would be back to cut the cord and tie it off. I grabbed a new surgical gown and mask, washed up and put on my rubber gloves to find my father and mother sitting with a cup of tea talking. I ran back out without saying anything and took care of my patient. When done, I returned to the surgery center and my father smiled and asked me if I learned anything. I replied, "I had to determine where my priority existed. I decided it had to be with the patient I was with since I was needed immediately. Had I abandoned my patient, the nurse would have had to deliver the baby and that isn't allowable. I ran into here to assist as quickly as I could and I kept your nurse informed of my status." Both of my parents said I handled the crisis as I should. I survived my first of many training disasters and real disasters. The difference in my residency is that I am the decision maker in most circumstances, but I would always defer to my father if I needed help or consultation. That night I fell asleep on the way home. This time my father carried me into my bedroom and laid me down. I woke up at 4:00 am and didn't remember anything about getting home or going to bed. *I thought this is what the practice of medicine will be. How exciting. I love the challenge.*

Planning for my Residency

I reassessed my education and figured I could be a board-certified OB/GYN by age fifteen at the latest. I began to look at my last four years of training and what it would involve. Based upon my reading of a four-year residency training program, I learned that I would have broad exposure to the health care of women. I would receive intense exposure to general Obstetrics and Gynecology with specialization in (a) Family Planning; (b) Gynecologic Oncology; (c) Maternal Fetal Medicine; (d) Pediatric and Adolescent Gynecology; (e) Reproductive Endocrinology & Infertility; (f) Sexual Medicine; and (g) Urogynecology & Pelvic Reconstruction. I had to look up many of the topics due to a lack of exposure during my clerkship. I realized that I had a lot to learn and then wondered if I could do my four-year residency at the medical center instead of the medical school. I put that thought away for another day because my phone went off and I had to report to the surgery center.

    I walked in and my father said, "Resident, it's about time. Next time I expect you to run when you are called." I apologized to my father and he replied, "No apology needed. Just run when called." I was washing up and getting on my scrubs, mask and gloves. I turned and stood by my father and he introduced me to Ms. Fields. He explained that she has consented to you doing her C-section. She looked at me and asked my father, "You are kidding, right?" He replied, "Not kidding." She asked how I could deliver her baby when I couldn't see over the surgical table. I pressed the down button and said, "Like that and please don't worry, I have done three C-sections previously and my father will be standing right here if I have any questions." She asked, "You are a doctor, right?" I replied, "Almost. I am in my fourth year of medical school doing my residency." She reaffirmed her consent and I walked through the numbers with my father as she was being put under anesthesia. I delivered the baby exactly the way I was trained. I went to close, but before doing so, I asked the charge nurse if she accounted for all of the sponges, gauze pads and instruments. She counted three times and was missing a gauze pad. I looked at her gown and it was stuck to her. I closed after delivering a healthy little girl.

    My father was talking with me about my residency when my nurse called me to hurry to delivery room 2B. I got in and the woman was already dilated and ready to deliver. I looked at her chart and my father noted the oversize head. I made the decision to do an episiotomy to allow an easier delivery. I used a topical and then I injected the perineum and cut it. The baby passed easily. I cut the cord and tied it off and then sutured the perineum. My father checked my work and smiled. When he found out that I had to cut the perineum, he rechecked the woman and smiled again.

A Gift from God

I started to talk with my father when I was called to delivery room 1A. I ran to the room, put on my lab coat over my surgical scrubs, washed and new gloves just before delivering child number three in one day. We lived in a small community and I wondered where were all these babies coming from? My father said, "We are growing and that is why we will need you here."

The following day I was back to seeing patients and doing gynecological exams. My first patient was a pregnant thirteen-year old. The mother asked for an abortion. I knew that we didn't do abortions, but I called my father to handle the patient. He politely explained that we do not do abortions and gave her the name of a Planned Parenthood Clinic. The mother complained because the nearest PPC was one hundred and sixty-two miles away. She demanded my father do the abortion and he replied, "Unless your daughter's life is at risk, I will not abort the fetus. That's final." She said we would be hearing from her lawyer. *I thought, go ahead and you will hear from my lawyer.* My father said, "Good decision to call me."

My next patient was experiencing severe pain in her abdomen. The mother asked, "Is my daughter pregnant? She denies she has had sex with anyone." I replied, "I need to look and do an exam. We can talk after I am done with the exam. I checked her and she was grossly inflamed and I couldn't believe she was even walking. I asked her how long she has had the pain. She replied, "It started after my last period and it has been getting progressively worse each day." I said I want my father to take a look too. I explained to my father that it appeared to be pelvic inflammatory disease and possibly a urinary tract infection. He looked and I properly diagnosed the PID, but there was no indication that a urinary tract infection also existed. He asked me to take a swab and send it to the lab. I took the swab and then he asked, "How do you treat PID?" I suggested a strong antibiotic for five to seven days and then follow up. In the meantime, we will know if there is more than PID. My father wrote the prescription and I was done.

I was cleaning up when admitting said they had an emergency. I asked, "Why isn't the patient being sent to emergency?" She replied, "This young woman is bleeding out of her vagina and it looks bad." I directed them to send her to me. I changed and washed up waiting for the woman. It turned out to be a seventeen-year old girl who had a spontaneous abortion. I called my father and confirmed my diagnosis and then assisted in removal of the fetal tissue. She was six weeks pregnant. Her mother wanted the fetal tissue tested for DNA. She wanted to know who got her daughter pregnant. I looked at the woman and asked, "Have you asked your daughter?" She replied, "Hell no. I am about to kill her for what she did." I made the decision to move the daughter into inpatient care overnight for observation and to let the mother cool off. I tried Jim's recommendation of breathing ten times deeply holding your breath each time, but the mother would have no part of a breathing exercise. Just for safety, I notified security of the potential threat.

My next patient was a twenty-week pregnancy check. My father ordered an ultrasound and I looked at it, but kept my mouth shut. I asked the expecting parents if they wanted to know the sex of their babies. I heard back in unison, "Babies? Did you say more than one baby?" I replied, "You are having twins. I asked again, "Do you want to know the sex of your babies? He said, "Yes"; she said, "No." He replied, "It's up to her. I'm sure you know the saying, "Happy wife-happy life." I asked if they would like to hear the babies' heartbeats. That they agreed upon. I used the Doppler and both heart beats sounded healthy and strong for twenty weeks. I was getting ready to leave the room when she asked, "What are the sexes of our twins?" I replied, "You are having twin boys and they look very healthy. I showed them the ultrasound and printed out a picture for them to take home.

I stepped into the hallway and my father said, "Follow me." We went to the surgical center and he said, "Suit up. You are going to learn about laparoscopic surgery today. I watched my father remove a cyst and cauterize the wound. He withdrew the cyst and put it into a tube for the lab. He explained that he wanted to make sure the cyst was benign. It looked so easy to do, but I knew I was a long way from doing laparoscopic surgeries.

I finished out my week with three gynecological exams for pills and one urinary tract infection. Surprisingly, my family was all done for the day at the same time I was done. I looked at my watch and we had been at the medical center for almost fourteen hours. I couldn't believe it was almost ten o'clock. My mother reminded me that the next day was Friday, my day off. She wanted to know if I wanted to spend the day talking with Marcus again or stay home and sleep. I chose sleep for the first time in my life. I woke up around noon and couldn't believe I slept so long. I called Teri to see if she wanted to get together. I received no answer. I called

Cynthia and remembered she was in school. I asked my grandfather to drive me to the medical center. I might as well talk with Marcus.

I was sitting in the cafeteria when my mother walked in and asked me how I got to the medical center. I replied, "Grandpa drove me and said to call him and he would pick me up when ready. My mother asked, "Will Marcus be here today?" I replied, "I have no idea." My mother just smiled and said, "Have fun."

I brought my book bag full of journals that I needed to read. I was reading and sipping my orange juice when I heard Marcus say, "Hi Hayden." I replied, "Hi." Marcus immediately apologized for his negative behavior at the horse barn. He said, "The way I acted was out-of-line, but I was a little jealous of your relationship with Jeremy." I replied, "I can have multiple friends. I don't need a boyfriend. I told you we are ten years old. I don't have time for a boyfriend; however, I do have time for a friend that is a boy if you understand what I am saying." Marcus replied, "You just want to be friends, right?" I touched my nose and said, "Exactly."

We ordered lunch and I asked that I not wear my lunch today. We both ordered plain cheese sandwiches with hot chocolate. That was one of my favorite lunches. As we talked, Marcus asked me if he would ever fit into my world. I replied, "Until I obtain my certification as an OB/GYN, which by the way is five years from now, I will have little time to share with anyone including my parents. Right now, my father is letting me have Friday through Sunday off. However, when fall semester comes, I will be working six days a week as a resident. I am trying to limit to five days with a study day at night or on weekends, but so far I am scheduled to work six days a week." Marcus asked, "I suppose that means no Friday lunches together anymore?" I replied, "I still need lunch. I don't see why I can't have lunch with you, provided I am not dealing with a patient." Marcus looked at me and teared up. He said, "I guess I shouldn't have dumped my girlfriend for you." Marcus got up and left without saying good-bye or anything."

I spent most of my time riding horses or swimming with Teri and Cynthia. Both were low stress and weren't looking for a girlfriend or fussing over boyfriends. It was just girls which was a welcome relief after Marcus. We were swimming when Cynthia offered to have me and Teri spend the night at her house. I had fun the last time and said, "I will go, but I need my parents' approval first." Cynthia asked, "Why? You are almost a medical doctor. Why do you need parental approval to spend the night with me?" I replied, "Regardless of my education, I am still only ten years old and I have an obligation to obtain my parents' approval before I go anywhere." Teri replied, "Same goes for me. My mother will ask if there will be boys there. What do I tell my mother?" Cynthia paused, so I spoke and said, "The truth please." Cynthia replied, "I invited three boys over to be with us. I thought we could play games." I asked, "What kind of games?" Cynthia replied, "Like spin the bottle; five minutes in heaven; you know, big kid's games." I asked, "What is five minutes in heaven about?" Cynthia replied, "You do lead a sheltered life. A boy and a girl go in the closet and do what they want for five minutes." I replied, "No thank you. I will stay home." Teri said, "Ditto for me." Cynthia got mad at me and said I was no longer her friend. I responded, "Cynthia, for your sake I hope you don't become a pregnancy patient at the medical center." Cynthia just laughed at me.

Teri came to my house and spent the night. We discussed Cynthia and the concerns I had about boys at our age. Teri promised me that she would abstain from sex with boys and I gave her the same promise. Teri and I were close friends once again.

I consumed myself with my residency. I had Teri as a friend. All of my other friends dumped me which was alright given what they wanted to do. I worked my twelve to fourteen hours a day completing my residency. Fall semester arrived and I made sure I mailed my registration and fees to the medical school. This time I mailed each separately by certified mail.

Teri stopped by to inform me that she was going to be enrolled in the public school. She was too bored and lonely doing home school. I gave her a hug and wished her well with a promise to see her on my day off. The next time I saw Teri she had acquired a boyfriend at school. At ten, Teri explained to me that she really liked Thomas and so did her parents. Teri mentioned a date with Thomas at the pizza parlor and swimming and she was hoping for many more dates with him. Teri whispered, 'Thomas kisses nicely too. Hayden, you should have a boyfriend too and we can double date." I replied, "No thank you, but please remember your promise to me." Teri replied, "I know." Every time I called to talk with Teri she was with Thomas and didn't want to talk. *I thought to myself… there goes another friendship. I am now officially without any friends.* I teared up and then kicked my own butt and said, "Girl, you have work to do so quit feeling sorry for yourself."

I was at work when my father called his monthly staff meeting. The meeting was mandatory unless urgent patient business kept a doctor or nurse away. This morning my parents introduced Dr. Edna Stephens, a board-certified Endocrinologist. She would be handling our diabetes and many of the internal medicine issues. She introduced herself and explained that she had two boys, twelve and eleven and a daughter ten. She looked at me and said, "About her age. What are you ten or eleven?" I replied, "I will be eleven in April. She looked at me and said, "You are beautiful. My boys are going to want to meet you. What is that you are wearing? Are you playing doctor or what?" My father explained that I was in my fourth-year residency in O&G. She looked at me and laughed, before saying, "That little girl, I doubt that. My ten-year old can barely choose her clothes and tie her shoes." I replied, "This little girl is in my fourth-year residency. I have delivered thirty-five babies by natural birth and I have done four C-section deliveries by myself, but of course under my father's supervision. She looked at my father and asked, "She is kidding, isn't she?" My mother replied, "No kidding and you will find that she is a very dedicated resident and brilliant." She replied, "Now I know my children will want to meet you. Maybe some of your smartness will rub off on them." I looked at my father and said, "I need to get to work. I have a full line of patients waiting for me today."

True to her word, Dr. Stephens brought her children to the medical center Friday and they hung out all day in the cafeteria. They were bored and disruptive to the staff and patients using the cafeteria. I was done with my patients and only had a simple procedure to do with my father at 4:00 pm. I asked to go to the cafeteria and meet Dr. Stephen's children. I walked into the cafeteria in my lab coat and stethoscope. I walked over to their table and asked them to please keep their voices down. The cafeteria is the only place in the medical center where staff can come to relax outside of their office. What you are doing is not relaxing for anyone. I introduced myself and got their names. Thomas was twelve, Stewart was eleven and Mindy was ten. Thomas asked me where they could get white coats and play doctor with me. I straightened them out immediately and received an apology. Thomas was boisterous and arrogant and I didn't care for him too much. Stewart was quiet and reserved. He listened more than talked which I liked. Mindy was sweet, but she was a lot like Teri. She was into dress up, make believe and ....boys!

I spent two hours visiting with the family. Thomas kept trying to convince me that we could go for a walk outside; just the two of us. I replied, "That is not going to happen. I am on call right now and I do not date boys." Thomas replied, "Your loss." Mindy explained that she had a boyfriend going into seventh grade. I asked, "Are you going into sixth or fifth grade?" She replied, "Fifth. I got held back in first grade because I was hyperactive." I asked her if her mother knew about her older boyfriend and she replied, "Of course. My mother takes us to the movie or wherever we want to go on a date together." I have even stayed overnight with my boyfriend's sister. That is always fun." I apologized and excused myself. Later I told my parents that Edna's children are a bunch of losers and explained why.

At my ripe old age of ten I began to understand my parents' plight when it came to dating others. I often found myself sitting with someone like Marcus and having nothing much to say or talk about. We only had horses in common, but he wanted a girlfriend and I wasn't ready for that part of my life. I was too busy to even consider boys at this point in my life.

Help Me Father for I am Lost

My fall semester officially began and my father agreed to let me work Monday through Thursday, but I had to put in ten hours of reading and studying O&G journals over my three days off. I replied, "Why not. I have nothing else to do. I have no more friends to be with anyway." On my days off, I would sit and play music with my grandparents and I developed a liking for chamber music because it reflected the dark, loneliness and sadness I felt inside my heart. I would sit in my bedroom and play the violin for hours at a time, while hearing my grandparents discuss me in the background. They knew I was lonely and hurting, but admitted they didn't know how to help me through this personal struggle.

I was in tears, out of control of my emotions and angry at the world that I no longer felt a part of. I was alone and couldn't fit in socially with others my age. I blamed God, my Father for creating me and then leaving me alone to suffer. I asked my Heavenly Father, "Is this your will that your daughter suffer like Jesus?" My grandfather held me and prayed, "Lord Jesus, before you is my granddaughter who we believe was created in Heaven through your grace and delivered to earth by Archangel Michael. I ask that you lift my granddaughter's burdens and heal her heart and mind and through your grace help her to find her way through these troubled times; Amen."

I thanked my grandfather for praying for me. He asked, "Did prayer help?" I replied, "I don't know. I am still lonely and hurting, but prayer never hurts. Maybe the answer to my prayers is that I will become a healing physician and help others while I exist in social isolation and alone. I will wait and see if our prayer is answered."

I prayed to my Heavenly Father and prayed again and again, but I received no answer. Like my friends, my Heavenly Father apparently abandoned me too. I fell upon my knees in pain as tears ran down my face. I was crying when I prayed again, this time asking Jesus to send my guardian angel because I needed help and I cannot cope further in my quiet solitude. I sat through Saturday wondering if my prayers would ever be answered and my burden lifted. As I waited, I experienced more anger, rage and then self-pity. I looked in my mirror and I did not recognize the face looking back at me. I asked, "Who am I?"

I dropped to my knees again and I prayed, "Lord God, my Father, please hear my prayer. I am your creation. You sent Archangel Michael to deliver me to my parents to help fill their loneliness and now I am in need of help too. I too am alone and angry for I am lost in a place I do not understand or cannot remain. Within my heart and soul exists a raging battle and I am feeling nothing but sadness, emptiness and isolation. I am a prisoner in the body you created through your love and I have feelings and desires I cannot understand or satisfy. I no longer recognize who I am and I don't know what to do, or where to turn except to you, my Heavenly Father. Please help me and guide me through this period of my life. Amen."

My body was shaking uncontrollably and I was in tears when I decided to grab my laptop computer and sit outside amidst the colorful deciduous and evergreen trees. I stopped crying and I marveled at my Father's handiwork and remembered that I too was a product of God's handiwork.

The day was warm and the air was still. The leaves on the deciduous tree I sat under were motionless and hung like ornaments on a Christmas tree. I watched and waited for another leaf to fall, but the remaining leaves were securely attached and provided me shade and cover on this warm day. I wore shorts for the first time this year and my new medical center polo shirt.

I sat alone and when I looked upon the ground I saw one red leaf lying amongst a pile of yellow and orange leaves. The red leaf represented me. It lay quietly on the ground; alone and separated from the orange and yellow leaves that filled the ground around me. I am different, just like the red leaf in contrast to the orange and yellow leaves. I do not belong any more in this life than the red leaf belongs to the yellow and orange leaves. The red leaf was alone, different and unwelcomed by the other leaves which is how I feel most of the time. *I wondered, do I pick up the red leaf to rescue it from being overwhelmed by the rest of the dropping leaves; isolate it and protect it; or is it better to push the red leaf into the diverse pile of leaves showing that the little red leaf can fit in with the others.* I then realized and accepted that I can't fit in with friends. I had no friends left. Like the red leaf, I am alone, and I am different from all the others I once knew and cared for as my friends.

I decided to rescue the red leaf from its isolation and obscurity and I carefully mounted it in my study. I would look at the red leaf daily, hoping that it will turn color just enough to fit in and I could return it; But what of me? Where do I belong? How or where do I fit in? How do I communicate with others outside of my isolation when they have ears, but do not hear my cries for help? Should I exist alone, or should I change who I am to be like my former friends? Is my isolation and solitude a result of my inability to accept love or friendship from a boy? Am I to conform or remain isolated? Would I like me if I conformed and became someone I should not become? I am lost and pray my Heavenly Father picks me up and protects me as I have protected the little red leaf.

I self-diagnosed acute depression that affected who I am. I was becoming a nonperson, isolated by my learning ability and inability to relate to others at my age and education level. *I wondered, Am I arrogant? Astute or just unwelcomed like the little red leaf lying so quietly beneath the tree. I wondered if the tree discarded the red leaf like my friends discarded me as a friend.*

I walked out to the mailbox, just to walk. When I arrived, I screamed as loud as I could scream and I did so ten times and then thought of Jim and said, "I hope you are happy now." I teared up and realized that I was angry with the world. I felt no love and I wasn't old enough to be in love, much less date a boy or engage in inappropriate games. But then again, am I the red leaf? I am an outsider because I haven't caved into peer pressure and found a boyfriend. I have no time for a boyfriend and it would be cruel to even consider such a relationship with the demands upon my life. I cannot accept who I am becoming; however, I cannot accept who my former friends have become either. I am lost and cannot recognize who I am, or who I should become.

Symbolically, I knelt before my Father's creation and I prayed again and asked my Heavenly Father to take my burden now. I told my Father that I could go no further in life unless I was shown the way and my sadness was lifted. I cried out, "Help me Father! Please hear and answer my prayers. I am lost and don't know who I am anymore." I looked up and a sudden gust of wind moved the remaining leaves on my deciduous tree and I felt the sunlight shine upon my face through the leafy tree. I am not sure how or why, but I felt an immediate sense of relief as if my burdens were lifted and my prayers were answered. I remember my grandfather saying, "Put your troubles at the foot of the cross." For me, my Father in Heaven created me; the trees and grass; in fact, everything I could see. I didn't need the cross. My Father in Heaven lifted my burden and healed my heart in a simple moment of me trusting in him and allowing him to take my burden. As I knelt before my Father, I am certain, without any hesitation, that I heard my Heavenly Father say, "Go my child as I will be with you always."

My grandparents observed me come back into the house. I hugged and kissed both and I was my happy self again. My grandfather held me tightly and said, "You put your troubles at the foot of the cross, didn't you?" I replied, "I did metaphorically. My Heavenly Father heard my prayers and accepted my burden. I look in the mirror and I know who I am and I feel wonderful and alive again." I hugged my grandfather and thanked him for loving me and helping me when I was lost." I asked my grandparents to please take comfort in the simple fact that my Father said, "Go my child as I will be with you always." I walked forward in life that day knowing that my Father would be with me always and through his love and grace, I would be set free to move forward and not dwell in the past. I would no longer be lonely or isolated and I thanked my Father daily through prayer.

James A. Gauthier, J.D.

Time for Giving Thanks

No one needed to give thanks to God, my Heavenly Father more than me. I trusted in God, who just happened to be my Father Creator, and I was positive and motivated to finish my medical degree. My attitude changed and I no longer felt the darkness in my heart. I was alive and thankful for all of my Heavenly gifts, my parents and the opportunities I will have to help others. I was once again a force for change and accomplishment. I realized that I wasn't alone. My Father was with me on my journey and I truly believed my Father sent one of his angels to watch over me. I have never felt alone again. I am learning to heal bodies, but my Father healed my heart and soul.

My parents chose to shut down the medical center for Thanksgiving leaving minimal staff to meet inpatient care and emergencies. As with all physicians at the center, we were all on call for any emergencies that arose. I was excited because my father gave me Thursday through Sunday off of work. My mother suggested I call Teri and see if she wants to get together with me. I tried, but Teri was riding with her new boyfriend. I learned from Teri's mother that she was on her third boyfriend in three months.

Thanksgiving was a wonderful time for sharing and giving thanks for the blessings each of us received. As with every year I could remember, my grandmother adorned our dining table with a large, perfectly cooked turkey, mashed potatoes and turkey gravy, stuffing, corn, cranberries, rolls, four kinds of salads and enough pie for ten Thanksgivings. I especially prayed and gave thanks to my Heavenly Father and then gave thanks to my family who cared for me. I ate my fourth piece of pumpkin pie just before bed when I knew better. I was five-foot four inches tall and weighed one hundred and four pounds soaking wet. My mother gave me a hug and asked where I put all the food I ate. I replied, "I have a good metabolism." I was changing for bed and decided to weigh myself. I looked down and the scale read one hundred and fourteen pounds. I looked in the mirror and I felt slovenly and disgusting and immediately regretted my overeating. *I wondered what kind of doctor I would become with such poor eating habits. Doctors should lead by example and I am currently the example of what not to do.*

My parents were standing near the bathroom and my father asked, "Did you put on any pounds, Dr. Hayden?" I replied, "It can't be, but the scale can't lie. I put on ten pounds from dinner." I was deeply concerned and embarrassed. My mother could see and feel my embarrassment and suggested I eat less pie next time. I agreed to be more responsible with my eating habits. My father couldn't keep a straight face and started laughing at my weight gain. I was about to comment on his insensitivity when he said, "Hayden, get off the scale and read the weight." I looked and the scale read ten pounds before I stepped on it. My father's prank made my Thanksgiving and I enjoyed the levity even though I was the brunt of the joke. *I thought – thank God!*

Friday morning arrived and my mother and grandmother planned to shop for Christmas. I asked to be dropped off at the public indoor pool. I felt like swimming and for some reason, the water sounded refreshing and pulled me to it. I grabbed twenty dollars and wore my new yellow bikini swimsuit underneath my pants and shirt. I brought two towels just in case I needed both. When I arrived, there were two adults swimming, but most of the pool was wide open allowing me space to improve my swimming ability. I undressed down to my bikini and stood by the pool looking at the water. I wasn't sure so I put my foot in the water and it felt good and I immediately relaxed. I tightened my bikini ties and was ready to jump in when I felt someone poke my ribs and say 'Hi' to me. I was a little upset that someone would touch me without my permission. I turned around and I met Michael, an eleven-year old boy that had just finished taking the GED and was headed off to college in the fall. I immediately felt comfortable with Michael, almost like I was at peace within my being. I smiled at Michael and we introduced ourselves. I experienced an immediate attraction to Michael which was unlike how I felt with Marcus and Jeremy. I felt like I belonged with him as a friend.

Michael and I sat beside the pool, dangling our legs in the water as we talked about who we were. We talked for about thirty minutes when Michael asked, "Do you like hot chocolate?" I replied, "I love hot chocolate and plain cheese sandwiches." We walked over to the snack bar and each of us ordered a dry cheese sandwich and hot chocolate. We sat and talked while eating our lunch. Michael was different than Marcus and Jeremy. He wasn't trying to compete for my attention and I didn't feel like I had to change my vocabulary, or who I was in order to communicate with him. I would sit and stare into Michael's eyes as he talked about who he was and where his life goals were headed. His eyes were different, almost steely in appearance and his mannerisms were gentle and soft spoken. *I wondered if this Michael might be Archangel Michael here in answer to my prayers.* I knew the name was a mere coincidence, but I had to ask, "Are you Archangel Michael?" Michael smiled and replied, "Do you know that Archangel Michael is one of the seven Archangels of God. Michael is a messenger angel carrying out God's will. Why would you ask me such a question?" I replied, "Just curious." Michael replied, "Please tell me why you needed to ask that question." I replied, "Once I tell you, I expect you will walk away from me like I am nuts or something." Michael replied, "How could I think you are nuts. I don't even know you yet." I agreed to give Michael the short version of my miraculous birth.

I explained to Michael that it was two days before Easter 2007 when a young woman dressed in a white nightgown without shoes or a coat, stood on the entry steps to the Wilderness Health Outreach Medical Center. It was snowing and freezing rain. The young woman entered the medical center and said, "I am here to deliver this child." She was asked for identification and she produced a card with the name Michaele and an address – nothing else was readable.

My father is now and was then the OB/GYN at the medical center He determined that he would need to do a C-section delivery because of the way the baby was positioned in the uterus. The anesthesiologist administered the anesthetic and the young woman died instantly. My father delivered the baby girl and obtained DNA samples of my birth mother and me." Michael interrupted and asked, "You are the baby he delivered?" I replied, "Yes, that's me."

"The sheriff checked the young woman's address and it turned out to be a vacant lot. She was considered a Jane Doe and was sent to the morgue for a coroner's autopsy. My father sent some of the DNA samples he collected to the local lab who reported that the birth mother's DNA was contaminated because it contained both male and female sex chromosomes. The lab results indicated that my DNA didn't match my birth mother suggesting she was a surrogate. My biological family wasn't found within six months and my parents adopted me. My body chemistry is identical to my adoptive parents. My heart and the hearts of my parents beat in one single rhythm and I have many of the skills my mother enjoys like premonitions and remote viewing.

My father and mother were curious about me and decided to send their DNA and my DNA to the lab for analysis. The results showed my parents were 100 percent identical and I was 99.892 percent of my parents' DNA. Medically speaking, I was not from my parents like most children that are born. I was of my parents suggesting that I was created of their likeness. My parents have 160 IQs and mine is 154. When my birth mother's body was to be returned to my father for additional DNA evidence, the young woman was no longer in the morgue. An exhaustive search only found her surgical gown that she wore in delivery and her body has never been found. Our neighbor looked at the given name of my birth mother, which was spelled Michaele. Take off the 'e' and you have Michael. Michael is an Archangel whose DNA is both male and female because he is a creation of God to serve God's will."

Michael commented, "You must have been a gift from God. The connection between you and your adoptive parents is remarkable. I don't know if I should kneel before you or what." I replied, "If you kneel before me, I will kick you in the head. I may be a creation of my Father in Heaven, but I am all girl here on earth."

I talked more with Michael and learned that he wanted to become a pediatrician. He indicated that he loved children and couldn't wait to get married and start a family. He then asked me, "Please tell me a little about you. We have only talked about me and that was rude on my part." I asked him, "What would you like to know about me?" He asked, "How old are you?" I replied, "I will be eleven April 6th." Michael asked, "What grade are you in at school?" I replied, "I don't want to say and please do not ask." Michael replied, "That's fine. I am not pushy. I am above-average and like I said earlier, I obtained my GED and I am starting college next fall." I replied, "Very nice–good job."

Michael took my hot chocolate and said, "Answer my question and I will return your hot chocolate." He was laughing as he played keep away from me. I agreed to say so he would return my hot chocolate. I asked that he not over react and he asked, "Why?" I explained that I was a fourth-year resident in medical school. I am in training to become an obstetrics and gynecology type doctor. I work and am currently in my residency at the Wilderness Health Outreach Medical Center. My parents are both doctors and they run the medical center."

I was genuinely pleased that Michael didn't react to my education. He wanted to hear more about what I had learned so far. I shared that I had delivered babies, sutured wounds, fixed broken bones; a little bit of everything. Michael replied, "You are amazing." Michael indicated that he just moved into the area and his parents were looking for work. He explained that his parents had to get out of the big city because they felt smothered and they wanted more of a wilderness lifestyle.

I asked Michael what his parents do for a job. Michael explained that his father was the administrator of the largest teaching hospital in the state. He eventually burned out with the changes in medical coverages, fees and funding and decided to find something smaller to manage. Michael said his mother was an ER nurse, but also trained in O&G and general surgery. I asked, "Where are they looking for work?" Michael replied, "We have only been here for four days. We are still getting settled in. My parents plan to start job hunting next week. I replied, "Our administrator quit several months ago to return to big city life. I will check with my parents and see if they are interested in hiring another administrator. In terms of nurses, we can always use a good nurse." I asked for Michael's parents' names and his phone number. I don't fully understand why, but I drew a heart next to Michael's name.

My mother arrived at the same time as Michael's mother. Michael blurted out, "Look at that. It's a helicopter landing in the parking lot. I wonder if they are in trouble." Before I could explain the helicopter, Michael said, "Let's go see what is happening." I replied, "Don't bother. It is just my mother." He replied, "In a helicopter?" I replied, "All the time."

My mother walked into the snack bar and asked, "Did you swim or just spend the day in here?" I smiled and introduced Michael to my mother. He introduced his mother to me and my mother. Michael said, "Mom, Hayden is a fourth-year resident practicing at the medical center that you and dad talked about. Hayden's parents operate the center. You should talk with her about possible jobs."

Our mothers sat at another table and discussed the medical center while Michael and I ordered another hot chocolate. I was a little hungry and I bought an oversize oatmeal cookie that Michael and I shared. My mother offered to take Michael's mother and Michael for a tour of the medical center and meet my father. Michael was thrilled to ride in our helicopter. I was polite and sat with Michael in the back allowing his mother to sit up front with my mother. We took the tour of the facility, but my father was in the middle of another C-section delivery. I asked the nurse if my father needed any help. She replied, "No. I think your dad has it all under control. Are you going to be here for a while, just in case he needs you?" I replied, "For a little while. We are giving a tour and should be leaving within thirty minutes." I was disappointed that my father was too busy to say hi, but I knew first-hand what it is like. I smiled when my mother invited Shirley and her husband Scott over for dinner that night. I asked, "Michael is invited also?" My mother replied, "Of course."

I wondered if Michael was my answer to prayer. He was smart, kind and accepting. He wasn't pushy or judgmental and I really liked talking with him. On our way back to the swimming pool Michael placed his hand over mine and I didn't yank my hand away from his. I keyed my headset and asked my mother privately if Michael could fly home with us and his parents could arrive by car. I explained that I would like to show Michael my study. I followed up by saying, "So long as Michael is in my room, the door will be left open." My mother replied fine and then obtained Shirley's approval."

We landed in front of the house and Michael said, "Sweet". I assumed that was slang for nice or something. I brought him into my bedroom, library and laboratory and he was fascinated with my science equipment. He looked through my library and he had read many of my literature books. He loved science and hoped to do pediatric research and practice pediatric medicine when he finished medical school.

We talked about horses and he wanted to know who the girl was on the jumping horse. I took down the picture and he said, "That's you isn't it?" I replied, "It is. I was eight when I did that run." I promised to take Michael to the barn and also to meet Tempest. As the night progressed, I naturally began sharing my life with Michael and including him in my planned activities outside of work. It wasn't love because I was too young to be in love with any boy, but it felt really nice to have a friend again who just happened to be a boy.

My mother peeked inside my room and said, "Dinner in twenty." I walked into the living room and introduced myself to Michael's father. He was gracious, like Michael, and complemented me on my educational achievement. I listened to my parents discuss the medical center and the need for a full-time administrator. My parents and Michael's parents talked for four hours after dinner and then agreed to meet at the medical center Monday morning for a full tour. My parents indicated that they would have a decision made on hiring an administrator and another nurse. Michael asked if he could also attend. I replied, "Sure, but understand something; if I get called into an emergency, I am going to dump you like a bowl of tomato soup until I resolve the emergency." Michael just laughed and said, "I understand. Patients will always come first."

Monday morning arrived and I greeted Michael wearing my white lab coat and stethoscope. I was working and had Michael walk with me to the O&G section so I could check with my nurses to see if anything was pending. I was told that a delivery was on the way. The husband called in twenty minutes ago and he estimated thirty minutes for arrival. We have already prepared a birthing room and we are ready to receive her. Do we call you or your father?" I replied, "Call me. My parents are busy right now interviewing a possible administrator." I looked at Michael and suggested we remain close to delivery room 1B since the patient is on the way. While waiting, I grabbed the patient's chart and noted all of the conditions for a normal delivery. I told Michael, "This could be slow or fast. It is her first pregnancy."

Michael offered to pick up a hot chocolate for me while I waited for my patient. We sat in the waiting room talking about delivering babies. Fifty minutes and two hot chocolates later and the patient arrived. I excused myself and closed the door to the delivery room. I checked my patient for dilation and position of the baby. Everything looked good. I listened to the baby's heart beat to determine if the baby was in distress. I let the expectant parents know the baby's heart sounds good. I inched my way out of the room so Michael couldn't see in. I visited, but left every five minutes to check on my patient. I was explaining how to do a C-section when my nurse said, "Hayden, it's time." I stepped in and delivered a healthy baby girl. I left the clean up to the nurses and I rejoined Michael on a tour of my department. All Michael kept saying is, "I can't believe you just stepped in, delivered a baby, and you are out again." I replied, "Once you deliver fifty babies, it is pretty much routine."

I sat with Michael in my waiting room and we talked some more. I explained that I liked Michael as a friend and indicated that I am not old enough to be having a boyfriend and too busy to maintain a boyfriend type relationship. Michael responded, "Thank you Hayden. I feel the same way. I like you as a friend, but I have a lot of learning to do and I do not need distractions." I felt instant relief. Michael and I agreed to meet in the cafeteria every Friday for lunch and to be with each other to share our stories and adventures in the world of medicine. When Michael's mother arrived, Michael said, "Good-bye. Please call me if you can. Here is my phone number." I don't know why I did it, but I kissed Michael on his cheek and promised I would call him.

My father talked with me after Michael and his parents left the medical center. He said he wouldn't lecture me about right and wrong because he knew who I was. He asked me if I liked Michael and I replied, "Yes. He is very nice. I like him a lot. He is so different from Marcus and Jeremy. Michael is a motivated student who is starting college early like I did and his goal is to become a pediatrician." My dad hugged me and said, "I hope he turns out to be a true friend." My father then said, "I know you need time for friendships. You may have Friday through Sunday off, but be prepared to run Monday through Thursday. By the way, thank you for doing my delivery today so I could meet Michael's parents." I asked my father, "Are you going to hire them?" He replied, "I hired Michael's mother. I need the foundation's approval to hire another administrator. I offered the job subject to approval." I hugged my father and said, "Thank you. I would like to see more of Michael on my days off. I think meeting at the cafeteria is a good and safe place to meet on Fridays." The following morning my father hired Michael's father as the medical center administrator. He worked for my parents which kept the medical staff happy.

SIX

Planning for my future as an OB/GYN

It was almost Christmas again. Outside the freezing rain and snow blanketed the ground and painted everything in its path white. The deciduous trees stood tall, but bare as the final leaf fell and hit the ground. I knew that my fourth-year residency would come to an end in May, 2018 and I began receiving literature from the medical school identifying my course of study in order to receive board certification as an OB/GYN. Based upon the O&G specialty, I was looking at four more years in a residency training program focused on women's healthcare issues. The literature identified the goals and objectives needed to receive my OB/GYN certification and fellowship.

Under the four year residency program, I will receive training focused exclusively on Obstetrics and Gynecology with subfields of study including, but not limited to (a) Family Planning; (b) Gynecologic Oncology; (c) Maternal Fetal Medicine; (d) Pediatric and Adolescent Gynecology; (e) Reproductive Endocrinology & Infertility; (f) Sexual Medicine; and (g) Urogynecology & Pelvic Reconstruction. I had to look up many of the topics due to a lack of exposure during my clerkship and fourth-year residency to date. I realized that I had a lot to learn and I was anxious to get started.

I was reading the O&G residency training highlights and areas where fellowships were currently being offered. Early Friday morning I discussed the fellowship areas and asked my father which focus would best benefit the medical center. He replied, "I need you to learn everything. Your fellowship is something you will approach in your third year of residency so please don't get hung up on a fellowship right now. It will happen in due time."

I was sitting in the cafeteria reading and decided to get another hot chocolate because Michael was late as usual. *I wondered if he forgot our Friday get together.* I returned to reading when I heard Michael say, "Sorry doc, but I depend on my parents to get me here and my father was doing administrative things at the time we were to leave." I smiled at Michael and said, "I forgive your tardiness this time." Michael replied, "What about next time I am late?" I looked at Michael's steely eyes and said, "No problem because there won't be a next time!" We both got a good laugh.

Michael bought two more hot chocolates and two plain cheese sandwiches to be consumed around our fourth or fifth hot chocolate for the day. Michael sat by me and asked, "Are you studying right now that I should leave you alone?" I replied, "No, I am reviewing the requirements for my O&G residency." Michael asked, "Don't you mean your OMG residency?" I smiled and said, "No. It is O&G which stands for obstetrics and gynecology." Michael asked when my residency would start. I explained, "My four-year O&G residency will start after I graduate from medical school." Michael replied, "That gives me more time to be with you on Fridays until I start college in the fall."

I journalized my hours for the day and Michael asked, "How many hours of work do you need to graduate from medical school? I see you studying all the time." I was curious and pulled my laptop out of my backpack and pulled up my excel spread sheet and added up my hours in residency and studying at home. I pointed out to Michael that I had already exceeded the needed hours to get my medical degree. I replied, "Thanks for asking. I wonder if the medical school will confer my medical degree prior to the formal graduation ceremony in May." Michael replied, "It can't hurt to ask." I kissed Michael's cheek again and thanked him for his wisdom.

I wrote Dr. Sorenson a letter inquiring about my OB/GYN residency.

Dear Dr. Sorensen:

I have completed my minimum hours to fulfill my fourth-year residency. Attached is my resident's journal which includes my hours of work and study hours. The combination of hours exceeds the minimum hours by seventy-four hours. I have diligently documented my hands-on training, work experience and where I identify areas requiring more training like laparoscopic surgery and of course surgical reconstruction.

I am writing to request the medical school confer my medical degree now; however, I do plan to participate in the formal graduation ceremony this coming May.

My father is an OB/GYN and he has a Teaching Fellowship as well as a Fellowship in Maternal Fetal Medicine and Female Pelvic Medicine and Reproductive surgery. I am asking to complete my OB/GYN residency at the Wilderness Health Outreach Medical Center using my father as my instructor.

There exist three significant reasons why I should complete my O&G training at the medical center. (1) My father holds the credentials necessary to instruct and provide training necessary to certify my completion of my residency; (2) I will be eleven when my specialty training starts, which is too young to take course work on campus; and (3) The number of births has doubled over the last year as the wilderness community keeps growing. Having one OB/GYN is inadequate to meet patient need. I filled the need this year and the Foundation expects me to remain and complete my O&G residency in their medical center.

Please let me know if the medical school will approve this requests at your earliest convenience.

Hayden Gehardi

I recognized that I was jumping before I finished walking, but that is who I am. If there was to be a problem with doing my O&G residency at the medical center then I wanted to know early and have time to resolve any issues. I received the Dean's letter in three days. He wrote:

Dear Ms. Gehardi:

I am in receipt of your letter seeking approval to complete your O&G residency off campus. After careful consideration by the board, I must inform you that your request is denied. The medical school's hospital is a teaching hospital. The fact that your father has a teaching fellowship in the O&G field is not persuasive. Your request to have your degree conferred prior to graduation is also denied. The board believes it is appropriate to graduate with your class.

You may register and attend your training at our medical center. However, until you are twelve years of age, you will be required to have a parent or guardian present during your hours fulfilling the residency requirements.

I trust I have fully responded to your inquiry. My recommendation to you is to slow down and enjoy life. Please confirm if you intend to participate in the fall term of your residency.

/s/Chair

I was very unhappy with the board's decision. I was going to call Jim, but I thought I could handle this myself. I prayed my Father was still watching over me because this would become a battle if not handled correctly. One strength and weakness I have is my combative attitude when road blocks are placed upon my education. I have difficulty accepting 'NO', especially when the option I proposed will mutually benefit both parties. I thought through the problem and then called Jim for some feedback. I explained to Jim that the wilderness medical center needs me working as a resident for the next four years.

Jim's first question was, "Hayden, have you contacted the Foundation representative to determine if the Foundation will back you?" I replied, "Not yet. I was trying to work out the problem with the medical school. I don't think the Medical school wants me to graduate early." Jim recommended I stop wasting my time petitioning the medical school for reconsideration. Jim recommended I set up a meeting with the Foundation representative and my parents. He suggested that I might find out if the Foundation has some pull with the medical school. I thanked Jim and asked my father to help set up a meeting with the Foundation to address my O&G residency. My father replied, "Dr. Stephenson is the director of the Foundation and he will be here tomorrow to discuss the addition of a new administrator. Let's talk with him then."

My father and I met Dr. Stephenson at 7:00 a.m., which was before the medical center was fully open for business. At that time of day, the emergency room was open, but that was it. My father discussed the need for a replacement administrator. Dr. Stephenson replied, "Ian, you and Eli are doing a great job with the medical center. Your reviews are all outstanding and patient care has nearly doubled over the last year. You and Eli are the medical center directors. You may make the decision on who you employ without seeking my permission. Please make sure the new administrator understands his relationship with you and Eli. He works for you and not the other way around." Dr. Stephenson asked, "Did we cover what you wanted to discuss?" My father replied, "Yes, but my daughter wants to speak with you too."

I introduced myself and gave a firm handshake and explained that I am a fourth-year resident this year, but with the increased population, births doubled this year. My father and I kept up with the deliveries and examinations, but demand for quality O&G care is increasing. I have asked the medical school for permission to complete my O&G residency at the medical center because one OB/GYN is not going to be able to take care of all the patients. I work well with my father and I am asking if you, or the Foundation, have any pull with the medical school. The medical center needs me and I want to serve the health needs of the wilderness community and I plan to remain working at the medical center following certification." Dr. Stephenson asked me what type of work I did for my fourth-year residency. My father started to explain when Dr. Stephenson asked that I explain my year.

I replied to Dr. Stephenson that I did routine school physicals, gynecological exams and I diagnosed multiple woman's issues, such as an ectopic pregnancy, endometrial tissue removal, and I began some exposure to laparoscopic type surgeries, I delivered more than fifty babies by natural child birth and to date I have completed four C-section births under my father's supervision. I have studied the majority of the medical conditions affecting women's health like PID, STDs, and urinary tract infections; I have done two episiotomies and diagnosed multiple issues from cancer to inflammation. I have written more than two hundred prescriptions for birth control pills as well. I can also read and interpret ultrasounds and correctly use the ultrasound to determine if a natural child birth may require an episiotomy. I have also had three cases of child abuse/rape. I have learned a lot in one year and I look forward to being able to continue my O&G residency under my father's direction. I will become a great medical doctor like him if given the chance.

Dr. Stephenson replied, "Very impressive accomplishments for someone who I understand will be eleven in April." I replied, "Yes, April 6th." Dr. Stephenson stood up and said "Good-bye". I asked, "What about my request. Can you help me?" He replied, "It's already approved. You will do your residency at our medical facility under your father's direction." I asked, "How?" Dr. Stephenson smiled and said, "I am a professor emeritus at the medical school. I am the chairman of the Board of Regents that owns the medical buildings and even the medical school. My foundation provides the medical school with a lot of money every year. This year the medical school received 2.2 million dollars from my foundation. The medical school can either work with you or lose their funding." He then said, "I will do one better for you. Dr. Stephenson called someone and said, "Jack, this is Phil Stevenson. If necessary, will your medical school sponsor a young lady doing her O&G residency at my Wilderness Heath Outreach Medical Center? Her existing medical school is requiring her to train out of the school's teaching hospital, but I need her at my facility. Dr. Stephenson put Jack on the speaker and I heard him say, "It's done. Just let me know if she needs us." Dr. Stephenson shook my hand and said, "Is that good enough?" I replied, "May a future doctor give you a hug as a thank you?" I gave him a bear hug and he told me that I could give him hugs anytime. He wished me well and gave me his card should I need to contact him. Two days later I received this letter:

Dear Ms. Gehardi:

Upon reconsideration by the board, your request to complete your O&G residency at the medical center is approved. The board is concerned that your absence from the medical center will create a vacancy that could not be easily filled and patient care is the highest priority in outlying medical centers. Please register and pay your fees each semester like usual and I will see you at graduation.

/s/ Dean Sorenson, Chair

I received Dr. Sorenson's letter and I was so excited that I ran into my father's office, dropped onto my knees and prayed. I thanked my Heavenly Father for helping guide me in the right direction. That afternoon, my father and mother took my hands and walked me down the hallway. While I was seeing patients, they had assigned me my own office. On the door glass read, "Hayden E. Gehardi, M.D". (almost). The next line read Obstetrics and Gynecology Resident. My father asked me to look in the closet. I had ten new white lab coats with my name, Hayden E. Gehardi, M.D and underneath read 'Obstetrics and Gynecology Resident. My mother said, "That's not all. Look in your drawers." I looked and I had ten pair of scrubs including mask, shoe covers and my size surgical gloves. That day I felt my Father's hand on my shoulder. My future was set and I was excited to embark on my residency as soon as I could. I called Jim and thanked him one more time for guiding me in the path I needed to follow.

I was planning on writing the medical school again asking for my medical degree to be conferred early when I received a page directing me to delivery room 2B. I ran into the room and was shocked that I didn't have a patient waiting. Instead of a patient, Dean Sorenson was there with four other doctors and my parents. Dr. Sorenson smiled and said, "Ms. Gehardi, on behalf of the medical school, and in recognition of your personal achievements and commitment to the field of medicine, the medical school has decided to grant your request for early award of your medical degree. I am very pleased to confer upon you the degree of Medical Doctor. By this grant, you may begin your O&G residency upon any schedule you and your father work out. I extend to you the heartfelt congratulations from the board." I was so excited that I personally scrapped off the word "Almost" from my office door and I couldn't wait to tell Michael that I am a MD.

SEVEN

A Strong Case of Like

My life was back on track. For the rest of the week I was up early to greet the sun and say good-night to the moon. I was happy and I thanked my Heavenly Father for caring for me and guiding me through my darkness and into his light. I knew I was a creation of God and I lived my life in great reverence to him.

I got up Friday morning and I stood in the morning sun for several minutes before I showered and dressed to meet Michael at the medical center. I wore a light blue spring dress with white leggings. I fixed my hair and even tried my hand at a little makeup, and I do mean a little or I would never get out of my house. I may be a medical doctor, but I was still my parents' almost eleven-year old daughter and I too had limits.

I hadn't seen Michael for three weeks because they were moving and getting set up in their new home. Michael lived about twelve miles from me, but meeting at the medical center cafeteria eliminated the mileage issue since both of his parents worked at the medical center.

I arrived and ordered a hot chocolate and sat reading my journals waiting for Michael. Our arrangement was 8:00 a.m., but Michael didn't show up until 9:20 a.m. My irritation showed a little when Michael explained that his father was on the phone talking with a man from the foundation and he is why I am late. I replied, "He was probably talking to Dr. Stephenson. He is a really nice man." Michael said, "My dad was approved to be the new administrator of this facility." He likes the fact that your parents remain in full charge and my father works for them."

Michael asked me, "How is it that your parents look like identical twins. Are they married to each other? My mother said they are identical and they are partners. Is that true? Are your parents like husband and wife? How can they do that if they are brother and sister?" I asked Michael to read the book, "Ian and Eli" Near Identical Twins. That book will explain everything to you. I just have one copy left in my bag and you can have it." Michael accepted the book and suggested that my parents were a little weird. I replied, "They are good parents and wonderful doctors. I love my parents like every other child loves their parents. Being a little different is alright and I am not on this earth to force my values onto someone else. If that bothers you, we can go our separate ways right now." Michael replied, "It makes no difference to me. I just want you as my friend." Michael reached over our table and held me by my hands. He tried to kiss my hand, but I withdrew and let him know that I am still not looking for a boyfriend, but I am excited to have him as my friend that just happens to be a boy.

I mentioned to Michael that my birthday was just around the corner and asked if he would like to join me at the bear restaurant. My parents want to celebrate my medical degree and my birthday at the same time. He asked, "What is the bear restaurant?" I explained that when I first came to the restaurant, I had a premonition that a little bear was in the restaurant. Nobody believed me until a little brown bear pushed open the door and walked into the restaurant. He left just as quickly and since then we call it the bear restaurant." Michael hugged me and said, "I would love to share your birthday at the bear restaurant. Who else is coming?" I replied, "Just you, me, my parents and grandparents."

Michael was a little shy and didn't want to join in on the activities. I grabbed his hand and said, "You are coming with me so move your butt." I made Michael sit on a chair and I painted his face like a happy clown. He looked and laughed as he said, "My turn to paint your face." Michael carefully painted my face and I almost appeared angelic. His use of the paints was well done and he received complements from everyone that saw my face. Michael explained that he liked painting, especially on a cute canvas like my face. We stopped at the balloon section and Michael surprised me by making a halo out of four balloons. Even the clown doing the balloons liked the halo and asked to have Michael show him how to make it. The restaurant had added a couple new games. Michael and I played a form of bowling where we tossed balls into openings for points. He did well, but I couldn't get the wooden balls to go where I wanted them to go. Michael stood behind me, took my throwing arm and gently guided my arm and the ball fell into the fifty-point hole. It was fun and I kissed him on his cheek again. I got up from my chair and Michael held my hand and we continued holding each other's hand as we joined my family. I looked at my parents and they simply smiled and asked, "Having fun? Your painted faces are adorable." My mother used her phone and took a picture of me with my painted face and balloon halo. She told my father that she would use that picture to post on the medical center's physician's wall. My mother then took several pictures of me and Michael. She sent the pictures to Michael's phone so he had a copy as well. My father commented, "You are a cute couple."

I explained to Michael that the fun part was here. The clowns brought out a cake with my name on it "Hayden E. Gehardi, M.D." The restaurant all joined in singing for me the 'Happy Birthday song. When that was done, several people asked, "What do the initials mean behind her name? Is she a medical doctor?" My mother replied, "Yes, she just received her medical degree and we are celebrating that and her birthday." The woman followed up and asked, "How old is she?" I replied, "I am eleven, or will be in a few days." My mother offered to cut the cake and the restaurant brought out a one-gallon tub of my favorite vanilla ice scream. My family ate the entire cake and gallon of ice cream over a four-hour period. I think Michael and I ate half of the cake, but then it was my eleventh birthday and I was having fun with a very special friend named Michael.

I learned that Michael was familiar with horses and I arranged for my mother to fly us to the horse barn so we could ride. Michael rode my father's horse and I rode Midnight. I made us ten cheese sandwiches and my mother bought two gallons of chocolate milk. We heated the chocolate milk in the microwave and enjoyed our lunch together. The barn was surprisingly quiet and I asked Michael if he liked dry cheese sandwiches just because I do. Michael replied, "I am embarrassed to admit, but every time I eat something with mustard or mayonnaise on it, I spill some down my front. I don't want to look stupid in front of you." I replied back, "I spill down my front all the time. That is why I order plain cheese sandwiches. No mess. Michael laughed and said, "See Hayden, we have a lot in common." I think I rolled my eyes and laughed at him.

We were almost done with our lunch when Teri showed up with Kelly who she described as boyfriend number four. Teri was surprisingly friendly and asked if Michael was my boyfriend. In front of Michael, I replied, "No, Michael is a friend that just happens to be a boy. None of us are ready for a serious relationship." Teri French kissed Kelly and said, "I am ready for kissing and Kelly is really good at kissing." I cleaned up our lunch and prepared to go riding again. Teri asked if she and Kelly could join us. I replied, "I don't see why not." I felt a glimmer of friendship with Teri, but I knew I could never compete with a boyfriend. I prayed Teri protect herself and I don't see her at the medical center.

My mother landed and I let Michael know it was time to stow our tack and brush out our horses. As I was brushing Midnight, Cynthia Peters showed up and asked to talk with me privately. I was curious why she wanted to talk with me. The last time I saw her was two years prior and she was really rude to me, Teri and my friend Cynthia Tewes. I replied, "I'm listening." Cynthia asked, "I missed my period from last month and it hasn't started this month either. Do you know why?" I explained that several medical conditions can stop or interrupt a period. I would need to do an exam and have my father look if I have questions. Why don't you come into the medical center and I will examine you there?" Cynthia asked, "Does pregnancy stop periods?" I replied, "It is the biggest reason why periods stop. That is an indication that your body is using the blood to help in the gestation of the fetus." Cynthia cried and said, "I know I am pregnant." I hugged her and said, "I can't check out here. You should purchase a pregnancy stick and see for yourself." Cynthia replied, "How? I get an allowance and my mother will know if I spend my allowance all in one place." I handed her my twenty dollars and asked her to please check, and if she is pregnant, then she needed an examination and a discussion about adoption or keeping the baby. Cynthia Peters asked that I don't say anything to Teri, Cynthia T. or her mother. I replied, "What you have told me is medically privileged. I will ask your mother to wait in the waiting room if you come in for an examination."

Teri whispered in my ear, "Cynthia is pregnant. She told me yesterday what happened with her boyfriend. I am not that stupid to have unprotected sex." I replied, "Our promise was no sex until we were out of school at least." Teri said, "I don't want to wait that long. You can, but leave me alone. It's my decision, not yours."

Michael asked, "What were you and that girl talking about?" I replied, "It is confidential". Michael said I heard her talking about pregnancy. Is she pregnant?" I replied, "She might be and she is afraid to tell her mother." Michael looked at me and said, "I hope you understand that if we become boyfriend and girlfriend, I want to be a virgin when I marry. I will not have sex before marriage. I believe that is wrong and I feel sorry for that girl." I hugged Michael and said, "Thank you. That is how I feel too." I don't know why, but when I hugged Michael, I kissed him on his lips. I felt stupid and I wiped my mouth. Michael replied, "You kissed me once. I get to kiss you once and no more." Michael hugged me and kissed me on my lips and we both wiped our lips and said, "No more". That night I thought about Michael's kiss and I smiled and thanked my Heavenly Father for his answer to my prayers.

Cynthia's mother brought Cynthia into the medical center for a check-up. She said Cynthia is complaining of bad cramps and painful burning and she has been lethargic for nearly a week. I am concerned about her. She then asked, "Why are going to examine my daughter. You don't look any older than Cynthia." I replied, "I am a MD and qualified to examine Cynthia. I am an O&G resident at this facility. I politely asked Cynthia's mother to wait in the outside waiting room while I examined Cynthia. Her mother was unhappy, but did as I asked. The first thing I had Cynthia do is pee on the pregnancy indicator. I expected it to be positive, but she wasn't pregnant. I did an exam and diagnosed a bad case of pelvic inflammatory disease as well as a urinary tract infection. I prepared two prescriptions for her and recommended she come back in one week. I asked Cynthia if she was sexually active with her boyfriend. She replied, "We have done it a few times." I recommended that when her PID is gone that she get examined for birth control pills. I looked in her eyes and said, "No sex until this is cleared up and you are on the pill." My father stepped in and confirmed my diagnosis, signed the scrips and I said, "Please set another appointment for one week so I can check you further. I brought her mother in and explained the PID problem. She replied, "Thank God she isn't pregnant. I had Cynthia when I was thirteen years old."

I finished a short week because my father gave me December 22nd through December 26th off. I asked my mother if I could shop and find a present to give to Michael for Christmas. My mother replied, "You must really like Michael to want to buy him a Christmas present. Do you believe he feels the same way about you?" I replied, "I think so. He talks about us being boyfriend and girlfriend in the future, but I think he would like the title 'Boyfriend' now. I should tell you that Michael and I talked about sexual relations"; my mother interrupted me and said, "That isn't going to happen. You are almost eleven years old." I replied, "Before you interrupted me I was going to explain that Michael and I are of the same opinion that we will be virgins when we marry. Michael doesn't believe in premarital sex. He told me that he respected my position and asked me to respect his as well. My mother apologized and softly said, "Thank you Hayden." I replied, "You are welcome." My mother pried a little and asked me, "Have you kissed Michael?" I replied, "I kissed his cheek three times and once on his lips. I wiped off my mouth and he kissed my lips and we both wiped our mouths. I liked his kiss and I think he liked mine. Did you know that Teri is French kissing her latest boyfriend? I told her to be careful so I don't have to see her in the medical center."

Christmas was almost here and like most kids, I too was excited to share in the joy of the season. I liked to receive presents, but my true joy is in giving to someone else. At ten years old I met my goal of graduating from medical school. I am a M.D. I know this because it is written on my white lab coat next to my name and ingrained in my heart to be a healer of bodies and souls. My Heavenly Father created me and I walk with him where ever I go and he is with me always in whatever I do.

I decided on day one of my residency that I would bring prayer into my medical practice to honor my Heavenly Father. Before examining a patient, or in delivering a child, I would ask if the patient would like to share a short prayer. Some patients refused for personal reasons, but for most of my patients, they appreciated a short prayer for them and their unborn child. I could see and experience my patients relaxing after our prayer. I knew that my Father's healing hands would work through me and often I would hear my patient say, "I feel better already". My response is that my Father in Heaven is the divine healer. I am merely his tool in which I too carry out his will. Am I an angel of or for God? Of course not, but through the grace of my Father in Heaven, all things are possible. To give glory to my Father in Heaven I started the medical prayer program at the medical center. In just one short week of prayer; praying became contagious as other practitioners no longer feared bringing God into the practice of medicine. By Christmas Eve, fourteen medical doctors at our medical center prayed with their patients. In the back of my mind, I truly felt that prayer never hurt a patient. Like foxholes in the military and patients in the hospital, there are few atheists in either venue.

Christmas was in four days. I excitedly opened my bedroom curtain and I felt the warmth of the morning sun. I said "Good night" to the disappearing evening moon that highlighted the horizon and I thanked my Father for another opportunity to heal the sick and share in his love. I walked out into the kitchen, stretched in my pajamas, and said, "Good Morning" as I yawned. I looked at my mother and she was cooking breakfast when I felt two fingers poke my ribs and I heard that familiar voice of Michael. I turned and Michael was standing there fully dressed. He said, "Good morning to you too." My mother had arranged for Michael's parents to drop him off to spend the day with me. I was a little embarrassed and excused myself to get cleaned up and dressed. When I returned Michael commented that I was cute in the morning. He whispered to me that he hoped in time we would become more than friends. I replied, "Anything is possible, but you and I have some educational hurdles to jump before that day arrives. Until then we are just friends who happen to be a boy and girl that really like each other. I spent the day with Michael and we talked about everything; our likes and dislikes; our families and our personal goals in life. Like my mother, I have certain abilities beyond the norm of human development. I have premonition abilities and I could see me and Michael together for years to come. Was it a true premonition or simply my hope and desire to have Michael in my life? Who knows? My Heavenly Father knows, but he isn't telling me either. *I thought to myself – time will answer all questions.*

My mother informed me that she had invited Michael's family to Christmas Dinner. I hugged and kissed my mother and said, "Thank you for inviting Michael." My mother replied, "I thought it was better to have him here to share Christmas with you. Otherwise, I knew that your body would have been with us, but your mind would be with Michael and quite frankly, I wanted my entire daughter with me at Christmas. I hugged my mother again and was excited to have Michael to share my day.

My family opens presents on Christmas Eve and I learned that Michael's family followed the same tradition. To accommodate my desire to share an early Christmas with Michael, he and I arranged to meet Thursday and exchange Christmas presents. I never thought we would be meeting at my house. Michael went into our living room and appeared with flowers and a present for me. I opened it and it was a desk name plate "HAYDEN E. GEHARDI, M.D. I thanked Michael and he replied, "Just because I bought you a present doesn't mean you are obligated to buy me a present." I got up and handed Michael his present. Inside were two pediatric medicine journals and a subscription for four more years. Michael asked, "Why buy me this publication now?" I explained that it is never too soon to plan for your future as a pediatrician. I then handed him my MCAT test booklet and the ten practice tests and suggested he start preparing for the MCAT now. I explained that I spent three hours a day studying for the MCAT and the rest of my time doing my other school work. I thought Michael was a little disappointed in his gift so I handed him a wrapped 8 x 10 photo of me that he could put anywhere he wanted including the trash can. He replied, "I will cherish your picture and take it with me when I start college. It will help me remember you." I smiled and said, "You can call me and I can call you so remembering me won't be too difficult." I handed Michael two wallet size pictures of me; one in my gray pleated skirt, mauve stockings and pink blouse and the other in my white breeches, jacket and helmet sitting on Tempest. Michael told me I was beautiful and I nearly cried when he hugged me.

Michael and I were standing in the living room when he put his arms around me and I shared my first real kiss with him. I think we were both a little awkward and uncomfortable, but we couldn't stop talking about our first kiss. Michael said, "I will miss you when I start college this fall." I replied, "We have all summer to do things together and remember, "Absence makes the heart grow fonder." Michael asked me if I would wait for him to graduate. I replied, "I am almost eleven years old. Our friendship has nothing but time on our side. If you study hard, you may be able to complete medical school by the time you are nineteen or twenty years old. Pediatrics has a one-year residency requirement and you are in business. Please don't worry about me. I am going nowhere." *Michael appeared relieved by my comforting words.*

My mother and I flew Michael home. On the way back, my mother smiled and asked how I liked my first kiss. I asked, "Did you see me kiss Michael?" My mother laughed and said, "Remote viewing." I replied, "Not fair." She replied, "I am your mother. I peeked and saw you kissing Michael. Just remember doctor, you are ten; not twenty." I replied, "I know that and so does Michael; and remember birthday number eleven will be here in no time."

EIGHT

Epilogue

Christmas was two days away and I was able to spend each day with Michael. I will start my O&G residency right after Christmas. My father explained that babies have their own timeline and I am needed to meet our ever-growing patient population. It was nice that I no longer required a patient's permission to treat them; well, almost anyway. I still needed my medical license and my first application was rejected due to my age. This time I was armed for a fight if needed. I handed the licensing agent the letter I received from the Director of Professional Licensing which confirmed that I could receive my medical license once my medical degree was conferred. She found the file copy along with a letter from Dr. Stephenson. She looked at me and asked, "What makes you so special anyway?" I smiled and asked, "When was the last time you approved a medical license for a ten-year old?" She replied, "Oh, you are that girl." I have a note in your file that instructs my department to issue you your medical license over the counter. If you will please have a seat, I will get the forms for your signature." She handed me the forms and I indicated that I will fill them out and have my parents sign. She replied, "I only need your signature Dr. Gehardi. You are the licensed professional; not your parents. I also received my Drug Enforcement Agency DEA license to prescribe controlled substances. My father had insisted I send that application in once my degree was conferred and I was ready to go. Dr. Stephenson apparently spoke with the licensing agent for the DEA because my license to prescribe medication was waiting for me.

I walked into the medical center Christmas Eve and handed the administrator my medical license and my DEA license to prescribe medicine. I wanted everything ready for my first day of my residency. I began to leave when the administrator asked me to sit down. He informed me that I couldn't start work until I had completed my W-9, whatever that was; my 401K set up; my health and life insurance; and my errors and omissions (E&O) insurance was updated. I replied, "I gave you my licenses and I have got to go to work. I have a full morning of unscheduled patients and two deliveries. I was to have today off to be with your son." He replied, "Until I change your status with our errors and omissions insurance carrier, you are not working as a physician in this medical center." I was sitting in the administrator's office and I strangely felt like what I perceived Jeremy and Marcus would feel like when seated in their principal's office. I nervously looked around and had a foreboding sense that I had done something wrong, even though I knew better. I prayed, "Father, get me out of here please. I have patients to see." After twenty minutes of waiting, my father arrived and asked me why I was sitting in the administrator's office instead of seeing my patients. He said, "I asked you to come in today because I need you." I pointed to the administrator and said, "He won't let me practice until my E&O insurance is updated and I have completed all his other paperwork."

My father thumbed through the paperwork and said, "Get the E&O verified now. Dr. Gehardi is needed in patient care. You can handle administrative matters with professional staff during slow periods or after work. I need Dr. Gehardi now." I thanked my Heavenly Father and walked out of the administrator's office and wanted to look back and sneer at him for his attitude; however, he is Michael's father and I would do nothing to separate me from my time visiting with Michael. My father caught me in the hallway and confirmed that my E&O insurance was updated and I was now fully insured for five million dollars per incident. I hoped I would never need to make a claim under my insurance.

It took me a little time to adjust to the name, 'Dr. Gehardi' and every time I heard a nurse or patient say, 'Dr. Gehardi' I had to consider where my parents were. On my first day of my residency my nurse said, "Dr. Gehardi, you are needed in exam room 1C. She repeated, "Dr. Gehardi" and finally she grabbed my arm and said, "Dr. Gehardi I am speaking to you." I then realized for the first time that I was "Dr. Gehardi." To avoid confusion around the medical center, my family went by Dr. Ian Gehardi, Dr. Eli Gehardi and Dr. Hayden Gehardi. That worked well when everyone followed the same procedure.

I was talking with my parents when the PA system announced, "Dr. Gehardi, you are needed in emergency stat." All three of us ran to the ER. Sitting in the exam room was Cynthia and her mother. I mentioned to my parents that I would handle this. Cynthia was crying and explained that her boyfriend took away her birth control pills and he refused to do protected sex. I examined Cynthia and confirmed that she was indeed pregnant this time. Cynthia was almost twelve and her mother somewhat laughed and said her daughter would deliver earlier than she did. Cynthia wanted to keep the baby and I set her up on our schedule for monthly checkups. I prescribed several vitamins and said "Good-bye". Cynthia made me think of Teri and Cynthia T., my other friends, and I still wondered if Teri would follow our agreement. I wished the best for my childhood friend.

I was scheduled to work between Christmas and New Year's Day. I was so excited to see and visit Michael on Friday. I dressed in my favorite gray pleated skirt and wore my mauve tights and a new pink blouse. I fixed my hair a little nicer than usual by putting it up on the top of my head. That accented my slim neck and my facial features that Michael called "Cute". I made sure my fingernails were clean and painted with a clear polish. I carefully applied some makeup with the help of my mother and I was ready to spend the day at the medical center cafeteria. My mother and father both said I looked beautiful and Michael was lucky to have me as his friend. I didn't feel like I was ten years old and I wouldn't be eleven until April 6th, approximately twelve weeks away. I looked at myself in my mirror and I felt my Heavenly Father's hand on my shoulder. He had kept his promise of always being with me. I couldn't see my Heavenly Father, but I could feel his grace and love for me as he kept his promise of being with me always.

My mother called and said, "Hayden, it's time to go." Today was my day off and I walked like a young lady instead of running like an intern. I was excited to get going and see Michael; just because he was my friend. Like the little red leaf that I rescued from obscurity and isolation, Michael saw that I was also a red leaf; he knew I was just a little different and he accepted me like I accepted my red leaf. Michael helped me to feel alive and never alone. Had I conformed to the peer pressure of having a boyfriend when I wasn't old enough to be dating boys? I looked at me again in my mirror and the girl I saw was still me. I exist because I was created of my parents; I live for my desire to work and to love one day. Will that love be Michael or maybe someone else? I cannot see that far into my future. However, I do live in the present and today was Friday; a day to tip my toe into the water of life and be with Michael, a friend that just happens to be a boy. Michael looked at me and said I was truly beautiful. He touched my face and kissed me as he freed my hair allowing it to fall upon my shoulders. He looked again and said, "Now that is the girl I will love one day."

This is my life and I thank you for sharing in my life's story, at least to almost age eleven. I asked my very special friend and Lawyer to please write the story of my life. This book is a culmination of hours of telephone calls between me and Jim. Jim says the book is a collaborative effort, but I know that he has learned to use words like I have learned to use the tools of my occupation.

I hope that the reader is convinced that I was created by my Heavenly Father, who through his grace and love sent me to earth for delivery to my parents who couldn't have children. The medical evidence confirms that I am a part of both of my parents. Angel Michaele, who carried me in her womb to my parents, was a hermaphrodite, meaning she had male and female sex chromosomes or DNA. The DNA test confirmed that Michaele was a hermaphrodite. For those in doubt, I ask, "Where does the body of an angel go when his or her task is completed?" Of course, the angel would return to Heaven until needed again to carry out God's will. Michaele disappeared after completing her mission to deliver 'this child'. That child was me. I was and am a true gift from God, my Father in Heaven. There are no other conclusions to be drawn. Identical twins have a one hundred percent DNA match. My parents' DNA confirmed that their DNA was identical. Explain how my DNA is 99.892 percent of my parents. According to the DNA experts, I am not a child of my parents; rather my DNA proves that I am of my parents and not by my parents. Sounds confusing? Not really. As God took one of Adam's ribs to create Eve; I wonder if God took a little part of Ian and Eli Gehardi and created me in heaven to become the person I am today. All I can humbly say is, "Thank you Father."

I am Hayden and I am prepared for my future, whatever that will bring. I am almost eleven and I have a lot of future left, God willing. I will pray to my Heavenly Father and hopefully he will answer my prayer and guide me through the rest of my life as he helped me through my dark times. I feel my Heavenly Father's love and I firmly believe that my Father has a guardian angel accompanying me on my life journey. I see my Heavenly Father in all of his creation and I know he is there with me and me with him. I have learned to slow down long enough to look into a mirror and thank God for making me in the image of my parents. I am blessed because I have two fathers that love, guide and protect me in my walk-through life.

I was asked, "Hayden, what is your most important lesson that you have learned." I replied, "I am the little red leaf. I don't need to be isolated, alone or even afraid if I believe in my heart that my Father is with me and remains with me through the darkness of the moonlit sky until the light of the morning sunshine. I am therefore not alone nor should I feel isolated. My Father answered my prayer and I have a very special friend in Michael. His love and grace sometimes make me wonder if he may yet be Archangel Michael whose original job was to deliver me; now he may be my guardian angel. All I know is that I like being with Michael regardless of his actual being. Michael brings me comfort, happiness and that occasional kiss.

I am Hayden, a medical doctor. I understand hormones and human development. Does a battle continue to exist within me between right and belonging? Of course, it does. I am human and vulnerable. My Father blessed me with free will and self-determination. I can overcome my hormonal desires because I have found a friend that may become more than a friend in my future as we share and support each other.

I am Hayden, a gift from God, my Father, and I thank God for who I am and who I will become one day. I know my Heavenly Father walks with me and he protects me as he fulfills his promise to be with me always. My Father in Heaven gave man and woman free will and how you exercise your free will is important to your future as it is to mine.

I am Hayden because I am. I will pray for you and ask that you too pray to God, through our Lord Jesus Christ when you find yourself in darkness. When you compare yourself to the red leaf upon the ground, remember that my Father in Heaven will guide you and never abandon you for he walks with anyone who accepts his love.

I am Hayden and I thank you for reading my story. I hope you believe in angels after reading about my miraculous birth and my life. My future is yet to be written. When that time comes, I hope and pray my friend and lawyer will be with me to share the rest of my life with you.

Hayden

Author Biography

Author James A. Gauthier, J.D. is a lawyer licensed to practice law in Washington and Idaho. He has published "A Gift from God"; "Emily" and "Emily 2"; "Unacceptable Expectations"; "Kid's Court"; "Ian & Eli"; "Interstitial Beings"; "Surrealeum Dreams"; "Inside Out Trilogy –New Beginnings, Rise of the Monarchy, and Final Conflict"; "Until Tomorrow" and Anna Banana, the Golden Yellow Banana Slug". The author has no preset genre and enjoys presenting exciting story lines that keep the reader from putting down the book until it is finished.

Edwards Brothers Inc.
Ann Arbor MI. USA
February 27, 2018